How ~~NOT~~ to Date a GRIFFIN

CAUTIONARY TAILS BOOK THREE

LANA KOLE

✿ Formatted with Vellum

CONTENTS

CONTENT INFORMATION

For a complete list of content information pertaining to How Not to Date a Griffin, please refer to my website.

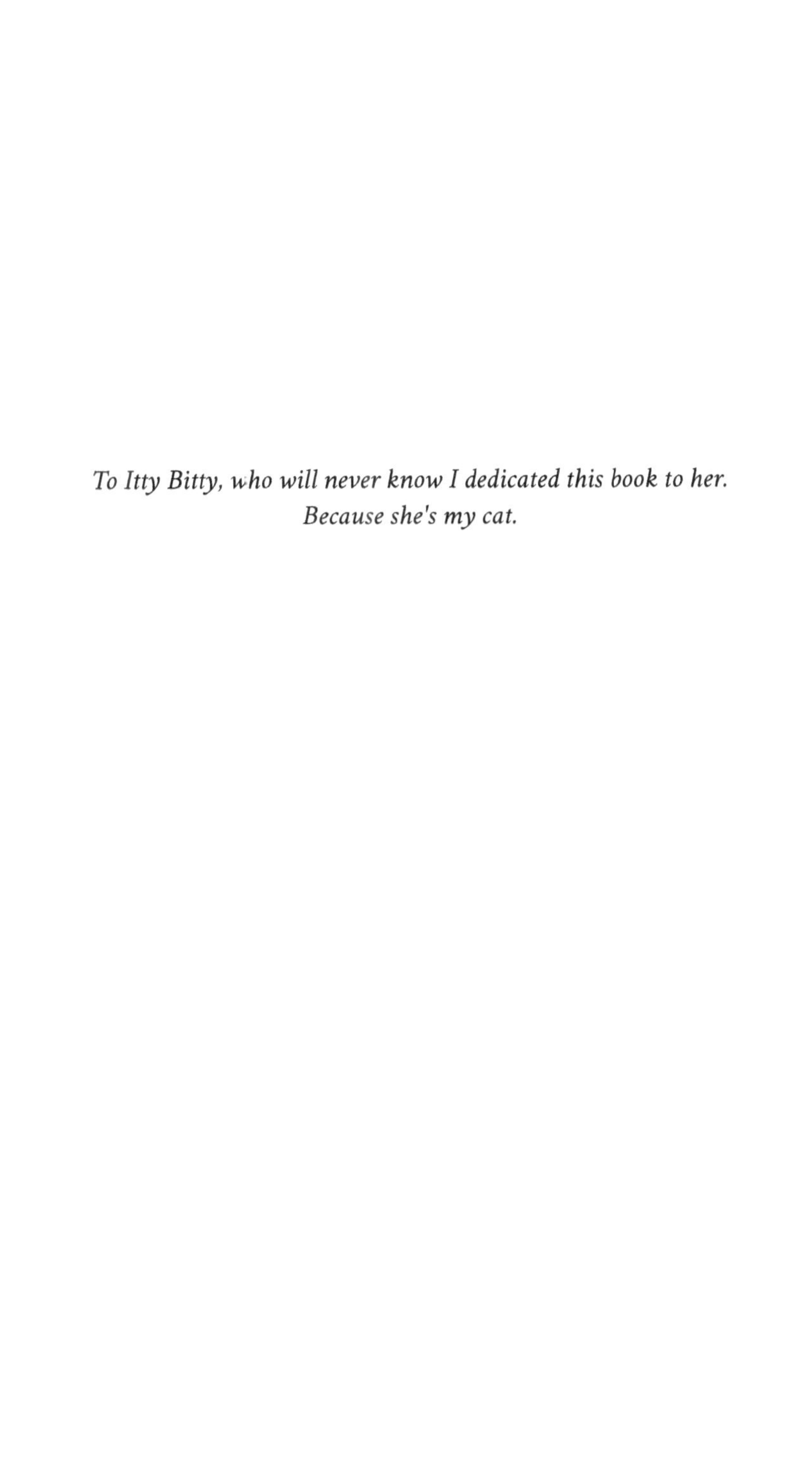

To Itty Bitty, who will never know I dedicated this book to her.
Because she's my cat.

DREAD ON ARRIVAL

The warm, muggy air assaulted Nolan as he stepped out of the frosty glass of the hotel entrance.

A line of ride shares blocked the drive as the small crowd of well-dressed men and women awaited their rides, and Nolan had no choice but to wade into the swells.

He'd much rather be decompressing in his hotel room, but work conferences rarely afforded him the precious time.

The suit jacket he'd chosen for this evening of interactions—which blended him seamlessly into the masses—was already too warm, and he considered skipping back up to his room to change. But he feared if he returned to the silent oasis of his room, he might not want to leave.

And well, the dinner wouldn't be on his dime, would it?

However, his dinner party was nowhere to be found in this mess, so he figured they must have gone ahead without him.

Fine.

Pulling his phone from his pocket, he pulled up a rideshare app on his phone and… stared at the prices.

It may have been a Friday evening in a very large city, but surely a taxi shouldn't cost this much? The driver would only get the smallest fraction of it, anyway. Completely unfair, since they were the ones doing the driving and all.

Nolan scrolled through the options, and paused, thumb hovering over something he'd never seen before.

A flight? An icon of… was that a griffin?

"No, surely not," he muttered to himself, and clicked the option more out of curiosity than anything.

Surely they wouldn't send a real, live griffin to his location? That just seemed…

Well, actually quite ingenious.

Sure enough, it located a *real* griffin by the name of Reid. He would be arriving in four minutes.

A guilty, giddy flutter of excitement and apprehension struck him, and he almost canceled the ride immediately. But if his father and the rest of the crew had gone on ahead, they would not glance kindly on his tardiness.

Never mind the fact they could have just waited for him. It probably never crossed their minds.

Murmurs disturbed the mass as their attention was drawn to the sky, bracelet-adorned hands lifting and ringed fingers pointing. Following their interest, Nolan's eyes widened as the half-lion, half-eagle creature flapped his wings and lowered himself to the sidewalk.

And waited.

Nolan supposed he couldn't exactly call out the name of his rider, not with his beak, and—dear lord, Nolan was going to have to straddle the creature, like on horseback, wasn't he?

How terribly embarrassing.

The last time he'd ridden a horse, he was twelve. It had not gone well. In fact, he'd fallen off and broken his arm. He'd had to wear that garishly green cast—they hadn't exactly told him it would be *neon* when he chose it—embellished with immaturely drawn dicks for six weeks, thanks to his classmates.

Not that he still held a grudge. Of course not.

With a wince, Nolan made his way through the crowd and approached the creature from the side, hiding his apprehension behind a polite smile as he stepped into his eyeline.

"Hello there," he greeted.

Silence answered him, and he chuckled awkwardly before holding up his phone, highly aware of the stares he was receiving from the throng of elegant couples.

"Are you Reid?"

The creature huffed through his very large beak, and Nolan stared. "Right. You *are* the only griffin in the area, I suppose, so you must be, right?"

He huffed again.

"Right. Better get on with it then. Don't want to be late for dinner. Well, *more* late," he mumbled, and pocketed his phone. The creature's head was eye-level with Nolan, and he stared at the tall, wide span of his back and the simple saddle with something akin to dread.

He had the feeling he was about to embarrass himself.

"S'pose you don't have any tips for how to, uh… get in the saddle, eh?" he asked, chuckling to ease the stitch of panic weaving through his chest.

The creature—Reid, Nolan could just refer to him by his name—shuddered, and a single roped step unfurled itself from the side of the saddle.

"Oh thank god," he breathed, and placed his hands on either side of the leather, then hooked one foot into the single step before throwing his other leg up and over the creature's back. The first time he didn't get enough momentum, and his foot fell back to the ground with a thump, and Nolan sighed as heat rushed to his face.

The second time, though, he settled into the dip of the saddle effortlessly, and marveled at his athleticism.

"Well, that was easier than expected. Oh shit, you are

rather large, aren't you, there? Oh god," he rambled, as the wings bracketing him began to flap.

There were no seatbelts. What if he fell off?

Heart racing, he gripped onto the saddle with both hands and squeezed his eyes shut, unable to find the fucks to give about how ridiculous he may look.

"This might be a bad time to admit how terrified I am of heights." He gulped as they lifted away from the ground, ignoring the flash of devices from the crowd of people as they captured the rare sighting.

Rare for him, at least. He'd most certainly never taken a ride on a griffin. He didn't even know it was a *thing*.

His father would probably have something to say about this whole situation, but as the griffin drifted higher into the sky and away from the swanky circle, Nolan found he didn't particularly care.

The griffin didn't quite take him to the clouds, but they might as well have been spattered with their condensation for all the difference it made. They were *flying*!

Nolan's heart raced in his chest and his fingers tightened around the saddle, but he spied the moving cars and the walking people, little ants from way up here, with a grin.

"Wow!" he shouted, voice lost in the wind. "This is amazing!"

Reid dipped into the next turn, cutting between buildings with a *whoosh*, the rushing air all white noise in Nolan's ears as he stared at everything from this new, impossible perspective.

All too soon, Nolan spotted the name of the restaurant, but not even the dread of the evening, the whole week, could manage to spoil his excitement as they drifted lower to the ground.

The gentle landing surprised him, and if his eyes had been closed like earlier, he would've hardly noticed they'd touched the ground. He waited a few seconds to make sure the creature was still before he clambered off, and locked his knees to keep from wobbling as he readjusted to the cement beneath his feet.

"That was magnificent," he breathed, running a hand through his sure-to-be-unruly hair and pulling his phone from his pocket. "Oh, do let me tip you, uh…" As he fumbled for the setting in the app, he grumbled about new technology and his inability to keep up. "Sorry, just let me figure this thing out," he said, gaze flicking to the rather unimpressed looking griffin before him.

His eagle's eyes were shrewd, and until that moment Nolan hadn't considered that eagles could look *annoyed*, and yet somehow, this one managed.

Just as Nolan discovered the rating, review, and tip section of his past rides—honestly, did they have to make it so hard to find, were they trying to make these people's lives harder?—a notification appeared at the top of his screen, and his heart sank.

His cheeks went red at the words his coworker had sent him.

Dinner canceled. Decided to schedule for another night, give everyone downtime in their rooms. See you tomorrow. 9 sharp.

Well, fuck.

That would have been nice to know fifteen minutes ago.

Nolan was so focused on his annoyance, he didn't notice the slight vibration in the air until someone cleared their throat.

He startled as he glanced up to find a man standing in place of the griffin, arms crossed and brow arched.

Nolan swallowed.

"Everything alright?" the man asked in a deep voice that scratched the inside of Nolan's brain like something special.

"Reid?" he asked, rather coherently for someone who's

just come face to face with the hottest person they'd ever seen. Reid's long and unruly blond hair curled around the nape of his neck and framed his face, blending with the mustache and short beard that softened the sharp line of his jaw. Nolan would like to clock him around mid-thirties, but with the lengthened lifespan of most Others, there was really no telling.

Healthy. Sure, let's go with that. Reid looked… healthy.

Reid nodded, and motioned to the phone still in Nolan's hand. "Figure everything out?"

"Oh!" Nolan's attention jerked back to the screen, the offending message now hidden from sight but very close in mind. "Uh…"

His thoughts spun. He could go back to the hotel, but now he needed another ride, and how embarrassing if he booked another griffin only for it to be Reid again. And yet telling him he'd been ditched by his coworkers seemed rather humiliating, and he'd rather directly avoid having to admit it aloud.

He could, however, panic about what to do after he paid the handsome gentleman for his time.

Even internally, Nolan realized how that sounded, and winced before typing a few numbers into the screen. "Yes. Tip sent. Thank you for the ride—uh, flight?"

Where did the saddle go? Nolan wondered as Reid pulled his own phone out and blinked at the screen.

"Is that a typo?" he asked, a frown marring his features as he looked back up.

"Hmm?" Nolan was distracted by the long, lean line of Reid's figure, and snapped his attention back up.

"The zeros. That's too many," Reid said, and turned the phone to him, jaw grinding.

Nolan's cheeks reddened further. "Ah, no. That's correct."

"What?! Why would you tip that much? Are you crazy?!"

Nolan held his ground as Reid stepped forward, and tried to get his tongue to work. "W-well, those rideshare apps kind of price gouge, don't they? Especially during busy hours. And the drivers only get a small fraction of it. Plus, well, you quite literally flew me here, and that's tiring manual labor, and I thought you should be paid as such. Is that… alright?" he asked, his tirade falling to a more suitable volume as his passion and embarrassment faded to a simmer.

"No, man, it's just… a lot. I mean, you were my last of the night anyway, but now I can take off without feeling bad. Thanks."

The smile he offered Nolan left devastation in its wake.

"You're quite welcome."

And then Nolan was stalling, waiting for Reid to leave so he could—

"So… you gonna go in?" Reid asked.

"What?" Nolan blinked at him.

"The restaurant? Now that you're here."

The text message ran through his mind again, and he cast a dubious glance toward the ritzy restaurant. "Uh… actually—"

Just then, he caught sight of familiar faces gathered around a table through one of the windows.

A few others from the office, all here for the event. Chase, the assistant, for god's sake, the one who'd texted him. And his own *father*.

Nolan supposed *giving everyone downtime in their rooms* really only referred to Nolan himself.

The table laughed at something, and Chase clapped Nolan's father on the shoulder, jovial smiles all around.

Figures.

Swallowing the confusion and frustration, he turned back to Reid. "Actually, no. I won't. Something's come up."

His brow furrowed as he nodded. "Well, alright then. You sure everything's alright?"

Nolan considered walking into the oncoming traffic. "Certainly. Why do you ask?"

"You're gonna break your phone, man," Reid said, and pointed to the tight—too tight—grasp he had on the device.

Nolan loosened his grip and winced at the stiffness of his fingers. "Right. Yes, well, I meant to do that. Don't wanna drop it," he muttered, and tapped the damn screen back to life.

Reid crossed his arms again. "What, your date stand you up?"

Nolan saw not why it was any of his business, but his eyes were twinkling and Nolan couldn't find it in him to tell him to fuck off. However, the longer he stood there making small talk, the more of a chance Nolan had to spill the whole unfortunate incident at his feet.

"Something like that. I'm just going to order a car for the ride home," he informed him, staring down at the glaring light of his phone. He didn't want the poor guy to think Nolan was ignoring him. He did seem rather kind, after all. No reason to be an asshole.

"What? Why? I could just give you a lift," Reid said, tossing a thumb over his shoulder.

Nolan lifted only his gaze. "Never. I couldn't ask that of you."

"You didn't ask. I offered."

Indeed, he had. And why?

In his tight black pants and the layering situation with the coral-colored shirt and faded graphic tee beneath, this man was leagues above some posh snob. He *oozed* coolness, or whatever the kids were calling it these days.

Though no matter how old or young the man may actually be, he did appear closer in age to Nolan than he'd first assumed.

And he couldn't very well argue with his logic, could he?

"You already tipped me more than enough. It would be no big deal to drop you back off."

Ah, so that's what it was about.

"Don't worry about that. Really, its nothing—"

Reid laid a hand on his shoulder, shaking him just a little and freezing Nolan into silence. "You tipped more than enough to cover another ride. Let me take you back to your fucking hotel."

Nolan's lips twitched at the man's vehemence, and he nodded, still reeling from the familiar touch. "Well, alright then. If you insist."

Reid squeezed once, a *well-done*, before releasing him altogether. "You're sure you don't wanna look around, get something? There's some pretty great spots around here."

Nolan glanced around at the multiple signs and the passing crowd. "Ah, no, thank you. I wouldn't even know where to start, anyhow."

"Let me ask again," Reid said, voice firmer, and held up a hand to garner Nolan's attention. As if he'd been unable to do anything but match the precise kind of chocolate truffle to the darkness of Reid's eyes for the past several minutes.

Maybe that dark chocolate rose truffle from that one place in… oh, what was the city?

Nolan tilted his head forward to show he was listening. Kind of.

"Do you *want* something to eat?" The forceful way he asked made something warm unfurl low in Nolan's gut, and it had nothing to do with wanting *food*.

Though he hadn't eaten since before the flight that morning, so really, something to eat would be lovely, and he guiltily told Reid as such.

He startled as Reid clapped his hands together. "Great. Well, lucky for you, I'm from here, so I know all the good secret places that don't require a reservation six months in advance," he drawled, rolling his eyes in the direction of the exact restaurant Nolan was going to walk into ten minutes ago.

"I see," Nolan said coherently. "Where to, then, my unofficial guide?"

He tripped over referring to Reid as *his* anything, but covered the blunder by sliding his phone back in his pocket.

Reid leaned in close, and Nolan was overcome by the earthy, spiced scent of him.

"Do you like pizza? And I mean the greasy, *dripping* with cheese kind of pizza?"

Nolan's cheeks went warm again, and he couldn't exactly blame it on the heat of the summer evening any longer.

"I think I could be persuaded," he murmured.

"Good," Reid purred—was that a griffin thing?—and grabbed Nolan's hand before pulling him through the crowd. Away from the crowd. To a slightly quieter street, and then kept leading him.

String lights and ivory pillars disappeared in favor of cracked sidewalks and small businesses. The scent of grease and salted food filled the air, and Nolan breathed it in.

He was still dazed by Reid's casual hand holding, when Reid finally released him to pull open a glass door beneath a sign proclaiming Crustworthy's was home to the *Best Pizza EVER.*

"That's quite a title," Nolan mused, and stepped inside the building.

"They live up to it, promise. I wouldn't bring you somewhere mediocre, would I?"

Nolan eyed his temporary companion, his black boots

with the yellow thread, and—yeah, that was an earring that glimmered in the terrible lighting.

Mediocre was the last word that came to mind when Nolan looked at Reid.

BITE TO SAVOR

This guy was insane…ly hot. Emphasis on *insane*.

Who let some stranger drag them around the city? Reid could be a serial killer or something. He wasn't, but how could Nolan know that?

Drag him along Reid had, and now he was watching Nolan devour a slice of pizza from his favorite place.

Nolan moaned *again* as he took a bite, the cheese threatening to slide right off the huge triangle and onto his paper plate.

Reid had been a little hesitant to bring someone like Nolan, in his fancy little matching pants and suit jacket and shiny watch, to his favorite place… and yet.

And yet not even the harsh fluorescent lights and scratched metal top of the counter could diminish this guy's appeal. He had seemed a little alarmed when the cook had slid two paper plates across the counter.

In the moment, he'd glanced to Reid for… well, Reid wasn't sure, really. Approval? Doubt? But it'd made his heart do a little flip in his chest all the same.

"I take it you like the place, then?" he asked, amusement twitching his lips as he adjusted in his seat. They had found a bench not even a block away, and Reid's cheeks kept turning red every time Nolan groaned when he took a bite.

The man was shameless. He looked like a weirdo, moaning around his pizza no matter who was walking by and shooting them odd looks.

Nolan leveled him with a dry look, jaw working before he swallowed. "You were right. And the sign. It's quite literally the best pizza I've ever had in my entire life. I could... I could marry this!"

Too bad it won't be here for much longer, Reid almost said, but didn't want to spoil the mood.

He snorted. "Might wanna try taking it on a date first. You skipped a few steps."

Nolan's lips twitched, and Reid wanted to give himself a pat on the back for drawing amusement from him. "You're quite right, wouldn't want to rush things," he mused.

"Oh no," Nolan suddenly said, and dropped his pizza to the plate.

Reid arched a brow, watching curiously as Nolan grabbed one of the ten thousand napkins he'd required before leaving the shop.

"See? I knew these would come in handy," he said, dabbing at his palm. "I'm going to ruin this shirt, and honestly, I can't be fucked to care," he muttered.

Reid didn't know why the curse surprised him, but it felt out of place from Nolan's lips.

Nolan shrugged off his jacket, and Reid gulped as he revealed the broad expanse of his shoulders, somehow hidden beneath that one layer. Then he did the unthinkable, and began rolling the crisp white shirt sleeves up.

Dear god, Reid began, swallowing sharply. *It's me. I don't ask for much.*

Nolan's actions proved he actually *could* be fucked to care about his probably expensive shirt, but he still picked up his pizza once his sleeves were rolled appropriately, and back to moaning he went.

Reid sent a few more prayers north, and finished off his own slice.

After folding his paper plate down, he leaned back in the bench and stretched his legs out, crossing them at the ankle and watching Nolan.

"What is it?" Nolan asked, glancing down at his shirt as if he expected a stain.

"What happened at the restaurant?" Reid finally asked, prepared for the way Nolan suddenly stiffened, as if just recalling whatever had happened was enough to set him on edge. "Can't imagine anyone standing you up," he continued.

Sure, it was a little bold, but it was true, so fuck it.

Nolan finished his pizza before he answered, and picked up another napkin. "Nothing so scandalous as that, I assure you," he admitted, dabbing at the grease covering his hand. "I'm here for work, and the group I was supposed to meet for dinner canceled via a text message."

"Oh, that—"

"But they were already seated inside. I saw them."

Oh.

Fuck, that was just *mean.*

"Sounds like a bunch of assholes, if you ask me," Reid grumbled, with half a mind to return to the restaurant himself.

"Oh, they most certainly are. Not news to me," he said, and folded his plate in the same way Reid had. "Probably wouldn't smart quite so much if my own father wasn't with them."

Reid schooled his expression, kept his eyes from widening. The guy's own *dad* ditched him? Fuuuck.

"That's really fucking shitty," Reid finally said, eloquent as ever.

But it made Nolan's lips curl, so he counted it as a victory. "Yes. Really fucking shitty," he echoed.

Reid pulled his legs back into the bench, and stood up with a clap, the paper plate muffling the sound. "Since I introduced you to the best pizza *ever*, do you trust me yet?"

Nolan, the little shit, tilted his hand back and forth. "Jury's still out on that one."

He scoffed, and grabbed Nolan's trash to dunk it in the bin nearby. "Well, how do you feel about ice cream?"

When he spun back around, he almost wheeled right into Nolan, and had to steady himself.

"Please, don't... don't pity hang out with me, or something. That's worse than going back to the hotel alone."

Crossing his arms, Reid tilted his chin up before saying, "Who said I pitied you? Maybe I pity them."

Nolan rolled his eyes, but they eventually trailed back to him, a question glimmering in their depths. "And why's that?"

"I don't know, man, you seem pretty cool to me."

Nolan snorted.

"Okay, so like, maybe you don't know how to work your phone, which is— are you, like, seventy-five or something?"

"Seventy-six, actually," Nolan interjected with a soft smile.

Reid kind of wanted to taste it.

"Wow. I have to say you look great for your age," he drawled.

Did Nolan just blush? Why did that make Reid's chest tight? Who *was* this man?

"It's a family secret. I'd tell you, but..."

"You'd have to kill me?"

Nolan nodded solemnly. "At the very least."

"Well, I'd like to avoid that, so fine. Keep your secrets."

The moment hung there, suspended between them in

silence, and they might have been standing by a trash can, with noisy cars passing by and dawdling strangers giving them a wide berth as they stared at each other, but Reid couldn't find it in him to care. He finally spoke. "So, ice cream?"

Nolan studied him, probably searching for that pity he'd expected. But empathizing with someone's shitty situation and wanting to make their night better was different than pity, yeah?

Whatever Nolan found in Reid's gaze was enough for him, and he finally nodded.

Reid didn't even realize he was holding his breath until Nolan said, "Yes. Alright, let's get ice cream."

He *just* stopped himself from bringing his fist down in a *fuck yeah*, but *couldn't* stop himself from grabbing Nolan's hand again, if only to watch his cheeks flush and his gaze drop to where they touched.

Then he dragged him down the street, back toward the pizza place, and past it, around the block.

"How long have you been here?" Nolan asked, waving his unoccupied hand around them. "You sure know your way around," he continued as Reid tugged them down the sidewalk.

"My whole life, since before the Big Reveal," he said.

"And have you always been a rideshare, uhm, taxi?"

Reid chuckled at the title. "What is this, a job interview?"

At Nolan's sputtering, he chuckled and gave his hand a squeeze. "Relax, I'm teasing."

It was probably weird to be holding this guy's hand, right? But he didn't want to let go, and likewise, Nolan wasn't trying to release his hand either.

So he didn't.

And he zigzagged them around a few pedestrians, until the faded pink sign of a local ice cream shop called Chippy's came into view, and he grinned, sharing his excitement with Nolan.

What must this fancy schmancy guy think of Reid bringing him to all these rundown places?

Their hands finally did part as Reid reached forward to hold the door open for him.

Nolan *smirked.* "Why thank you, kind sir."

"After you, sir," Reid retorted, and his dick absolutely showed interest in the way the word made Nolan's cheeks go red.

"Everything is made in house, even the cookie pieces you can mix in," he explained, and motioned to the case full of chilled metal containers, and the plastic bins holding all the toppings. On top of the case, the different bowl sizes and cones were lined up.

"There's so many choices – how the hell do you decide?" Nolan asked, eyes wide as he took it all in. Very much like a kid in an ice cream shop and not a refined businessman in a suit.

"I have my go-to's. But it's fun to try something new," he teased, nudging his shoulder into the back of Nolan's.

Nolan shot a grin over his shoulder, and Reid wondered if needing three to five business days to recover from his smile was too much.

Nolan's gaze dragged greedily over the chocolate dipped waffle cone and all the toppings. Reid pointed out all the flavors, and called his favorites off by heart.

So when they finally reached the counter, only for Nolan to order a plain vanilla scoop on a sugar cone… Reid was surprised. Slightly disappointed.

But he didn't let that hold him back. He asked for his favorite combination on a waffle cone, and shot a wink in Nolan's direction.

Before Nolan could assault the napkin station, Reid

grabbed a handful as they waited for their cones. The hum of the air conditioner was loud, the shop was small, a little dingy, and Reid felt perfectly at home there.

His double-stacked cone was cold to the touch as he accepted it from the employee, and Nolan gathered his with two fingers daintily curling around the paper wrapper.

Reid held the door open for him and groaned as the humid air poured through the door.

Nolan's jacket was tossed over one arm, and they stalled out on the sidewalk. "Where to now?"

"We're not too far from the park. Wanna take a walk?"

"Sounds lovely," Nolan agreed, and motioned with the hand holding the jacket for him to lead the way.

Reid pointed ahead and walked alongside Nolan as the cars passed, splashing them with light and casting their shadows along the concrete, side by side.

"So I have to ask. Bubblegum *and* chocolate?" Nolan asked, and Reid could hear the doubt in his voice.

"Hey, don't knock it til you try it, Mr. Vanilla. Who gets vanilla?" Reid teased.

Nolan lifted his hands in innocence. "There was too much to choose from – vanilla is easy."

Rolling his eyes, Reid scoffed. "Everyone knows what vanilla tastes like. You could've picked the ribbon one, with the caramel and dark chocolate mixed in. The best of all three worlds."

"I could have. But what if I didn't like it?"

"Trust me, you can't go wrong with anything in there."

"Fine, fine. Next time, maybe," Nolan acquiesced.

Next time? Reid's heart did a little flip at the idea of it.

Next time.

The iron gates of the park entrance came into view, and *this* area did have the twinkle lights and fancy lamp posts reminiscent of the hoity-toity district he'd flown Nolan to.

"This is one of the nicer parks in the area," he explained. "Perfect for eating ice cream on a gross summer night."

"Oh, it's not that bad," Nolan said. Except his sleeves were still rolled up, and he kept shuffling the suit jacket from arm to arm when it got too hot against his skin.

"Maybe after, we can find somewhere with air conditioning," Reid suggested haltingly. As if he expected Nolan to end their night, to decide he'd spent enough time with the lowbrow griffin taking him to shops that had seen better years, maybe even decades.

But the smile Nolan sent him was the complete opposite, as if he was... excited about the prospect of spending more time together.

Reid refrained from narrowing his eyes. Could this be a...?

Surely not.

He'd know if it was a date.

No. Nope, this was just two strangers, casually spending the evening together, getting pizza and ice cream and... sitting under the romantic string lights of the park.

Reid studied Nolan for a moment. *Was* this a date?

No. They'd just met, barely knew each other. So what if they were doing date activities? Didn't necessarily mean it was a date. They were just strangers turned friends. Yeah.

And for all Reid knew, Nolan could be straight.

Did straight just-friends hold hands for blocks at a time?

Oh, give it a rest.

Reid had been burned by his fair share of straight guys, and knew better than to read too much into any kind of interaction. But how couldn't he?

"So, you like plain cheese pizza and vanilla ice cream. What other daring things am I gonna learn about you tonight?" Reid asked, unable to bear the silence and his thoughts any longer.

Nolan chuckled, and—

Reid's brain white-screened as a dollop of melted ice cream landed on the back of Nolan's hand. He didn't even pause as he tilted his hand slightly and licked it off, tongue extending to let the creamy drop stain it before he swallowed, throat working as his hand returned to the upright position.

Jesus fucking christ.

"There's not much that's interesting about me," Nolan began.

Reid highly doubted that.

"Just a business guy stuck in a career he never picked and hates, but is chicken to do anything about it."

"See, that *is* interesting, believe it or not." Reid wanted to ask Nolan more, but something in his expression made him choke it back.

"I don't want to talk about work. I want to think about anything *but* work, actually. Tell me about yourself."

"Where do you want me to start?" Reid asked, strangely happy to indulge in whatever Nolan wanted.

"From the beginning?" he asked.

Reid winced. "Oof. Well. It's going to sound a little strange, but my upbringing *was* probably different than what you grew up around. What with being a griffin and all."

Nolan's eyebrows arched in interest, gaze intent to show he was listening. Unfortunately he was still making sweet, tender love to the fucking ice cream cone, and Reid had to remind himself what the hell he was talking about.

"We had to hide what we were, obviously, because this was all before the Big Reveal. And being a kid makes that a little harder, y'know, to control the shift and everything. So I was homeschooled for a while. Like I said, born and raised here. Dad was shit. Mom was awesome." He grimaced and chewed on the bubblegum piece that was too hard to be safe, but still a sweet treat all the same. "That ice cream place is actually where we used to go when I was little. Bubblegum was my favorite, and my mom always said I was going to crack a tooth one day." He winked. "Haven't yet."

"Was the Big Reveal a relief for you, then?" Nolan asked, lowering his ice cream cone.

"Yeah, kinda. I was used to hiding my griffin by that point, but it is nice to see everyone be more open about it. Like, that pizza place? The ice cream shop? All run by Others."

"Always thought that was kind of a stupid name. Rather exclusive."

Reid frowned. "Yeah. The media ran with it and it stuck. But whatever. Better than, like, freaks or weirdos."

"Oh, I hope no one ever called you that," Nolan said with an angry twitch to his brow. "That's not nice."

Reid laughed and tried not to let the bitterness seep in. "Newsflash, man, the world isn't all that nice to Others. Though it's getting better, bit by bit."

"How so?"

"Well, like the app. So." He scrubbed a hand over his thigh, suddenly nervous. "Even though it's a service position, it's integrating us into society. The insurance was stupidly complicated, but we finally figured out the fine print and now it's, like, a normal thing."

"Normal?" Nolan teased. "I'm pretty sure our picture is floating around on the internet somewhere. The crowd seemed rather scandalized."

"Hey, any publicity is good publicity."

"I'm… not sure that's true," Nolan argued.

"Aw, come on. You just gotta spin it right." Holding up his hands, ice cream cone included, he framed the shape of a square. "*Inventive new travel medium spotted in the city.*"

Nolan chuckled, and copied the square with his own hands. *"Idiot falls off griffin to his death."*

Reid gasped. "I would never let one of my patrons fall. But that *is* what the majority of the fine print is for," he grumbled. "Accepting the ride makes you liable for any injuries, et cetera."

"The ladder trick with the saddle was pretty nifty, though!" Nolan suddenly said, as if to make Reid feel better.

"Seemed like you needed the help," Reid teased, if only to watch his cheeks flush.

They went rosy pink, and it was like a reward all for him.

Silence settled again, and it dawned on Reid that getting ice cream had been a terrible idea.

They had to be quick, because the humid air was melting it faster than they could eat. Which meant Nolan was going at his ice cream with a fervor, licking around the edges to keep it from melting down the cone and onto his hand. Then, of course, he'd have to even it out by licking a circle around the top.

By the time Reid reached the chocolate part of his ice cream, he was trying not to get a fucking hard-on in the middle of the park with this hot, oblivious business guy sitting next to him.

This was going to be a *very* long night.

And part of him didn't mind at all.

BANANA SHARK

Ice cream had been a terrible idea, in hindsight.

It was impossible to eat politely, and if Nolan looked anything like Reid did, trying to catch the melted drops before they could meet his skin, it was downright indecent.

But he tried not to focus on that. Instead, he eyed the string lights and avoided the gazes of passersby who might glance twice at two grown men eating ice cream cones.

The wafer cone crunched and crackled between his teeth and for a brief moment, it was a flashback to his childhood.

Then finally, blissfully, he was done with his ice cream, and balled up a napkin to dab at a sticky bit on the back of his hand.

Against all odds, with *two* scoops of the strangest combination to work through, Reid was right behind him, and they chuckled at the loud crunch of his waffle cone.

Nolan checked the time on his watch and deemed it late, but not late enough that he was willing to sacrifice more time with his new…

Well, referring to Reid as a *friend* after only a few hours together seemed presumptuous, but *acquaintance* inspired a distant quality that didn't ring true, either.

"You've got something… there," he said, waving a hand in

the general direction of Reid's face. Reid mimicked his hand with the napkin and tried to swipe at the spot. "No, on your nose, to the right—"

"Here, you do it," Reid interjected and handed him the napkin.

Their fingers brushed as he passed the napkin, and even though Nolan had straight-up held Reid's hand not a half hour ago, it made something in him flutter with excitement.

He brushed at the smudge of chocolate on Reid's hooked nose, and slowly warmed beneath his gaze.

"There you go," he murmured, and scrunched the napkin up.

"Thanks," Reid responded, gaze heavy and alight with something Nolan was certain meant he wasn't ready for this night to end, either. "So. Dinner, dessert. Drinks?"

Nolan failed to keep his smile to himself. "I assume you have a place in mind?"

"Do I ever. Do you like games?"

Please, not sports. "What kind of games?"

Reid stood and offered Nolan his hand, and by god if his cheeks didn't flush *again* at just the thought of the casual contact.

He laid his palm in Reid's and was pulled from the bench in one swift move, and then Reid was leading him through the park, beneath the twinkle lights. They shone gold against his skin, and Nolan let himself stare as it reflected off his burnished blond hair and copper beard.

The man was attractive, yes. But continuing the evening had nothing to do with the small—tiny, even—crush that was developing.

Averting his gaze to the archway of the park, he let Reid pull him through the streets, who seemed uncaring and clearly unaffected by the simple action of holding his hand.

Maybe this was something friends did? There was no

reason for Nolan to look so far into it. This was just a chance meeting of strangers who were having a decent night out on the town.

Shamelessly, Nolan realized he much preferred his time spent this way than at some long, suffering dinner where his father complained about the perfectly decent service and snubbed his nose at the delicious food, telling stories of other places he'd been and had *better*, only to impress the "lesser" men at the table whose approval he sought.

No, Nolan didn't feel a certain type of way about that group of men. Not at all.

"I can hear you thinking. What's up?" Reid asked.

Coming back to the present, Nolan glanced at his new companion and winced. "Just thinking… I've had much more fun so far than I ever would have had at dinner."

The crinkles around Reid's eyes softened, and inexplicably, a pang took root in Nolan's chest. "Glad to hear it, man." He paired the softly uttered words with a squeeze of his hand, and Nolan wondered if he'd ever be able to take a full breath again.

Before he knew it, they'd come to a stop outside of a building that had probably seen better days—he was sensing a theme.

"This might not be as fancy as your usual joint," Reid rushed to explain, pulling open the door.

Cool air rushed over them as the air conditioning pumped full blast. A low-lit din awaited them, the ring and clatter of arcade games, glasses meeting tables, murmurs of excitement.

"Shush, I'm sure I'll love it like I have every other place you've taken me to tonight," Nolan said, raising his voice a bit to be heard over the noise.

If Reid blushed, Nolan couldn't quite tell because of the low lighting. It was warm inside, not in temperature, but in the way that the lighting was gold and everything was made of wood in some way, shape, or form.

Tacky beer signs littered the tinted windows and lined the wall behind the bar, which is the first place Reid directed them to.

"What'll you have?"

Nolan tried not to mourn his touch when Reid finally released his hand to tap a beat into the bartop. Nolan wasn't quite sure that was sanitary, but refrained from saying so.

"Ah…" A wine menu seemed out of the question, but without any guidance, he was a little lost. "Any kind of whiskey will do," he said, clearing his throat and eyeing the bottles and shiny labels.

It was quite a few seconds before he realized Reid hadn't responded, and he turned to his left only to stop short at the stare he was leveled with.

"Cheese pizza. Vanilla ice cream. Basic whiskey."

Nolan felt nervous all of a sudden, and twisted his hands together. "Uh… yes?"

"What do you *really* want to drink? They'll make anything."

His lips parted, but in the end he floundered. "Uh…"

"This isn't some business meeting where you have to fit in," Reid reminded him.

Nolan let his eyes drift shut briefly. He was right. This was… Reid.

"Fine," he announced. "I'll have… a tequila sunrise. With three cherries."

Reid's eyes *sparkled* in the dim lighting, but not from laughter. At least, not laughter at Nolan's expense.

When the bartender drifted closer, Reid flagged them down with a flick of his wrist and bravely requested, "We'll have two tequila sunrises, please. Three cherries."

The bartender smirked, but offered no commentary other than "I'll have that right up."

"Oh, and can we get ten chips apiece?" he added, nudging Nolan's shoulder.

Nolan was confused until the bartender—Guy, by his name tag— reached under the bar and lifted a small, branded cup with little fake gold coins inside.

"These are for the games."

"Games?" Nolan asked, and glanced over his shoulder. He was met with glowing blue lights, an entirely different atmosphere than what surrounded them at the bar, and arcade machines he hadn't seen in *years.*

Pac-Man. Pinball machines. "Is that *Frogger?*" he asked, and pointed to the classic arcade game. A group of men were cheering as the little green frog hopped from traffic lane to lane, avoiding the pixelated cars on the screen.

"I take it that's where we're headed?" Reid asked.

Nolan nodded absently. He hadn't played that since he was a kid!

A clink of glasses caught his attention, and he turned back to watch Reid hand over his card, and slide a bright yellow and red concoction his way, three cherries and an orange slice topping the tall glasses.

Nolan's cheeks flushed as he accepted the drink, but he couldn't deny the little fissure of pleasure that bubbled in his chest. He took a sip from the black straw and smiled. "Now that's a drink," he admitted.

He lifted his gaze to find Reid staring at him, lips quirked in a little half-smile that sent his heart racing anew.

"What?"

Reid blinked, lifted his own drink, and sipped from the straw. "So you like the sweet ones," he mused.

"I... guess so."

While they waited for the crowd by the Frogger game to disperse, Reid motioned for him to follow.

"I'll have you know, I'm a legend around here," he said, voice dramatic and low and daring.

"A legend? At… air hockey?" he clarified, following Reid's lead and setting his colorful drink on a barstool he would not be using.

"Yes. Very serious business," Reid claimed.

"So what you're saying is, I should give up now?" Nolan wasn't going to give up. Where would—

"—be the fun in that, man?" Reid finished his thought aloud and a flare of excitement erupted in Nolan, uncontainable in the form of a smile.

Nolan gripped the pusher and reveled in the nostalgic, harsh clack of the plastic against the table.

"It really has been years since—"

Distantly, Nolan registered the clang of the puck against metal as it slid into his goal box.

The digital numbers on top of the post shifted in Reid's favor.

Glancing up, Nolan found a sly smile on Reid's lips as he stared at him in anticipation.

"So that's how it is," Nolan called over, chest splintering open and something bright spilling out.

Reid grinned, then paused for a quick second before he shrugged off one shoulder of his coral button-up.

Nolan slapped the puck on the table and tried not to stare as he pulled the sleeve off.

Maybe Reid was giving him the chance to make his point back. It had been a sneaky move, getting it in while Nolan wasn't paying attention.

Nolan slid the pusher across the table with a loud, resounding crack of plastic against the puck. Without missing a beat, sleeve halfway down his right arm, Reid blocked it, sending it ricocheting from side to side. *Then* he went on to slip the sleeve over his wrist and hand, seemingly unconcerned about being distracted.

But the puck was taking its sweet time to get down the table – how did he *do* that, hit it so it went both fast and slow at the same time?

Nolan bounced on his toes in anticipation, gaze flicking to Reid again and again after every clack of the puck. He reached forward, extending his arm to flick the pusher against the plastic, sending it skating across the table once again.

Reid had half his shirt hanging off the left side of his body, short sleeves of his worn band tee wrapping snugly around his biceps, and were those tattoos—

Clang.

Oh shit.

Nolan glanced down and watched the puck appear in the retrieval slot, and lifted his head to glare at Reid, who seemed to be fighting his own battles in the form of a smirk he hid behind a sip of his tropical drink.

"Gotta pay attention, y'know," Reid said.

"That was a little unfair, wouldn't you say?" Nolan cut sharply, and sent the puck reeling across the table.

"What was unfair?" he questioned, a knowing little grin on his face, their banter echoing the puck.

"You—" Undressing to distract me? Nolan couldn't very well admit that!

He let the thought dissipate and lined up what he thought was a perfect shot into Reid's goal box.

But Reid slid the pusher into the puck, blocking it just as it neared the goal and sent it reeling back toward him.

Concentration took focus as they went back and forth a few times.

"Can't keep this up forever, Nolan," Reid called out.

Nolan wasn't thinking when he said, "I don't know, my longevity might surprise you!"

Nolan's puck clanged into the goal box, and he laughed with delight as the score changed to tie them. When he glanced across the table to his opponent, Reid seemed to shake himself, *blushing* as he retrieved the puck.

Gosh, it felt nice to be the cause of those pink cheeks, even if unintentionally.

When he replayed his words in his head, he realized it did sound rather suggestive, but chose to move on before he made the moment any more awkward.

"Oh, you're in trouble now," Reid promised, and before Nolan could move his pusher to block, he sunk the puck without pause.

When Nolan glanced over at Reid, he was met with a smug, sly curl of lips, and the promise of more to come.

"It appears so," he murmured, and began their next round.

Reid sunk another, and then another, and Nolan laughed hopelessly. He didn't even care that he was losing, because Reid positively glowed with delight whenever he scored a point.

So maybe it felt a little like he was winning anyway, even if the difference in their scores kept rising.

Nolan scored a point, and then Reid scored two more, securing the win with an excited fist pump. Grinning, Nolan picked up his drink as Reid joined him on his side of the table, and then they took the empty places left at the Frogger station.

The old school graphics were *just* the right touch of nostalgia he didn't know he'd needed.

He didn't get very far the first time, and Reid chuckled beside him.

"To be fair, I forgot you could move left and right," Nolan admitted, laughing with him.

Reacquainting himself with the buttons and the movements of the console took a moment, but by the time his third game queued up, he was more confident.

"You've got this one," Reid encouraged.

They drank and they laughed – god, Nolan hadn't laughed this much in forever – and Nolan got his frog across the street, then across the pixelated river. They cheered, and they hogged the Frogger game, but they didn't care.

At one point, Reid retrieved them more drinks, and they moved on to play some of the other games.

Nolan was shit at Skee-Ball, and Reid was the first to let him know. He laughed so hard his side hurt, and once they were done with their second drinks, they'd made it through their tokens. They traded their tickets for drink tokens and two Twizzlers, then redeemed their drinks at the bar and sat, watching the rest of the patrons groan and shout over the games.

Reid bit into his Twizzler and winced.

"Stale?" Nolan guessed.

"*So* stale," he groaned, and sat the rest of it, wrapping still intact, beside his drink on the bar.

Nolan lifted his and watched the light reflect off the plastic. "I might keep mine. Frame it. That was an impressive game of Frogger. I think that's where I won the most tickets."

"You got to put your initials on the scoreboard, of course it was impressive," Reid said, and clapped him on the shoulder.

"And to show for it… this Twizzler," Nolan announced, and held it up balanced over both his palms.

"A twenty-dollar Twizzler, right there."

Nolan's lips twitched. "Well, when you put it that way…"

"The prizes are never as fun as earning the tickets, anyway," Reid said, and sipped his drink.

"I don't know," Nolan disagreed and eyed the prize counter. "That banana shark was pretty cool."

"Banana shark is the coolest," Reid agreed. "Who even comes up with that?"

"Well, pear bear just didn't have the same ring to it," Nolan retorted.

Reid's smile was impossibly dazzling. "Watermelon armadillo?"

Oh, Nolan liked this game. Mostly, he liked Reid's smile as they played. "Pomegranate jellyfish."

Reid slapped the bartop, then pointed at him. "See? There's untapped potential here. We could make a whole ecosystem of fruit-animal hybrid…plushes."

"Who's to say it doesn't already exist?"

He scoffed, lifting his drink. "Ours are better."

"Why's that?" The words came on instinct, because Nolan was too busy staring shamelessly as Reid's lips curled around the edge of the glass, chasing a cherry as it neared the rim. With a shake of the glass, it tumbled into his mouth, and Nolan blinked himself out of the trance as Reid said, "'Cause they're ours, duh."

Nolan nodded vehemently. "Right, right, of course. I knew that."

"Everything's better at the Fruit-Animal Hybrid Ecosystem."

Nolan chuckled, absentmindedly stirring the last of his drink. "Is that the official name?"

"Yep. Already got the patent for it. Trademark pending, all that." He waved his hand in a very official manner, and Nolan was so besotted he couldn't breathe.

"I hope production starts soon, I've heard there's a high demand." He wasn't imagining it, right? The connection. The effortless way they matched the other's energy.

Nolan really couldn't have another drink. The conference was in the morning—*nine sharp*— and if he showed up late or, god forbid, *hungover*, he'd never live it down.

Reid bumped his hip into Nolan as they chuckled and finished their drinks, sharing a smile.

Unbidden, Nolan's gaze dipped to Reid's lips, reddened and shining from the cold, brightly-colored drinks.

He could've sworn it had only been a split second, but when he returned his attention where it belonged, Reid's warm, brown eyes were glittering.

"Ready to move on?" Reid asked, voice low and soft.

Never. "Yeah, suppose it's time."

It took until they left the bar for Nolan to realize he was right. It couldn't be one-sided.

If it was one-sided, would Reid trip over the lip of the door, stumble into Nolan, and wrap an arm around his waist to balance himself, only to leave the arm there as he corralled him down the street? Nolan froze, frantic in his desire *not* to mess this up.

What would someone who knew exactly what kind of situation this was do now?

And he did that, threading the fingers of his right hand through Reid's where they rested on his hip. Nolan couldn't look at Reid, but he didn't *not* look at Reid, either, and saw the ghost of a smile tug at his lips.

This is happening, right?

Reid wouldn't have dedicated his entire night to showing Nolan all his favorite places—places from his childhood, places that had meaning to him—if he didn't enjoy Nolan's company.

Reid slowed their pace before pausing in front of a restaurant and bar, string lights glowing warm in the windows, and waiters rushing to and fro as patrons laughed.

"What's this?" Nolan asked, glancing up at the sign. Essie's Place. It seemed familiar, but he couldn't imagine why.

"This is my place," Reid announced.

Nolan's eyes widened. "This is your restaurant?"

"Yep. For now." There was something sad in his eyes suddenly, but it disappeared with a blink. "She's all mine."

"Well, why didn't you bring us here for dinner, then?" Nolan asked, curious and strangely proud of Reid. He couldn't see much of the decor or the layout from the street, but inside, everyone seemed happy and content, the waiters smiling as they passed each other.

"I don't like them to feel like I'm keeping an eye on them. When I'm off, I try to stay away."

"That's sweet of you," Nolan mused.

"That's how I got the idea for the whole ridesharing thing, y'know? I've taken home plenty of drunks with no other options before."

"Clever. And good on you, watching out for them." It was Reid's day off, yet he'd been shuffling strangers around the city on his back.

"Hmm. C'mere," Reid said suddenly, and pulled Nolan into an alley.

"What— oh!" Reid shivered and Nolan blinked at the wings perched on his back, gold like his lion form and mahogany-tipped. He was human in every other way. "I – is that safe?" he asked. Nolan didn't know he could just... change parts of himself!

With a scoff, Reid rolled his eyes and grabbed Nolan's hand, pulling him closer. "Of course it is. Come on, man. You think I'd let you get hurt?"

Impossibly, after only a few hours, Nolan knew Reid wouldn't.

Nolan tried to remember to *breathe*. Especially this close

to Reid, practically sharing the same breath. Especially when everything he'd tried not to let himself want clearly wanted him back.

Especially when Reid wrapped his arms around him and murmured, "Hold on tight."

CRISES

Reid concentrated on the motion of his wings, the flex of his muscles as they moved through the air. *Definitely* not on the way Nolan's arms held him around the waist, how his knee slotted between Reid's own, how their chests pressed together as they breathed the same air.

"Oh, god," Nolan muttered, panic flashing across his face before he slammed his eyes closed.

A chuckle rumbled through Reid's chest as he took them higher, directed them above the traffic lights and between buildings, and then up, up, up. His feet touched down to the concrete of a roof, and Nolan stayed frozen, wrapped around him.

His lips twitched. "Nolan, we're here," he murmured.

Nolan opened one eye, glanced around, and slowly slid his arms from around Reid, stepping back and clearing his throat.

His awkwardness was so damned endearing, and Reid tried to curb his own. "You said you're afraid of heights, so this might not be the best place to take you, but—"

"Oh my god, the view!" Nolan whispered vehemently, rushing over to the edge, yet stopping several feet back from the railing to gaze out over the city.

"Oh, good. You like it?" Reid asked, not above a little fishing if the weather was right.

"This is amazing," he breathed, glancing over his shoulder. When he lifted his hand and motioned Reid over, he went without pause.

The back of their hands bumped. *Fuck it.*

Reid threaded their fingers together, heart oddly leaping in his chest. *Chill out,* he tried to tell himself, but the relief when Nolan didn't pull away made his knees weak. Nolan hadn't shied away from him all night, and this moment was no different.

Nothing like some PG hand-holding to get his heart racing, hm?

"Welcome to the city," Reid said, squeezing tight.

Out of his peripherals, Nolan tilted his head to look at him, but when Reid turned to meet his gaze, he snapped his head around and turned back to the view.

The city lights stretched before them, glittering sprinkles of light sifted over the ground. From their height, they could barely make out the people scattered below, or the cars lining the streets and honking and following the motions.

"Isn't it weird?" Reid asked.

"What?"

"How each of those people down there have their own lives. They have jobs and families and concerns and worries. Sometimes it's just…"

"Hard to imagine?" Nolan finished, with a lilt to his tone.

"Exactly. There's no way all those people down there have their own crises and complicated situations."

"But they do, don't they?" Nolan asked, tilting his head.

"Yeah. Probably."

Reid shifted his attention from the lights and people below to the man beside him. Dark hair, clean jaw, a nose that he wanted to bite. Perfectly coiffed hair that his fingers itched to mess up.

"What about you?" he asked, and waited for Nolan to look at him. "Any crises?"

Nolan's lips twitched, but it wasn't humor that sparkled in his gaze like earlier. "My whole life is a crisis," he said, and then winced. "No, that's... That sounds dramatic. There's people out there who don't know where they're sleeping tonight. I'm just stuck in a job I hate."

"Hey," Reid said, frowning, and nudged his arm into Nolan's side. "Everyone has different struggles."

Nolan smiled, though the lines were tight. "It's okay, you don't have to make me feel better."

"Why do you hate it so much?" he asked, and pulled Nolan over to the lounge chairs.

"Oh, this is lovely," Nolan remarked as he sat. Above them, string lights zigzagged over the lattice privacy fence, cocooning them in their own little world.

"This building belongs to some company, but they're never here at night, only during the day. Don't even know why they hung these lights if no one's here to enjoy them."

"Well, *we're* here to enjoy them. Thank you," Nolan said, his gaze suddenly heavy, and Reid's heart was in his throat as he swallowed back the urge to lean forward and kiss him.

Did Nolan's eyes just drop to Reid's lips? He didn't have time to decide before Nolan glanced down at his lap and spoke. "Why do I hate my job? Where do I start? I sit in an office all day. Not even a nice one. What I do doesn't mean anything. I'm just a paper pusher, or worse, for show. I'm there to make my father look good, and in his eyes, I still manage to fuck that up."

"Dads are dicks," Reid declared.

"Dads *are* dicks," Nolan answered. "Sometimes I wish I could just... say *fuck it*, and walk out. He doesn't need me. I don't really need him." His brows lifted, surprise sparking in his expression.

"You used to, though?"

"Yeah… yeah, I did." He frowned. "Well, isn't that something."

Reid wished he could read his mind better than he could read his expressions. "What's wrong?"

"My dad owns the company I work at, obviously. But I'm not… he doesn't… I don't get any favor, is what I'm trying to say. I'm just another schmuck who works there."

"This seems… revolutionary to you. Why?"

Nolan turned in his seat and faced Reid, the lines around his eyes tense. "At the risk of sounding like an awful, spoiled rich kid, I've been under his thumb my whole life. Everything has been mapped out from the moment I was born, and at first it all seemed designed to get me as far away from him as possible. I'm talking… pre-k, nannies, boarding school, college in another state. He spent my whole life trying to keep me as far from him as possible, and yet…" He frowned, and Reid hung on every word, only stared at his lips, like, twice. "When I graduated, it was understood that I would just slot into his little office like I'd always belonged there. But I was doing shit work, getting coffee and running errands like an intern for some rich guy I didn't even know."

"Did you ever have a rebellious phase?" Everyone had a phase. Reid's had been smoking weed at the park with his high school friends, thinking he was tough. Mom had not been very happy about it, and Reid was definitely *not* tough when it came to his mom.

Nolan dug the palms of his hand into his eyes, and Reid resisted the urge to comfort him. "My rebellious phase was just finally coming out to him. I'd hoped maybe it would be the last straw, that he'd throw me out or cut me off or something." He dropped his hands with a groan, shoulders slumping, oblivious to the way Reid was suddenly frozen. "Because at least then I would've been free. Instead, I've spent the last several years stuck by his side. I'm like a... like a polished little trophy he shows off, to try and prove that he's not a homophobic, bigoted asshole, so he can keep his shareholders and hold people's interests and make the business look good."

Coming out. Reid's breath hitched, and he disguised it by clearing his throat. "Well, shit," Reid murmured, chest swelling in sympathy. The dad stuff? Terrible. Having his own shit dad, Reid knew how hard it was to move on, to function with the weight of those expectations on your shoulders. That really sucked.

But at the same time, he wasn't just going to *ignore* the fact that Nolan clearly wasn't straight. Thank god, because it would've been awkward as fuck if he'd tried to kiss a straight guy.

Because what Nolan had just admitted meant... *I have a chance.*

Focus, Reid. Be normal.

Reid tried to remember what his face looked like *normally*, and gave Nolan his full attention.

Nolan seemed oblivious to Reid's silent panic as he continued. "You know, I've... being in his shadow, doing what I've been told, has afforded me luxuries I enjoy. Like the hotel we're at. Like the place we were going for dinner. But I've had more fun with you tonight, pizza and ice cream and that arcade and now... this," he said, waving a hand at the lights. Reid was hopelessly staring, studying the soft, twinkling glow over his features when Nolan finally glanced at him. "When I say *thank you*, I mean it. I wouldn't trade tonight for all the stupid, snobby, expensive dinners in the world. I just wonder, could it have been like this my whole life, if I wasn't on his leash?"

"Like what?" Reid asked, heart in his throat.

"Fun!" Nolan blurted, laughing bitterly. "Exciting and fun and random." His gaze snapped to Reid, who almost startled at the intensity in his eyes. "Lovely, like I said."

Fuck, I hope not, Reid thought. It's selfish, it's awful, it's shitty, but Reid wanted to be the only one who made Nolan sparkle like this.

"Maybe. With the right people," Reid answered. "Not those dicks at the restaurant."

Nolan shuddered. "Definitely not."

"So listen, man," Reid said, diving in, no holds barred. "I'm not trying to tell you how to change your whole life. But if you want it to happen, you gotta start somewhere. I mean, did you expect to live your whole life miserable?"

Nolan paused. "Actually… yeah. I guess I did." He chuckled, but there wasn't any humor in it. "There's not really anywhere else I could imagine myself. God, that's depressing, isn't it?" He shook his head. "I'm so sorry, I dampened the whole night with my sob story."

"Hey, no, don't say that," Reid said, placing a hand on his knee. "I asked. It's okay, I mean, I *want* to hear about it, alright? Don't feel bad."

His lips twitched, and fuck, Reid wanted to kiss him.

"You want to hear about my sob story?" Nolan questioned.

Reid was dangerously close to sounding pathetic. "Maybe?" Reid shrugged. "I certainly don't mind learning more about you."

"Well, same here," Nolan said, his gaze practically sparkling. "So, how about you? Any crises you'd like to share?"

Was it hot? Nolan's attention was like a spotlight, and Reid decided, yes, it was actually so fucking hot. He wiped a hand over the back of his sweat-slicked neck, beneath the collar of his shirt.

He wanted to reciprocate, maybe tell Nolan a little about his own shitty dad. But instead he stumbled into the silence, trying to decide if Nolan was purposefully staring at his lips, or maybe—what if Reid had something on his face? Oh god.

Nolan was leaning across the space between their two lounge chairs, their knees brushing, hands smoothing over the top of his thighs.

Was he nervous too? Reid snapped his gaze over Nolan's, wondering if *now* was the time. Was it too forward?

"Yeah, okay," he began, and almost lost his nerve as Nolan's blue eyes slammed into his like a tidal wave. For a moment, Reid forgot how to breathe. "So, I met this guy," he choked out, and Nolan's eyes widened, fingers digging into his dress pants. "He tipped me more than any normal person would. Then we spent the evening together."

"Y-You said this was a crisis?" Nolan asked, worried.

Worried, Reid's mind supplied again, louder. That was a good sign, right?

"After all that, I'm trying to decide if it's too much to tell him… I don't want the evening to end." God, it was *hard* meeting Nolan's gaze, and he had to force himself not to look away. "So I took him to this really tall building, even though he's afraid of heights. But it's getting late, and he's here for work, so I've got to return the prince to his pumpkin by midnight, or something like that."

"Well," Nolan glanced at his watch, lips curling. "I think you missed that mark by a bit."

He's smiling. Smiling! "See? I fucked it all up," he said, shaking his head, *tsk*ing.

"I wouldn't say that," Nolan said, shifting closer on the lounger. Their thighs touched, knees slotting together. "I bet it's still salvageable."

Could Nolan hear Reid's heartbeat thundering in his ears like Reid did? "Hmm. I appreciate your opinion. Very insightful." Reid's gaze dropped to Nolan's lips, inches away, as he asked, "Do you think it'd be too forward to kiss him?"

Nolan's lips parted once, twice, before he choked the words out. "N-no, don't think so."

"Great."

Great? Jesus, fuck.

Reid leaned in, and Nolan followed his lead, but paused, making Reid come to him in the end.

The kiss was chaste, their lips meeting for a split second before he returned. They lingered this time, and it was still the most pure kiss Reid thought he'd ever felt.

It was warm and sticky and humid and Reid was suddenly thankful for his mustache, but Nolan sure as fuck didn't seem to mind as he tilted his head. Their lips met softly and Reid pushed in for more, and then he tasted the salty tease of Nolan's sweat on his lips and suddenly didn't care about his own anymore.

Their lips parted, and heat pooled in Reid's stomach at the first brush of Nolan's tongue against his. Nolan let loose a short little gasp, and Reid tasted it straight from the source, the warmth and want going straight to his head.

Before he knew it he was leaning up, pushing Nolan back onto the chaise lounge, and Nolan's hand was sliding up into his hair, nails raking across his scalp. A moan spilled out before he meant it to, but shit, he *loved* that.

Now Nolan knew it, too, and he threaded his other hand into Reid's hair, tugging lightly.

Fuck. Reid slid his knee further between Nolan's, finishing what the other man had started moments ago. They both groaned at the friction as Reid rolled his hips down.

It was sloppy and fast and wonderful and everything that their tension-filled, flirty evening *should* end with—

The bang of a metal door startled them both, and Reid jerked up, spying the flash of a light in their direction.

Heart pounding, he ducked his head, and met Nolan's wide eyes. "Someone's here," he said.

At the same moment, a deeper, scarier voice said, "Who's out here?"

Nolan's eyes widened further, and it would've been slightly comical, with his red lips and redder cheeks, were it any other circumstance.

"We have to go – come on."

Reid stood, gripping Nolan's hand, and pulled him in the direction of the edge of the roof, letting his wings out. They fluttered, muscles tense as he shook them out, and spun Nolan into his grip. "Hold on," he said.

"Stop right there!" A beam of light hit Reid right in the face, and he lifted two fingers to his temple in a sarcastic salute before tipping Nolan right off the roof with him.

Nolan went instantly silent, where before he'd been quietly repeating, *oh shit, oh shit, oh shit.*

His arms wrapped tightly around Reid's waist and he buried his head into Reid's neck and Reid reeled, grateful his muscles moved on memory alone, because all his thoughts were consumed by the man in his arms.

He flew them back to the hotel in moments, landing softly between two buildings, in the shadows. Nolan slumped against the wall and covered his face with his hands. "Oh my god, that just happened," he breathed.

Like someone had kicked him in the chest, Reid's heart seized. "I'm so sorry," he said.

Here Nolan was, this stand-up, prim and proper guy, and Reid had almost gotten them arrested, or something possibly worse.

"I am so sorry," he repeated, uttering each word with sincerity, projecting it into his earnest gaze as he moved a half-step away. "I have been up there a million times and never before has there been security. I didn't mean to put you in a situation like that. Please believe me."

God, suddenly he felt like how he feared he looked to the rich twats that buzzed around them on the street only feet away. A troublemaker, a low-life, or *something*. It filled his chest and he hated it, and he hated that he'd made Nolan feel unsafe and scared and—

"It's okay," Nolan said, taking his hand—when had he moved to stand before him again? "I know you didn't do it on purpose."

"Oh," he breathed, his anxiety stuttering in its dramatic climb to a peak. Nolan's touch was firm, and Reid forced his shoulders to relax, his concern fading with each breath. "Right."

"You got us out of there, right? Pretty certain my soul left my body when you threw us off the roof, but we're alive!" His cheeks were flushed bright pink, as if they'd been kissing again, eyes wide and genuine as he squeezed Reid's hand.

"I didn't mean to scare you," he said softly.

"It was just a reaction," Nolan promised. "I knew you wouldn't let anything happen."

Fuck.

Reid wanted to kiss him again, because who *was* this guy? Who literally placed his life in Reid's hands hours after meeting him with this blind, addicting trust?

He didn't realize the silence had stretched out for so long until Nolan cleared his throat. "I think I have another crisis," he said suddenly.

Blinking, Reid snapped back to the moment. "What's wrong?"

"Well..." Nolan began, and ran a hand over the back of his neck. His jacket miraculously was still tucked over his arm, but the seams of his shirt *streeetched* at the movement.

"I spent the entire evening with this guy," he began, and Reid's heart rate picked up as he suddenly recognized the coy expression on Nolan's face, the way his gaze danced over Reid. "And I don't want the night to end, either. So I was wondering if it would be… indecent to invite him up. To my room."

Reid's breath exploded out of him. "I think he'd be disappointed if you didn't."

"Oh," Nolan said, lips curling. "Lovely. Well."

Without further ado—which sounded like something that would come straight from Nolan's brain, not Reid's—Nolan pulled him along, out of the alley and to the hotel entrance.

Nolan nodded at the doorman, who didn't even ask to see his room key for proof of entrance or anything, and led them through the lobby with the confidence of someone who belonged there.

Reid tried to fuss his hair into some semblance of order, suddenly nervous and certain it was fucked from Nolan's fingers.

The hotel was still busy, but the elevator loading area was empty, and as the doors closed on them, the air was suddenly electric.

In the mirror reflection of the doors, Reid let his gaze cut to Nolan, standing tall, dark, handsome, and fucking divine right next to him.

His lips twitched, and the next thing he knew, Nolan had him pressed up against the wall, a hand messing his hair up again and *almost* tugging another moan from him.

"I've always wanted to do this," he admitted, gaze dark and voice darker, before he lowered his head to Reid's.

Good god.

Reid parted his lips for the kiss, groaning softly as their tongues twined once again. He fisted a hand in Nolan's shirt, in case he even thought about introducing distance between them.

Nolan slid a knee between Reid's, grinding, shoving a thigh against his erection. In response, Reid shifted, rolling his body into the movement, wanting more, and huffed a breath at the pleasure.

"Fuck," he mumbled into the kiss, but it mostly came out as a hum because Nolan was barely giving him room to breathe, and holy *fuck* where had this come from and how did he get more of it?

The hand not holding onto Nolan's shirt for dear life landed on his waist, tugging him in close, and Reid rolled his hips into him again and again in a mimicry of what they both really wanted.

They were so caught up that neither of them sensed the elevator slowing, but the ding made them jump apart with a gasp, breath harsh as the doors parted, opening to Nolan's selected floor.

He grinned, tugging Reid out of the metal box with a flourish, and laughed loudly. His voice echoed down the hallway and Reid could hardly catch a breath for how abruptly smitten he was with Nolan.

Who was this man? Afraid to crawl out from beneath his father's thumb, but willing to run from security and make out in elevators?

Reid wanted him so, so badly.

The card had barely made the door light flash green before Reid was shoving him into the room, slamming the door closed and pushing Nolan up against it.

Nolan hummed, pleased, if the way he framed Reid's face was anything to go by.

His head thunked against the door, and he pulled Reid forward, mouths slotting together. Nolan slid a hand down his chest, his side, leaving chills in his wake until he shoved his hand in Reid's back pocket.

Reid almost swallowed both of their tongues, and pulled back for a breath, then decided he didn't need air anyway, and kissed him again.

"I know we're, like, having this moment," Nolan uttered between kisses.

"Mhm," Reid agreed, tipping his head up so Nolan could speak uninterrupted and working his way along his shaven, sharp jaw and nipping at his throat. "Sounds like there's a 'but'?"

"Oh, there is," Nolan said, and squeezed the hand in Reid's back pocket.

Cheeky shit.

"It was so hot outside, and I am so grossly sweaty, can we please—"

"Shower?"

"God, yes," Nolan agreed, cheeks flushing.

"As long as we can both fit," Reid responded, and was already dragging Nolan across the room, toward the harsh light of the bathroom.

SWEET DREAMS

Some of the urgency faded beneath the harsh lights of the bathroom. It was all marble, with a huge walk-in shower, including a rainfall shower head. Reid had only seen those in movies, and he would be lying if he said he wasn't in awe.

"So you're like, *rich*-rich, huh?" he teased.

Nolan sputtered, and it pulled a soft note of amusement from Reid. He stepped forward, fingers lifting to Nolan's shirt and sliding the first button loose. Against the counter, Nolan's hands gripped the marble behind him, gaze intense as their eyes met.

"My father is. I'm doing alright for myself."

Reid arched a brow at that. "If you ever did decide to tell your father how you really feel, you'd be okay?"

He didn't know why he cared. He shouldn't, not after only spending a few hours together. But the thought of Nolan having no one to lean on, no buffer, didn't sit right with him. In fact, it made his chest tight, and he had the crazy urge to—

"I'll be okay. I've saved enough over the years that I could make it work. Which still feels like cheating, because the only reason I've been able to save my own money is because I spend his, and—"

"Hey," Reid interrupted, stilling his fingers halfway down Nolan's chest. His skin was so warm against his fingertips, Reid couldn't help but skim them beneath his shirt, over his ribs. "That's perfectly alright. All that matters is that you'll be okay."

Nolan scoffed. "Yeah. If I ever find the courage to actually do it. Talking about it, imagining it, is so easy. But whenever I'm in front of him, the focus of his stupidly intense, disapproving lens…"

Reid slid both hands inside Nolan's shirt, cupping his waist and holding tight.

"He makes me feel like a kid again, just waiting for Dad's approval," Nolan admitted with a huff. "I *hate* that. I hate that even after all this time, even when I know I'll never have his approval, his opinion of me still matters."

"I think that's part of having a dad, man. I mean, I haven't known mine in a long time, but sometimes I still wonder—would he think I've done okay?"

Nolan's lips curled up slightly, considering they were so downturned a moment ago. His eyes were shiny under the lights as he stared at Reid, searching for something in his expression. "They don't deserve it. Their opinion shouldn't matter. But for the record, I think he'd be proud."

Reid scoffed, shifting his gaze away at the compliment, at the warmth Nolan's words stirred up. "You don't know that. We hardly know each other. I could still be a serial killer on the side."

"Wow, you're a busy guy. Taxi. Restaurateur. Serial killer," Nolan reflected, tilting his head to the side.

"Gotta pass the time somehow," Reid retorted.

Nolan finally lifted his hands from the counter, bringing

them to rest on Reid's waist. They were mirroring each other, Nolan half-dressed.

Reid shifted his hands over the expanse of his warm skin, falling back to the buttons to remedy this tragedy.

Nolan followed his lead, palming his shoulders, pausing over the feathers there.

"They're so soft," Nolan noted, voice quietly devastating. Continuing his exploration, he directed his hands beneath Reid's button up, slipping it off his arms. His breath caught as he spied the few tattoos scattered up and down Reid's arm, fingers gliding carefully over the dark ink. Chills spread out from Nolan's touch, and they chased their way up Reid's spine in a shiver.

Reid pushed Nolan's shirt off too, and then lifted his remaining tee shirt over his head. Nolan gasped softly, and when the shirt fell to the floor, Reid studied him. Nolan was pale in the way only office jobs could make you, and lean but perfectly soft around the middle. They moved at the same time, Reid curling a hand around the back of his head to pull him in for a kiss.

Their chests met, warm skin against warm skin as they chased the taste of each other. Nolan threaded a hand through Reid's hair again, and Reid couldn't decide if he hated that he was so transparent, but forgot what he was trying to decide as Nolan tugged and sharp, delightful pain lit up his senses.

Reid drifted his touch south, hesitating at the button of Nolan's pants, not wanting to overwhelm. But it wasn't Nolan that Reid should've been worried about, because it was in this moment that Reid... paused.

"Reid?" Nolan asked, lips brushing against his as he breathed his name.

Reid swallowed, pulled back, and let his hands fall to his side.

"What's wrong?" Nolan's touch ghosted up his arms.

"Not… wrong, per se. Just… something you should know?"

Nolan stared at him, sapphire eyes dark with arousal and glimmering in confusion. "What is it?"

"So, I'm a griffin. Have you ever been with an Other?"

Nolan shook his head, leaning back against the vanity, a finger still hooked in Reid's belt loop.

"Okay, well. Others tend to be a bit different. Below the waist." He formed the words carefully, motioning in that direction with a wave of his hand.

Nolan's eyes widened, curiosity pooling in the depths. "Is that so?"

Reid nodded, heat rushing to his cheeks the more he met Nolan's gaze.

"I can tell you're a little worried," Nolan began with a slight grin. "And while it's true I've never been with an Other, I don't care about any of the differences. In fact…" Nolan continued, tugging him closer by his belt loop. Reid's breath caught. "I'm *very* interested in these differences."

"Oh," Reid said, and swallowed. "Well, that's… good."

So much better than good, but honestly, Reid was struggling to find a better word.

"You're not weirded out?" Reid asked.

Nolan shook his head almost before Reid finished asking the question.

"No. Not by you, not by these," he said, trailing a hand along Reid's shoulder, gently fluffing the feathers that grew along the back of his shoulders. His gaze flicked to the mirror over Reid's shoulder as Nolan brushed his fingers along them.

"Pretty."

Reid's breath went weak.

"I'm like, half-and-half," he explained. "Feathery up top, furry below."

"Show me?" Nolan asked, leaning forward and pressing their lips together. It was so gentle, so easy, and Reid's heart actually skipped before doubling pace.

Reid nodded eagerly into the kiss, hands dropping to the button on his pants. He unthreaded the button, shoving them down his hips. Nolan echoed his movements, and they stumbled together in their haste to step out of them, catching themselves against the counter with a laugh.

"You *are* furry!" Nolan breathed, hand brushing over the front of his thigh, beneath the hem of his boxers. "And you're still soft," he observed.

Reid huffed out a breath, the light touch of Nolan's fingertip ticklish against the soft blond fur.

"I kind of expected paws," Nolan teased, chuckling as he glanced toward Reid's totally normal feet. Reid shoved him, a snort slipping out.

"No paws in this form."

"Can I ask—"

"Yes," Reid answered, because Nolan wasn't being judgmental, and he wasn't weirded out. He didn't flee at the first sign of Otherness.

"Is each form the same to you? Do you prefer one or the other?"

Reid cocked his head to the side. "It's kind of like... being naked versus wearing clothes, I guess. Being fully griffin is like being naked. And being totally human, or as human as I get, is more like wearing a comfy pair of pajamas. And when I have my wings out, it's like only wearing boxers or something."

Nolan released a sigh. "Good. So you're comfortable?"

Reid melted a little at that question, released a sigh from the depths of his chest and nodded, swaying toward Nolan, hands falling to the other's hips and tugging at the waistband of his boxers. "Maybe more so if these were off."

With a grin, Nolan led him over to the shower, turning the water on before they finished stripping. Utter delight battled with his nerves as the waterfall shower head sprinkled to life.

But it seemed he didn't have anything to be nervous about anyway, because Nolan tugged him under the spray.

"I've always wanted one of these. They look so fancy in movies and shit," Reid said.

"They're delightful," Nolan agreed, pulling him close.

The water pressure left something to be desired, but the water was hot and wonderful – and even better, his skin slipped and slid against Nolan's as they crashed back together, water dripping from their lashes to their cheeks and spilling between their lips.

Reid cupped the back of his head and squeezed his hand around Nolan's hip, placing a leg between his to push him back. Nolan hit the wall with a hum, and Reid molded it into a gasp as he slotted their hips and cocks together, hardening more with each touch.

"Fuck," Nolan muttered, and Reid pulled back to see him.

His cheeks were flushed, either from the steam curling around them or arousal. Either way, he was adorably pink, lips wet and red, eyes glimmering in the dim glow as they traced over Reid's figure.

"You're like, really hot," Nolan whispered, eyes flicking back up for a moment. "You have tattoos."

Reid's lips twitched, and he brushed his thumb over Nolan's hip, because he couldn't stand not to touch him. *More more more.*

"I take it you like tattoos?"

"I guess so," Nolan answered, swallowing.

Blinking the water from his eyes, Reid tilted his head. "Do I… do I make you nervous, Nolan?"

Nolan nodded. "I thought it was rather obvious."

"Well, for what it's worth, you make me nervous, too," Reid said.

Nolan's hair was sticking to his forehead, water running down his jaw, the side of his neck, over his shoulders as the spray grazed them both.

His nose scrunched up in the cutest way as Reid's words registered. "*I* make *you* nervous?"

Reid reached for the little travel-sized body wash on the inset shelf, took the offered cloth, and lathered the citrusy soap between his hands.

He reached for Nolan, pausing before he met his skin. "Yeah. You do," he answered honestly, and finally laid the wet cloth against his chest. "You're this fancy rich guy, and I'm basically your Pretty Woman," he teased.

"Stop it," Nolan scoffed, chest lifting beneath Reid's touch. "Though you *are* pretty," he said with a soft little smile that threatened to melt Reid where he stood.

Reid rolled his eyes to disguise how pleased he was by the compliment, his cheeks threatening to flush like Nolan's often did. Nolan lathered up his own cloth, and the citrus and floral scent filled the steamy enclosure.

"This is okay on your feathers?" he asked, and Reid swayed toward him.

"Yeah," Reid rasped, voice thick with emotion because he'd *cared* to ask.

It was intimate, showering with someone else, but most of Reid's attention was drawn to the way Nolan shifted under his touch. The way his chest rose and fell with each breath, the strong biceps he'd been hiding under his button-up, how his hands moved over Reid's skin.

How he threaded his wet hands through Reid's long hair

and pulled him forward when he clearly couldn't take it anymore.

They slipped and slid together, bubbles rushing down the drain as they kissed. Reid sipped the water straight from Nolan's lips and tasted the little noises he made, wondering if he knew what those noises were doing to him.

He pushed his hips into Nolan's, cocks slipping alongside each other.

"Oh," Nolan murmured, bucking against his touch. "That's…"

"Yeah," Reid nodded, slipping a hand between them to stroke them together, letting Nolan feel the swelled ridge beneath the head of Reid's cock against his own. They rolled their hips together, breaths drawing short, pleasure striking up his spine.

Eventually, between messy kisses and long glances, they deemed themselves clean and collected towels. They'd barely dried off before Nolan was tugging Reid into the next room, pushing him back on the bed and straddling his thighs.

"Oh," Reid said, echoing Nolan, the single word cut off again by Nolan's lips. Nolan ground his hips down, swallowing the groan that spilled out of Reid, and how—when had blushes-like-a-virgin-business-nerd Nolan decide he was going to take charge?

Reid squeezed Nolan's hips, dragging him in again, grinding and panting together. He slipped a hand between them, thumbing over the heads of their cocks and collecting the slick there before wrapping a hand around the both of them.

A broken sound poured from Nolan, and Reid grinned in victory against his lips.

"I can't stop thinking about how you'd feel inside me," Nolan whispered. "If you'd want that."

Reid's entire body flushed hot at just the thought, and he nodded jerkily.

"Condoms?" Reid asked, because that was the natural next step, right? His breath and chest were tight with anticipation.

Nolan froze and pulled back, his wide eyes foggy with lust, and Reid's stomach dropped. "Condoms," he echoed, neither question nor statement.

"Yeah. Condoms. Do you have any?" Reid already knew the answer from Nolan's response, but he couldn't help but ask.

Nolan sat back on his knees, fingers digging into his thighs, and Reid let his hand fall away. "I never do this, so I don't think—"

"Me either," Reid interrupted, oddly flattered and maybe a little relieved. He cleared his throat.

Nolan groaned. "Maybe… maybe I have one in my toiletries bag. I don't know. I'll go check."

"Great idea," Reid agreed. "Go look."

"On it," Nolan said, and leaned in for a kiss before crawling off the bed and marching into the bathroom.

Reid could hear Nolan rustling around, the clink of bottles and plastic taps, the hiss of a zipper. Some cursing.

This was something new, something different, for both of them. Was Nolan as adrift as Reid was, unsure in the waves of their desire?

They didn't *have* to have penetrative sex. With Nolan, Reid was sure it wouldn't even take that much more grinding to come, not with the sweet, eager noises he knew he made.

Yeah. As soon as Nolan returned, Reid would propose the alternate plan, drag him back to bed. Nolan wouldn't know what hit him.

"I mean, it *is* true that Others can't contract or spread diseases," Reid offered helpfully.

A second passed slowly before Nolan's head appeared around the frame of the door, mouth agape. "You—really?"

Reid chuckled, and suddenly *his* cheeks were the pink ones. "Really."

"So what you're saying is…"

"We don't *have* to have a condom. Unless that's what you'd prefer—"

Reid watched the thought hit Nolan, and he disappeared around the doorway again. While he waited, Reid sank deeper into the bed, turning on his side to watch Nolan's shadow cut across the bathroom light, and then back the other way. Clutching one of the pillows to his chest, he inhaled deeply, breathing in the citrus scent embedded in the pillow.

Was it weird to sniff his pillow? Probably. Did Reid care?

Reid maybe would have cared, but jesus christ, what kind of bed was this? He was sinking deeper by the second, and the sheets were so soft and lovely he didn't want to move. Ever.

His eyelids drifted closed, and he snapped them open at the clink of another bottle.

Shit.

Nolan was freaking out.

"Nolan, c'mere," he called out.

The clinking paused, followed by the soft padding steps of the other man.

Nolan paused beside the bed, and Reid reached out a hand, cupping somewhere around his thigh. Fabric brushed the back of his fingers. Nolan had put boxers on.

He should sit up properly.

"Why're you freaking out, man?" he asked, almost afraid to look up, to meet Nolan's gaze.

"I-I don't know," Nolan whispered.

Reid glanced up, found something too-big and a little bit

not-right-now in his eyes, and... shrugged, somehow relaxing in the face of Nolan's uncertainty. "Come lay down. This is the softest bed I've ever laid on."

Nolan didn't say anything, his hand fluttering over Reid's, which was still gripping his thigh. Reid released him, and shifted his arm behind his back to awkwardly pat the mattress. "Come on."

He nuzzled his face into the pillow, but watched Nolan round the bed. The bed dipped as Nolan joined him, and Reid waited patiently, fighting drowsiness as he got comfy.

Nolan's warmth seeping into him, his arm trailing over Reid's side, did not help.

"We have all week, yeah? Nothing has to happen tonight," he offered, and rolled over so Nolan could see the sincerity in his gaze.

Nolan huffed, breath disturbing the hair falling into Reid's forehead. "It's not that I don't—I want it. A lot. Is there such a thing as too much?" His voice was quieter as he asked.

Fucking flattering, is what it was.

"Never too much. Like I said, we have all week, right? You'll be here at your conference?"

Nolan nodded, and Reid reached up to tap at the spot his dimple usually appeared. "See? We have so much time. Nothing has to happen right now."

"Tonight was just... really fucking perfect," Nolan breathed.

"Still is," Reid told him, and meant it. "Dunno about you, but I haven't shared a bed with someone in ages. Feels nice."

"The other stuff would've felt nice too," Nolan returned, fingers tensing over his hip. Was he pouting?

Reid cracked one eye open and tried not to let his cheeks twitch. "You'll have to prove it."

"Next time," Nolan whispered, and both Reid's eyes snapped open.

Next time, next time, next time. The words echoed in his head, imprinted on his mind.

"I'll hold you to it," Reid promised, reminding himself to *breathe* even though he was stuck in the deep pools of Nolan's eyes again. "Hope you didn't plan on kicking me out. Bed's too nice."

"I would never," Nolan scoffed, sounding properly scandalized.

It should've been awkward, as wrapped around each other as they were, sinking into the bed like molasses. Instead, it was the most comfortable Reid could remember being with another person.

So when Reid's eyes drifted closed once more, they didn't open again for the rest of the night.

FAMILIAR FACE

Reid fell asleep quickly, lips parted as he breathed deeply, expression relaxing, one of Nolan's pillows still crumpled up behind him. Where he'd been *hugging* it, Nolan reminded himself.

His heart thumped against his ribs, and he settled into the embrace, a small smile curling his lips.

Reid was utterly, devastatingly handsome, blond hair spread across the pillows, tattoos stark against the white sheets. He wouldn't dream of waking him up, kicking him out. Maybe Nolan was crossing some invisible one-night stand line, but he couldn't find it in him to care. Not when Reid looked so at peace, so comfortable.

It was dark, the city lights casting the room in a soft glow. The citrus scent of his soap smelled divine on Reid.

Maybe don't sniff the attractive man while he's sleeping.

Nolan sank into Reid's heat, his skin smooth against his own. His heart thundered in his chest, each beat sure to wake the man in his bed, and he tried to calm himself down. His thoughts turned to their evening together, each touch they'd shared and the soft glances and even the conversations. Then to later, when arousal had burned low and hot, the embers sparking with every touch and kiss and god, Nolan *wanted* him.

Which had led to his *real* crisis. The night had been so perfect, *was* still perfect—he heard the words in Reid's voice, and felt the man shift in his arms—but what if he'd ruined it?

This wasn't some silly one-night stand, and he'd let his fear of it ending stop it in its tracks altogether.

But now *we have all week* and *next time* was echoing in his head, and Nolan knew this wasn't something casual for Reid, either. He found comfort in the epiphany, and finally, truly relaxed against Reid, the late hour and too many emotions catching up to him. The morning would come early. He should sleep.

Even with something to look forward to, the week still loomed. Nolan hated that he had to wake up tomorrow to go stand behind his father and give presentations for a business he hated.

Maybe Reid was right. Nolan couldn't be miserable forever, but when would he ever find the courage to tear himself away?

That thought chased the others around his mind until sleep finally claimed him.

When he awoke again, the first thing he noticed was warmth. Then light, and he blinked himself awake, wincing at the bright morning glare from the open windows, and buried his face in a pillow.

Except this pillow hummed. And smelled nice, all citrus like his own body wash, mixed with spice. And had blond hair that tickled his face.

Nolan's eyes widened, suddenly viscerally aware of the body he was spooning. He had an arm curled over Reid's side, and in turn, Reid had curled himself around his arm, replacing the pillow that had fallen off the edge. Nolan's knees were tucked into the curve of Reid's body, chest pressed to his back.

He would have loved to cuddle closer and push the almost-panic aside in favor of feeling Reid's body heat against him forever, but his gaze snagged on the clock, the numbers arranging themselves into an alarming lateness, and he froze.

Oh god. Oh fuck. He was so late. His father was going to be *pissed*.

He silently unwound his arm from Reid, who grumbled, but sank back into the pillows with a huff before sleep claimed him again.

With all the paranoia of a kid sneaking out at night, he slid from the bed and got dressed, tiptoeing around the room until he deemed himself ready to face the firing squad.

With the pen and hotel-branded notepad, he left a note for Reid and grabbed his badge before pausing by the door.

Reid looked like a dream Nolan didn't want to leave, but the clock was ticking. He just had to hope that Reid would put the number he'd scribbled at the bottom of the note to use.

The door clicked softly behind him, and Nolan sprinted down the hallway toward the elevators. His father couldn't have booked them in the same hotel as the conference, because that would have been too convenient. The rideshare line was far too crowded, so Nolan tossed his badge over his head and made for the front doors. It was already warm and sunny even so early in the morning, and he'd worked up a sweat by the time he made it down the block to the hotel hosting the conference.

With a huff, he adjusted his hair in the reflection of the glass doors and went inside.

It didn't take long to find his father, just coming out of the double doors of the conference room. Nolan steeled his expression as George Whittier's gaze landed on him.

"About time you showed up," he hissed, darting a glance to the passersby and pasting a smile on his face.

"I'm sorry, I overslept," Nolan admitted. Which wasn't a lie.

"Clearly," his father's assistant interjected, tone dismissive as always.

Nolan shared a tight smile with the both of them. "I'm here now. What have I missed?"

"Nothing of importance so far. Count yourself lucky," his father sneered.

Nolan wouldn't go that far. If he was lucky, he'd still be in bed with Reid. "What's next?" he asked, already pulling up his phone to view the order of events.

"You know we're really only here for one reason," his father reminded him. "And the city's officials won't be here until after lunch. Can I trust you to be there on time?"

Nolan nodded stiffly. "Where else would I be?"

"Yes, that's the question, isn't it?" he drawled before stalking off toward the complimentary coffee provided by the hotel. Would he be taking notes and comparing it to Whittier's Hotel coffee?

Chance, his father's assistant, rounded on Nolan and narrowed his eyes. "You know, you might be a pain in the ass, and utterly useless, but even I know that being on time is your favorite thing in your boring little life. So what was the hold-up this morning?"

"Wow, be careful there, Chance, that was almost a compliment," Nolan retorted, refusing to give into his line of questioning.

Chance bared his teeth in a mimicry of a smile. "When pigs fly. Just don't be late this afternoon."

"I will be there," Nolan repeated, and waited for him to walk away and join his father before releasing a breath. Late one time, and suddenly it's the end of the fucking world.

They both winced at the coffee before his father murmured something, and Chance dutifully marked it down on his device.

Nolan took the chance to escape, walking through the hotel, its tacky carpet muffling his steps, and mapping the area. He passed by the conference room they would be presenting in that afternoon, and he grimaced at the size of it.

How did so many people care about erecting another hotel? Was the one they were standing in not enough? Did this city really need another mini metropolis for the elite to throw their money at?

Nolan made it on time for the next presentation, some-thing about bettering customer service, offering rewards to employees for this or that. Nolan *just* stopped himself from rolling his eyes. No one cared about pizza parties and printed pieces of Employee of the Month papers. Give them a raise and maybe they'd be a little more enthusiastic about showing up to their soul-sucking, gut-wrenching job.

Maybe Nolan was projecting.

He held it together through the entire slideshow, tense and bored but on his best behavior, since his father was seated right next to him.

"I'm going to grab some lunch," Nolan said once the assembly began to break up.

"Next presentation is at—"

"One-fifteen, I know," he said, interrupting Chase, and walked off before they could stop him.

The morning was dragging, the day grating, and Nolan

was practically vibrating out of his skin. Restless, that's what he'd call it.

Granted, there wasn't much else he could be doing…

An image flashed through his mind of Reid sleeping soundly in the bed as he'd shut the door to the room that morning.

Well, maybe he could think of a few things.

The air was too warm and the sun too hot as he walked out the glass doors of the hotel, pedestrians on the sidewalk zipping around him.

He didn't know what made this day so different, what made him want to crawl out of his skin and leave it behind for a bit. But the urge itched at him, a pestering sensation he couldn't get away from.

Maybe it was the lack of sleep. He had been out rather late with Reid.

Forgoing the hot weather, he walked back into the hotel with a grimace and glanced at the signs, arrows pointing in different directions to the little shops and restaurants on the ground floor.

Burgers, salad, pizza…

He doubted any hotel pizza would live up to the slice he'd had last night. With Reid.

Aiming toward the salad and smoothie place, he smiled politely at passing faces and checked his watch, dreadfully counting down the time until the next assembly.

Were his presentations this boring as well? Or was it just different because he was another face in the crowd, instead of up on stage?

Mentally reviewing his own presentation, he followed the signs for the line and stood behind a businesswoman in a pale pink suit. Cute. Bold.

It suited her, and he imagined how he looked to anyone outside his own head, glancing down at his own suit for the day. It was sharp and expensive, at his father's insistence. It was also a boring, bland gray, and even though he tried to give it some life with a teal tie, he knew his attempt fell flat. As flat as his purpose.

God, that was rather depressing, wasn't it?

He recalled Reid's outfit, the coral button-up and the band tee and the boots. There was something about him, his style. A quality Nolan could only hope to exude one day.

He sighed, pulling out his phone to check the time again, because his watch wasn't enough. Disappointment laced through him as his notifications remained quiet, and he finally admitted to himself why he was so restless in the first place.

Either Reid wasn't awake, or he'd decided not to text Nolan. Maybe letting him stay had been the wrong move?

Was Nolan supposed to have awoken him? Sent him on his way in the dead of night? Nolan wasn't familiar with these unsaid rules of... of whatever was happening—had happened—with Reid.

He took a deeper breath, heart suddenly thumping against his chest with emphasis.

It wasn't a hook-up. No actual hooking up happened, had it? And if Reid wasn't going to text him, Nolan supposed it remained... nothing but a local showing an out-of-towner around.

Not a date.

Nolan wasn't daft enough to ignore the way the thought condensed into a dark gray cloud above him.

He was *really* expecting Reid to text him. Nolan was going to be in town for the week, so he... he'd hoped to slip out at some point and meet him for lunch. Maybe invite him to dinner. Repay his kindness.

Dear god, he felt naive suddenly, making plans with the guy when he hadn't even heard from him.

"Sir?" A voice suddenly interjected into his thoughts, and Nolan snapped his head up.

Shit.

"Sorry, sorry," he said, stepping up to the counter and smiling at the expectant woman behind the register. He hadn't even gotten to look at the menu, lost in his thoughts as he was.

He ordered the first salad he saw and paid for a bottle of water along with it.

The vibrant greens were tucked in a plastic box, handed to him over the glass counter, and off he went.

All the tables were full, so he continued on back to the presentation area, eyes scanning for a vacant seat.

He passed by a mostly empty room, and paused before backing up a step.

No… was that—

Reid?

That was definitely his long blond hair bouncing along his shoulders as he laughed and shook the hands of an official looking man in a suit.

Nolan was pretty sure his father had a meeting scheduled with that same man this week.

Nolan shook himself, glancing away before returning his reluctant attention to the blond man across the room. He couldn't believe he was here.

In the same way he couldn't believe last night was real. In the same way he couldn't believe *Reid* was real. In the same way Nolan couldn't believe his feet were leading him right to Reid, pausing with a caustic sort of grin. Was he welcome to say hello or not?

God, what if Reid was trying to ghost him—

Finally, Reid caught sight of him, a grin breaking out across his face, and the tension Nolan held in his shoulders dissipated. The pleased sort of surprise in Reid's expression was real, Nolan was certain. No regret visible.

"Hey, man," Reid said, and before Nolan knew it they were riding the wave of surprised excitement and letting it crash them into each other in a hug.

His cheeks went red at the intimate happiness they seemed to share at this unexpected turn of events, balancing his stupid salad and cold water bottle in his hands.

"What are you doing here?" Nolan asked as they pulled back, forcing himself to lower his full hands back down to his sides. In a flash Reid was pushing him against the shower wall, he felt the man's hips kick as he gripped those shoulders—

"Hey," Reid said, and waved his hand back and forth. "Where'd you go, are you listening?"

"Yes, of course!" Nolan answered, frantic.

Reid stared at him, waiting.

Nolan swallowed, noticing the businessman had made himself scarce. "But, uh, just perhaps, what was it you said?"

His lips twitched, one corner of Reid's mouth curling up. "I'm here to crash the hotel schmuck's hopes and dreams," he said proudly.

Nolan stuttered to a halt, tilting his head to the side. "Uh, what?"

"You know… Whittier. He's kind of an asshole, building his hotel empire on the bones of the businesses he's ruined, and—" Reid suddenly paused, gaze bouncing over Nolan's expression. "And you totally work for him, don't you?"

Slowly, a hand lifted to cover the lower half of Reid's face, his eyes twinkling in disbelief and amusement.

Nolan kind of wished the ground would swallow him up whole, and his hands tightened around the plastic containers. "Worse," he admitted, shaking his head.

"What's worse—no," Reid said, voice dropping. He even

took a half-step back as he studied Nolan, nose to toes and back again. Then he stepped forward, hissing, "You're his *son*?"

Oh, shit.

Mute with something akin to panic, Nolan nodded. Oh god, he'd *slept* with the enemy! Well, Nolan sure as hell didn't see him as the enemy, but if his father got wind of what had happened—

Wait, why would his father *ever* hear about this? He didn't give two shits what Nolan did, outside of looking nice for pictures to uphold the happy family bullshit and giving his presentations like a good little soulless employee.

No one would be the wiser as long as they kept their mouths shut about it.

He lifted his eyes, parted his lips to say just so, but he... stopped.

Reid was still smiling, even though it had softened, and it reminded him of last night.

No, not the making-out parts, though, trust him, that was still circling the forefront of his brain. But he meant... before even that. The greasy pizza and the ice cream and the confessions and the—god, Reid made him feel like a *person*, and not just a puppet to prop up when needed.

The night before had been such a gift, and Reid probably had no clue just how much it meant to Nolan. And of course, Nolan didn't think he could admit it aloud; it seemed rather intense for just one night. But he certainly wasn't about to snub his nose at the only person who'd ever... laughed *with* him and traded interests and was invested in what he had to say next, instead of counting down the seconds until the interaction was over.

He snapped his mouth shut, because no. He wasn't going to tell Reid any of the things crossing his mind—not the part about keeping it between them. Whose business was it of his father's who he saw?

God, he felt awfully old to be having thoughts like that, but he embraced them with a sort of giddiness, and a chuckle escaped him. "Yeah. Yeah, I'm the son," he said between chuckles.

Reid's grin widened too, and before he knew it they were laughing quite loudly, drawing the attention of a few curious onlookers, and he shushed them both.

"Quiet, quiet. We're disturbing the business moguls. Can't have that."

"Oh, of course, yep," Reid said, covering his chuckles behind a hand.

"So, how do you plan to crush all my father's hopes and dreams?"

Reid eyed the still curious onlookers, and took Nolan's water bottle before slotting their hands together. "Come with me."

Nolan let him lead, feeling sillier by the second with his salad clutched to his chest as he was pulled through the crowds of dawdling passersby, Reid's shockingly warm hand twined with his.

Reid found an actual empty room, and even went so far as to close the door behind them.

"I knew your name rang a bell," Reid said quietly, crossing his arms and leaning back against the door.

Nolan shrugged and set his stupid damned salad on an empty chair.

"What are you doing here?" Nolan asked, brain trying to connect these two seemingly random pieces. "You said you own a restaurant, ri—oh. *Oh*," Nolan breathed, eyes slamming shut in mortification. "Fuck."

"Bingo," Reid answered. "My little restaurant is in the way of your mega hotel."

"Not *my* hotel," Nolan retorted automatically, eyes drifting open.

"Did you know, last night?" Reid asked, brows knotting together. Nolan wished he was brave enough to step closer and smooth his thumb over them.

"I had no idea." Reid's restaurant was located on the same block as the ice cream shop and the arcade. Nolan scrubbed his hands over his face, the left one still slightly chilled from the bottle.

"Chippy's is part of the demolition?" he groaned. "And the arcade, then?"

"Yep," he said shortly.

Nolan lifted his head. "Did *you* know? Is that why you took me to all those places?"

Reid frowned. "No, man. I only connected the dots just now."

"Oh." A massive part of him was relieved. He felt connected to Reid because of those places now, because of their night spent together. The thought of it all being a sham, just as some ploy to…what? Make him feel guilty about his father buying those businesses out? Just the idea made his chest hurt. "I'm relieved," Nolan admitted, and paused, the words at the tip of his tongue. Maybe it *was* intense after just one night, but… "Last night was… special," he choked out.

Reid stepped forward, slid a hand to the back of his neck and held his head up, meeting his gaze. Warmth was reflected in those dark brown eyes; Nolan could feel it like the heat of the sun. He felt transparent beneath their light.

"I took you there because those are genuinely my favorite places in the city, like I told you."

"I don't have any control here," Nolan breathed. "I—

"Hate your dad. Makes sense now, knowing it's George Whittier, and all. We have that in common."

Nolan smiled wryly. "Yippee."

Reid grinned at that, a chuckle spilling out.

"I'm sorry," Nolan said. "Not that it means much, but... I wish I could change it."

Reid grimaced. "It's not like you personally selected the location of the new place, right?"

Nolan shook his head. "I'm only here to make him look like a family man," Nolan scoffed. "And to... sell the business to the possible shareholders."

"Nolan!" Reid hissed.

Nolan groaned, letting his head tilt back and wishing he was anyone else. "I know. I'm the one giving the fucking presentations." Nolan was the one in charge of convincing the shareholders to invest, persuading them to support the build of the hotel. If he did what he was brought here to do... if he succeeded, then...

Reid's business was done for.

And it would be Nolan's fault.

CONSEQUENCES

Fuck.

Fuck.

This *so* wasn't fair. Why hadn't Reid let himself explore the niggling in the back of his head the night before? When Nolan's name had struck a familiar chord in him?

He'd been so besotted with the weird man, he'd wanted to live in the moment with him.

Well, look where that fucking moment had lead him.

From his bed—much to Reid's surprise upon waking, and then delight when he'd seen the note next to his pillow—to this stupid conference he was literally here to protest.

"What do we do now?" Nolan asked sheepishly.

Reid's hand tightened over the back of his neck before he dropped it and ran his hands through his own hair. "You're here to convince them to bulldoze the business I spent my whole life building."

Nolan deflated before his eyes—not physically, his shoulders didn't sink and his expression didn't change—but Reid felt the tension shift, felt the guilt solidify within him.

"But that's not your fault. You didn't know. I didn't know," he said again.

"I'm sorry," Nolan replied, rolling those blue eyes up to him.

"It's... Nolan, I don't blame you. I had fun last night." More fun than he would care to admit, and like Nolan had said... "It was special for me, too," he admitted. But he still dropped his hand, Nolan's warm skin slipping away as Reid stepped back. "But this is my *life*, Nolan. I can't... I just wish we'd met under different circumstances."

Nolan nodded, steeling his expression and taking the water bottle Reid held out for him. "I do, too. For what it's worth, I hope whatever you have planned to make my father's life difficult works. Give him hell."

Despite the sinking feeling in his gut, Reid chuckled. Even to his own ears, it didn't sound as genuine as it normally did in Nolan's presence. "Oh, I will."

He nodded once more, and the silence settled between them, but unlike last night, it was rife with tension and uncertainty. Reid did *not* like the weighty disappointment that anchored in his stomach. He wanted to kiss Nolan, despite everything. He wanted to grab his hand and escape the hotel and – and *all* of this.

But his restaurant, those businesses he grew up with, they were important.

Surely more important than whatever crush he was harboring... on the enemy.

His gaze dropped to the sad-looking salad resting on the chair, and suddenly he jolted, checking his phone for the time. "Shit. I'm supposed to meet a friend for lunch. I guess... I guess I'll see you around, yeah?"

Nolan smiled, though it was polite and insincere, and Reid's chest twisted tightly once again. "I'll be here all week."

The promise did not have the same exciting buzz to it that it had when similar words had been whispered in the safety of Nolan's hotel bed.

"Alright," Reid responded, reaching behind himself to tug the door open. "See ya."

"Enjoy lunch," Nolan said, cordial as ever.

"You too."

Reid wanted to scream as he left the doorway and made his way down the hall. The further he went from the room, the tighter his chest got. He rushed into the main area, spotting his impatient-looking friend John, and hurried to his side.

John scoffed when he finally spied Reid. "About time you—"

"Hope you have time for a long lunch," Reid interrupted. "My treat," he added as he pulled John along by his shirt and not by the camera bag strap across his chest.

"What the hell is this about? You told me to meet you here."

"Something's come up, and I need to tell you about it. Can't do it here."

John's brows twitched in interest, and suddenly his feet were a lot more cooperative as they sped down the sidewalk.

Reid pushed into the first diner they came to, and marched his way to the back of the restaurant after waving at a waitress behind the bar.

"What's this about?" John asked as they settled into a booth.

Reid rested his elbows on the scratched metal table and dug the heels of his palms into his eyes.

The waitress appeared before Reid could organize his thoughts, and he dropped his hands while John ordered their usuals. Reid stared at the tabletop. Once she was gone, John rolled his hand in a *go on* motion, and Reid sucked in a sharp breath.

"I slept with Whittier's son."

John froze, eyes intent on Reid. "You... did *what?* Wait," he said suddenly, and reached in his bag to pull out a recorder. Reid slapped his hand down on top of John's, trapping the device against the table.

"No, John, you can't write about this. I just needed to talk to someone."

John threw up his arms, the device forgotten between them. Reid eyed it, making sure the light wasn't blinking for record. "Don't you have a therapist for that? What the fuck am I doing here, then?"

"Because you're my friend?" Reid guessed.

John ignored him. "You wanted me here to report on this little… *rebellion* you've got going on. Are the Whittiers not part of that?"

Reid crossed his arms, leaned back, and tried to wipe the stubborn pout off his face. "You know they are. But not this part."

John huffed. "Alright. You fucked the—"

"No, we slept together. Literally. It was…" Special. Kind of pure, in a way. He did not tell John these things, cheeks flushing hot.

John's cheeks went pink, too, and he stuttered before making to stand from the booth. "Alright, I don't have time for this school boy crush bullshit—"

"John, sit the fuck down," Reid demanded, exasperated with his best friend. "Quit being an ass for ten minutes and let me get the fucking story out."

John sat. "Fine. Clock started when we walked in."

Reid huffed. "I hate you."

In response, John checked his phone. "You have about five minutes left."

"Alright!" Reid hissed, and started from the beginning. John looked like he wanted the floor to swallow him whole rather than hear about Reid's love life, but the five minutes came and went and he didn't stand up and storm out.

Their food arrived and John stabbed his french fries in the ketchup like they'd personally wronged him while Reid finished his story.

"And then I just… walked off." Reid groaned, leaning back in the booth and glaring at his burger and fries. It looked much more appetizing than that sad salad of Nolan's, but that didn't mean he was in the mood to eat. "I already know what you're going to say, but I can't help but feel like…" Maybe it was a mistake? "…there's more to it." It had just felt so *big*, whatever he'd had with Nolan in the short time they'd been together.

"You've just got a measly little crush. It'll go away."

Reid didn't *want* it to go away, was the thing. He frowned.

"He looked so disappointed, J."

"Of course he was," John said with a pointed glance in his direction. "Look at you."

Reid rolled his eyes, but John continued speaking. "You're hot. And loyal. With integrity. Of course he wanted to see you again. It's not his livelihood on the line here. He's just a spoiled kid who's sad one thing didn't go his way."

Crossing his arms, Reid swallowed back the defenses rising to his lips on Nolan's behalf. That's not the vibe he'd felt from Nolan at all. But explaining that to John would just dig himself deeper.

John sighed, setting down a fry and leveling with Reid. "Look, I'm sorry if I'm not the most sympathetic to your cause," he said, grumbling. "But I thought you invited me to this thing to give me a story to run. I *really* need a story to run."

"Why?" Reid asked.

"Because I'm about to lose my job," he admitted, and Reid sat up a little straighter in alarm.

"What? Why? You told me your last evaluation went well!"

"It did, but they've decided to cut reporters anyway. And I haven't had any good, hard-hitting stories lately. If I don't find something to impress them, they're gonna think I'm not pulling my weight and axe me." John's head knocked against the back of the booth. "They need something by the weekend."

"Inside coverage on the conference won't be enough?" Reid asked. But he already knew what John was going to say.

"Not if nothing newsworthy happens. If the deal goes through, it'll be all over the news, and whatever I have to say about it won't be but a drop in the bucket." His gaze narrowed suddenly, and Reid shifted in the seat as his friend stared. A long moment passed before he spoke. "You wanna see that guy again?"

Reid did *not* like the tone of his voice. "Why?"

"Well, I mean, if you were hanging out with this Nolan guy… you'd probably be hanging around his dad a fair bit more, wouldn't you?"

Reid braced his hands on the table, shoulders rising up around his ears. "No way. I am not spying for you."

"Why would you think of it like that? Don't think of it like that," John insisted, pushing his plate away to give Reid his full attention. "Anything would be better than the nothing I have now. Even if it's… I don't know, he kicks dogs in his spare time or some shit. I don't know! We both know he's a piece of shit. There's got to be something that proves it. Now *that* would be a story."

"But I *like* this guy." Reid swallowed as the admission rang true, clanging through him with a start. "I don't want to hurt him."

"Yeah… but we're going after his *dad*, not him. From what you said, it sounds like the guy hates him too."

"But I'd be using him to get to his dad. That's not right," Reid argued, hands sliding from the table to fall into his lap.

"What's not right is what Whittier is trying to do to this community. You know these rich fucks are never innocent. Just… think about it. Please?"

Thinking about it wasn't committing to anything. Reid could think. Wasn't anything bad about that, right?

He nodded, and John laid a twenty out on the counter for their meal before gathering his recorder and bag. "I'm going to see if I can snap a few photos before heading back. Think about it, seriously, okay? I could use the help."

Fuck. John knew how to get him where it counted.

Using Nolan to get to his dad? He couldn't do that.

But helping a friend he's known for almost… god, ten *years*?

It was hard to say no to that.

He frowned down at the lukewarm burger and limp fries, sighing as he finally lifted one and dipped it into the ketchup before taking a bite.

The door jingled as John left, and Reid let his shoulders droop.

If he did this, agreed to hang around Nolan a little bit more in exchange for *hopefully* overhearing something damning about his father… at least he'd get to see Nolan again.

And maybe he wouldn't even find anything. It would suck for John, but no harm no foul.

Right?

Reid saw Nolan three more times that day.

The first was when Reid was talking to one of the city's

officials. The place had been swarming with them after lunch, and Reid made his move.

The city wasn't *that* large. Apparently big enough for its fifth mega hotel in the area, but small enough that he remembered *this* guy coming into his restaurant. He'd looked like a stuffy, black-tie asshole, and at first Reid had even thought he was a critic, but he'd had a genuine laugh, and most importantly, he'd loved Reid's food.

Reid was doing his best to remind the man of that fact. Lots of shoulder slapping and belly laughs, to the effect that Reid couldn't understand how this guy could support taking out his business – a whole block of them – if he loved the place so much that his recommendation had reached his sister-in-law's hairdresser.

"—who said she *loved* the crème brûlée," he finished proudly.

"Well, I appreciate that. Just because it sounds fancy, doesn't mean it has to cost fancy, too. That's why Essie's Place is so special," he said, meaning every fucking word and willing this man to pick up on his underlying desperation.

Don't back the hotel, man.

Everyone deserved to be able to treat themselves to a nice meal. Between the location of Reid's place and the prices he refused to raise, everyone could.

"It *is* special," the man assured him, and Reid smiled. He wanted this man's word, but that wasn't how you played this game. Politics and whatnot.

Reid hated every bit of it.

Reid shook his hand again, but his gaze got caught over the other man's shoulder.

Nolan's smile was blinding, aimed at a photographer off to the side as he posed with his father. But upon a second— and maybe a third—glance, Reid could make out the frame of tension around his lips, the tightness in the crinkles by his eyes.

The man in front of Reid took his hand back, and Reid snapped back into the moment like a rubber band against skin. Fuck, how long had Reid been staring?

"It was nice catching up with you. Maybe I'll see you in soon?" Reid suggested. He'd comp this guy's whole meal. Reid wasn't above bribery. He could make crème brûlée all day for his cousin's whoever.

As the man walked away after saying goodbye, Reid analyzed the interaction. Was what he'd said enough to make an impression, enough to make this guy think twice before investing in a hotel that would take Reid's business out?

God, he hoped so.

But he wouldn't know until the end of the week.

His gaze darted back to Nolan at the same moment they stopped posing. His father took a pointed step away from him, murmuring something to the assistant that was usually glued to his side. Nolan's smile faded instantly, lips twisting in a grimace before he was pulled back to attention at his father's words.

A pang of sympathy shot through him, and Reid turned away before he could give in to the urge to whisk Nolan away from all of this.

John's right. George Whittier looks like he'd kick a dog.

See? Reid should help John, if only to expose a possible dog kicker. Did the Whittiers even have a dog? He'd have to remember to look that up later.

You could just ask Nolan, a little voice in his head supplied.

It sounded a little too much like John's for comfort.

The second time he saw Nolan, however, was his deciding factor.

Nolan was at the front of the huge conference room, seats filled with more business suits than Reid had ever seen. The lights were harsh and cast Nolan in a pale glow that did him no favors, or maybe it was the tight frame of tension as he fake-smiled out at the crowd.

This was the first of the many presentations Nolan would be giving this week, all to convince these rich fuckers they needed a hotel with a spa and whatever other bells and whistles they could come up with to make it appealing.

Maybe the mud baths would help them sleep at night after bulldozing the livelihoods of the families who'd owned the businesses that once stood there.

It wasn't like they weren't offering the businesses money first. Buying them out.

But the lowball offer they'd sent Reid's way had made him *furious.* At thirty-four, he'd spent the last twelve years dedicating what meager education he had, as well as his time, passion, and love into that restaurant. That was worth more than the shitty numbers they'd offered him, and Reid had been proud to tell them so.

And if they'd given him a shitty offer, they'd probably given the other businesses shitty offers, too.

How long until one of them caved? And if one business caved, the others would follow suit like dominoes.

"And as you can see here, projected earnings based on the local economy will heavily outweigh the cost of production," Nolan said. "Which, I'm happy to add, will create as many as two *thousand* jobs."

Jesus.

That's a lot of people.

And unfortunately, that exceeded the amount of people

who would be out of a job if their businesses were shut down. Reid only employed around thirty people, if that.

Nolan's presentation was smooth, practiced, and effortless. The crowd clapped and he smiled politely before the room began to empty.

His father approached, and Reid watched from the back of the room as Nolan stiffened at the hand on his shoulder. George Whittier, from the outside, seemed like a normal dad congratulating his son on a presentation gone well. But from the tense line of Nolan's shoulders, the careful control of his expression, he was anything but.

That was the moment Reid made up his mind.

Which had led him to this current moment, riding the lift to the seventeenth floor of Nolan's hotel, nerves jangling inside of him like a set of keys.

His heel bounced against the floor as the elevator beeps filled the silence. It came to a slow stop before the doors opened, and the couple beside him stumbled out of the elevator.

Someone's started early, he mused, glancing at the time and finding the ripe hour of six p.m.

What if Nolan wasn't there? Would Reid leave? Or wait beside his door like a stalker until he returned?

What if Nolan *was* there? What would Reid even say?

He ran out of time to make up his mind, because the doors parted once more on Nolan's floor. With a deep breath, Reid stepped out of the elevator and made his way to the right, toward Nolan's room.

He tried to slow his steps, but his feet still carried him faster than he was prepared for. In seconds the brass numbers on his door seemed to be glaring at him.

Here goes.

He lifted his hand to knock—

And at the same moment the door swung open, revealing

Nolan for the third time that day. He stumbled to a halt, eyes widening at Reid's presence.

"Hello," he said softly, a note of wonder filling his voice.

"Hi," Reid said, staring back at Nolan and momentarily forgetting what the fuck he was there for. What single purpose he might have, other than to trace the way a perfect coil of Nolan's hair was falling out, a strand drooping across his forehead.

He had changed from his earlier suit into a short-sleeved blue button-up and dark wash jeans and sneakers, not a brand in sight.

He definitely looked more comfortable than he had the night before, yet the longer the moment stretched on, his broad shoulders began to tighten.

"Did you, uhm," he cleared his throat. "Forget something?" he asked, glancing over his shoulder, unsure.

"No, no, uh…" Reid trailed off. "Sorry, were you on your way somewhere?" he asked. "I can come back another—"

"No, it's fine!" he said, rushing the words out and lifting a hand as if to physically stop the suggestion from passing Reid's lips. "I mean, yes, I am on my way somewhere, but don't, uhm. What is it you have to say?" His cheeks colored with warmth as he babbled, and Reid's heart gave a loud, decisive thump.

"I changed my mind," he said softly.

Nolan's eyes widened.

"I don't wanna *see you around*," Reid said, the words tumbling out of him. "I want to see you right now. And tomorrow. And the day after. I know you're only here this week, and I don't know what will happen after Friday, but—"

"Yes," Nolan interrupted him, lips curling into a wide smile. It was real, unlike the one Reid had worn all day at the conference, dimples absent of the frame of tension, eyes crinkled in genuine joy. "Are you free right now?"

Oh thank *god*.

"Yep. All night," he said, reeling. *Is this happening?*

"Good. Come with me," Nolan said, stepping forward. Reid moved back to give him room, and the door shut with a decisive click, echoing in the hallway. Nolan grabbed his hand, and this time Reid was the one being pulled off in whatever direction. This one just happened to be toward the elevators.

"Where are we going?" Reid asked.

"It's a surprise," Nolan answered, that smile still stamped on his face.

Reid wanted to kiss him.

He barely refrained from doing so as the elevator doors closed on them, but he didn't know if that would be… welcome.

It had been less than fifteen hours ago that they'd been entwined with one another beneath the shower spray, but then again, it had only been about six since Reid had *stupidly* decided he wanted nothing to do with the man.

Stupid, because how could he deny himself this? This brightness in his chest, like coming home, as if Nolan was his North Star.

"I'm sorry," Reid said, and Nolan's head snapped around to him, his smile lessening in surprise.

"What for?" he asked, bewildered, thumb beginning to rub a pattern into Reid's skin.

Did Nolan know what he was doing to Reid? He struggled to catch a breath.

"I dunno, just… writing you off like that."

"Oh," Nolan breathed, as if only just remembering the way they'd last parted. "Well, that's… quite alright, I think."

Reid stared at him.

"I just mean, I don't blame you." He sighed, shaking his head just as Reid parted his lips to protest. "I don't mean that in a self-derogatory manner. I'm part of something that could end up hurting you, and that's very real, and something you have every right to feel any kind of emotion about."

Reid wanted to respond, even opened his mouth, but nothing came out. He flatlined, he was pretty sure. He felt like an old desktop that had been rebooted, the fans slowing to a stop and his memory going offline for a break.

Who *was* this guy?

Whoever he was, Reid *had* to kiss him.

He turned to face Nolan, hand sliding against his until Reid pushed him back into the mirrored wall, pressing Nolan's back then his hand against the surface. Reid could hear his breath catch, watch his eyes go wide as Reid erased the space between them.

"Any kind of emotion, hm?"

Nolan nodded frantically.

"And what if I was angry?" Reid asked, gaze dipping to Nolan's lips. The way he darted his tongue out to wet them.

"Oh. Well, that's certainly allowed. I would understand… that." Nolan's words trailed off as his attention dropped to Reid's lips, and then up to his eyes, and back down.

"What if I was mad? So mad I just wanna… fucking kiss you about it," Reid said, lowering his head to Nolan's.

Their lips brushed once – a tease, a test – and then again, petal-soft as neither of them moved away, and a third time, mouths crushing together like the other held the only air they'd ever need.

It was like the entire day had never happened, like it was last night all over again, on their way up to Nolan's room, horny and giddy instead of listening to the floors tick down.

Nolan threaded his fingers through Reid's, holding his hand as they made out like a couple of teenagers, and god, Reid *felt* like a teenager all over again, with butterflies in his stomach and heat swirling up the length of his spine as Nolan's lips parted beneath his and their tongues twined. They were holding *hands* and Reid melted into him as Nolan lifted the other, sliding it through his hair and holding on tight. Reid let Nolan tilt his head for the angle he wanted, a sliver of desire slicing through him at the firm action.

God, was it too late to put this elevator in reverse and take them back to the room?

The ding as they reached their floor apparently thought so, and Reid pulled away as the doors parted on the ground floor.

"Right," Nolan said – a little dazed, Reid noted with pride. "Where are we going?"

"I don't know, man, you tell me," Reid responded, trying to hide his smile and not succeeding at all.

It was hard *not* to smile when Nolan looked like he was trying to find his brain cells again, eyes dropping to Reid's lips twice before he cleared his throat. "Yeah. Right. I'll take it from here," he said, and stepped around Reid, grabbing his hand at the last second.

Reid grinned too, nodding his head at the two people waiting to enter the elevator with embarrassed glances. He wasn't even sorry.

Nolan refused to let Reid fly him to the location, not wanting to spoil the surprise.

"Now, you can't laugh," Nolan said softly. "When we get there," he clarified.

"Why would I laugh?" Reid asked. "We going to a comedy club?"

Nolan rolled his eyes, but his lips twitched up in Reid's desired effect. "You'll see."

What Reid *saw* was a cartoon painting of a dog and a cat along the blank white wall of a small building. The car came to a stop, and Reid followed Nolan's lead as he got out.

The tires of the ride crunched over the gravel as it left, and the headlights splashed over Nolan's unsure smile as he stared at Reid.

"It's stupid, right?"

"We're at a pet rescue place," Reid said.

"Yes."

"Are you getting a pet?" Reid asked, puzzled.

"Well, no, but—"

The creaky metal door to the building opened, and a woman in pink scrubs stepped out. "You must be Nolan, right?"

Nolan stepped forward, nodding as he went. "Yes! Are you Amanda?"

"That's me," she answered.

Reid stared as they shook hands, more questions forming in his mind. "This is a friend, Reid. Is it okay that I brought him along?"

Amanda smiled as she glanced between the two of them. "Of course. The more the merrier, as they say. Come on in, I'll show you around."

"Reid," he said in greeting as she held her hand out to him to shake.

"Good to have you. Come along."

He shot Nolan a confused look as they followed Amanda into the building. It was… small. Smaller than it looked from the outside, actually. In the background he could hear the muffled barking of dogs and a few meows, even from the reception area.

"It's a quiet night for us anyway, so you actually picked a perfect night to stop by. Just sign your names here." She swiped a clipboard off the counter and handed it over, and Reid's stomach flipped at the words on the top of the sheet. Nolan filled out his name, number, and time of arrival on the

Volunteer Sign-In form, and then handed it over to Reid, who did the same.

So this is happening?

Reid had never been to one of these places, had never been interested in pets, but the few cats he had come across around the restaurant alleys seemed to love the shrimp leftovers they had to throw out.

She led them down a hallway through a wooden door with… yes, those *were* teeth marks on the bottom of it. In fact, the whole corner of the door was chewed off, the dark wood littered with scratch marks.

"This is the cat room," she said softly, and pointed to their left. Through a screen door was a room the size of a living area, lined with cat trees in front of a giant window on one side, and metal crates stacked floor to ceiling on the other. Some cats were free and sat up at the sound of people, staring at them warily.

She pointed to the door opposite them. "Food, toys, and treats are in this closet, as well as fresh towels for the cages. Don't bother with the red-tagged cages—those are special cases, and they're best left alone."

"Surely not all the time, right?" Nolan asked. It could have been construed as a bitchy question, if not for the worry in his voice.

"No, of course not," she answered. "Those cats just have specific volunteers that handle their care and have been taken care of today already."

"Oh, that's wonderful. They've become attached?" he asked.

"Yeah, it just makes letting them go a little more bittersweet."

"What's your adoption rate here?" Nolan asked, and wow, he was really into this, nipping at Amanda's heels with question after question.

Amanda answered all of them with a smile as she led them to the kitten room, where they cared for healthy kittens, and the parvo room, where they cared for the sickly ones. They didn't go in that room, with different brightly colored papers taped to the front of it.

"This is surprisingly roomy, compared to some of the places I've volunteered at. I'm terribly afraid your place looks rather small from the outside," Nolan said at one point.

"I know, right?" she said, not offended at all. "It's a squeeze. We're actually looking at adding on a few rooms, which will be cheaper than finding a new place altogether."

"Oh, that'll be lovely," Nolan said sincerely.

Amanda led them back to the cat room, and clapped her hands together softly. "Okay, then, I think that's all you need to know. I don't usually leave first-time volunteers alone with the animals, but from your extensive reference list, I think you'll be alright," she said with a wide smile. "So, take your time, and if you need anything at all, I'll be up front. They're all yours."

"Thank you so much, Amanda."

Reid waited before she was out of sight before he elbowed Nolan. "You're a volunteer?"

His cheeks turned pink as he nodded. "I am. Shall we go in?"

Nolan unlatched the door after making sure none of the cats were trying to escape, and they slipped in before latching it back.

Instantly the cats, who had been waiting in silence, all leapt into action. They climbed to the tops of the cat trees, near the ceiling, and hissed in unison like a fucking choir.

Nolan froze. "Well, that's certainly never happened before."

"Uh..." Reid laid a hand over Nolan's shoulder. "I'm a griffin, dude."

He half-turned toward Reid, brows lifted in disbelief. "No… surely not! Is that what they're upset about?" he asked, eyes darting between the upset cats, their backs arched and tails flicking and hair standing up, and back to Reid, who slowly unlatched the door and slipped back out.

"I think so, man," he said, nodding at the cats who still eyed him suspiciously. With a door between them, they started to settle down again, tails snapping side to side in irritation. Reid watched in awe as Nolan shushed them with a gentle voice, high-pitched in the cutest way, soothing the army of cats like some magical cat whisperer.

Once they'd calmed down, Nolan turned back to the door and eyed Reid through the mesh net.

"Well, that's certainly disappointing."

Reid winced, running a hand through his hair. "I'm sorry. I mean, I guess I am half jungle cat. They can sense it."

Nolan huffed. "Do you want to leave?"

"Do you want to stay?"

Nolan's eyes were wide and round and… the only word that came to mind was *pouty*. "Yes."

"Then we'll stay. I'll just be your… your stuff grabber. From the closet. Just tell me what to do."

Nolan lifted his hands to his hips. "Are you sure? I didn't expect you to do any work. I just—"

Reid cut him off. "You came to volunteer, right?"

How his nod managed to be cute, Reid didn't know.

"So we'll volunteer. I'm happy to, honestly."

"You're sure?"

"Positive," he said, and leaned to the right side of the door, trying to see the cages. "How many new towels do you need?"

Nolan smiled – beamed, really, bright as the fucking sun breaking through the clouds – and nodded. "Well, alright, then. Let's see."

SECRET DATE

Nolan counted the kennels without red tags and called the number out to Reid.

He turned around to make sure Reid had heard him, and was greeted with the sight of Reid's ass. He was facing away from Nolan, the closet just across the small hall open as he gathered the towels, which—blessedly—were on a lower shelf for some reason. Reid had to bend at the waist to reach them, and Nolan's cheeks flushed.

He spun on his heel and faced the cat towers, the felines eying him from the tops in a manner as if to say, *We saw that*.

"You saw nothing," he whispered.

"What's that?"

Nolan jumped at the sound of Reid's voice, and twisted back around just as he unlatched the door.

"Nothing," Nolan answered far too quickly to be casual.

Reid's lips twitched. "You can talk to the cats, man, it's nothing to be embarrassed about."

"Right. Yes, I was talking to them," he admitted.

"What about?"

"Secret… cat stuff?"

"Fine, fine. Keep your secret cat secrets. I'm just the errand boy," Reid sighed.

Nolan winced, placing the stack of towels down and speaking low enough not to startle the cats. "I can't believe I never considered that they'd be set off by you. I'm so sorry, again. You'd think after volunteering around cats for so long, I would've known that."

He reached the first cage, spying a large orange tabby inside. "Hello, Citrus," he greeted gently, peering at him. He looked elderly, lounged out across a red towel that looked worse for wear. "Ready for a new red carpet?" he asked in his cat voice.

He couldn't help it. It just happened. His pitch went up as he spoke to them, almost an embarrassing squeak of a noise.

"How long?" Reid said, and Nolan turned his attention to the half-feline on the other side of the door.

His lips twitched. "How long what?"

"How long have you been volunteering?"

"Oh, uhm…" Nolan went over the different places he'd spent his time in his head. He grabbed a new towel to show Citrus, and slowly unlocked the cage, trying not to make the metal groan and screech. "A few years now, at least. Basically, ever since my father first started taking me on trips."

"So you volunteer all over?"

"I do. Every city we stop in, I try to find somewhere." It was his own form of therapy, in a way. Animals were way easier to talk to than people.

Citrus did not seem to care that Nolan was invading his space, even if he came with a clean, fluffy new towel.

"Hello, there," he said softly, removing first the food bowl, then the water, and finally the litter pan from the cage. "Just a little remodeling." Last but not least, the feline. Citrus stared at him in boredom as Nolan grabbed the edges of the towel and slowly pulled.

"What's that one's name?" Reid asked, and Nolan turned his head to find him peeking in through the screen door.

"This is Citrus. He seems friendly, or at least neutral. Have you ever had a pet?" Nolan asked.

Reid hummed. "No. Couldn't afford 'em when I was a kid, but there's a few strays that hang around the restaurant."

Nolan listened as he pulled the towel out of the cage. Eventually, Citrus rolled over to escape the movement of the fabric, and Nolan tossed the dirty towel in the hamper.

"Do you feed them?" Nolan asked.

"Of course. They love the scraps."

"And they're not scared of you?" Citrus wasn't offended when Nolan went to pet him, sniffing his hand curiously.

"I mean, they don't greet me when I go outside or anything. They just wait until I'm gone before they go after the food."

Nolan replaced the towel and then shut the cage, locking it behind him.

"What do you do now?" Reid asked.

"Well, for each cage we need to clean their water bowls and food bowls, scoop their litter, and replace it if it looks old enough."

"Every day?' Reid asked, eyes wide. "That's a lot of cats."

"Well, no. But I like to be thorough." Sometimes it was better to be safe.

"Here, I can wash the bowls while you replace the towels," Reid said, and unlatched the door. The cats on the towers hissed again, and Reid shot them a droll stare. "Oh, calm down. I'm doing you a favor, here."

Nolan chuckled at the cats' dramatics and handed over the bowls. "You remember where the sink is?"

"You mean the one that's five feet away? I think I can make it," Reid said, sending a wink toward him before disappearing down the hall.

Nolan moved onto the second cage, another elderly cat, who required a bit more pampering before he removed the towel. He didn't want to terrify the poor guy, so he let him warm up with some sniffs.

When he heard the clack of the bowls and the latch of the door, Nolan spoke without turning his head, keeping his voice soft for the cat. "Next, would you get me some of the treats out of the closet?"

He waited until the cat, Bobo, seemed less offended at his presence, and shut the cage to take the bowls from Reid.

"What's wrong?" he asked, unsure about the expression on Reid's face.

After a blink, lips parting in a distracting manner, Reid seemed to shake himself and said, "What? Nothing. Uh, treats?" His cheeks colored, and then Nolan flushed, and they both stammered as Reid left the room with another glare at the hissing cats.

He poked his hand through, the bag of treats crinkling, and suddenly the cats were a lot more eager to have their towels replaced.

"Hey, I have a question," Reid said softly, with a paranoid glance down the hallway. "Are the water bowls supposed to be slimy?"

Nolan stepped closer to the door, lowering his voice. "That's just a thing that happens. *And* it's why I insist on cleaning them when I volunteer. Does it gross you out? I can wash t—"

"No, I was just curious. I mean, ew, but it's fine," Reid insisted, and made a grabby hand for the next set of bowls.

They worked in tandem, the process flowing much smoother and faster with two people. The litter boxes took no time at all, a fresh scoop and a bit of baking soda that Reid kindly retrieved for him. Only a few of them needed full changes, which made his job easier.

"You're really good with them," Reid said suddenly, and Nolan startled, so focused on the sweetest cat, a tortoiseshell tabby, in the last cage. He ignored the blush on his cheeks from the compliment.

The cat was missing an eye and one of her ears was rather scraggly from old bites, but Nolan loved her with his whole heart right away.

It was intimate, even though they were in separate rooms with a screen door between them, to be showing this side of himself to Reid. A side he didn't share with anyone at all, really.

"This one's a fighter. Tough," Nolan said, scratching under her chin and welcoming her loud, vibrating purrs.

The cats on the towers made their way down at the promise of treats, and they were a lot more friendly from that moment forward. Earning their trust one treat at a time, he let them get their sniffs in, and behind him, Reid gasped at the first cat who nudged into Nolan's hand for a pat of the head.

"Well, look at you, cat whisperer," Reid called out in awe.

It made Nolan's chest tight, and he swiped his fingers between the gray cat's ears as he purred. Cats were easy. They only liked interacting as much as they could stand, and then they fucked off to be on their own. Nolan personally related, and knew to give them their space when they asked for it.

Together, they finished the rest of the cages, cleaning the last few bowls and litter trays. Nolan tied up the trash and brought the laundry tote with him as he exited the room.

"Bye, guys," Nolan whispered as he latched it back. It broke his heart a little as the gray cat followed him with his big green eyes.

But Reid was waiting for him at the end of the hallway, eyes locked on him, some unrecognizable emotion in their warm depths.

"What?" Nolan asked, cheeks flushing at the attention.

His question seemed to shake Reid out of his stare, and he shook his head, a smile quirking one corner of his mouth. "Nothing, nothing. Now what?"

He turned as Nolan neared and together they made their way back into the reception area. Amanda was nowhere to be found.

Setting the laundry basket down, Nolan leaned over the desk and grabbed the volunteer sheet. He signed his name and noted the time, then handed it over to Reid. "Now we sign out. Then we can find Amanda and tell her we're done."

He scooted the laundry basket out of the way and grabbed the bag of trash. "We can drop this off in the dumpster, too."

Reid grabbed the bag from him and waved a hand out. "Lead the way," he said.

Nolan huffed out a quiet laugh and pushed out the storm door, holding it open for Reid.

The wood creaked beneath their feet as they took the ramp leading down, and crossed the parking lot, gravel crunching under their shoes.

It was still hot, even as the sun began to set and cast the whole area in a golden orange glow.

After tossing the bag, they made their way to the attached building, following the sounds of excited barking.

"I'll wait here," Reid said.

Nolan was going to protest until he saw the sheepish grin on Reid's face. "Oh, the dogs, too?" he asked, disappointed.

"Unfortunately so."

Nolan shook his head in sympathy and knocked on the outer door. It sent the canines inside into a ruckus, and he grimaced at the noise level. Amanda called out to him, but it was muffled over the barking and through the door, so Nolan decided to risk it. He cracked open the door. "Amanda?" he called out.

"Come in," she shouted. "My hands are busy."

They most certainly were. She had two tug toys going, held at the other ends by a gray pitbull and a smaller terrier.

"We've wrapped up the cat room and locked everything up. Is there anything else I can do for you?" he asked, politeness winning out with the offer.

The terrier began growling and shaking the toy back and forth, making his lips twitch. Meanwhile, the pitbull was just snuffling as he gently tugged every so often.

"No, not really. You two work fast," she said, glancing over her shoulder. "You make a cute couple."

"Oh, well, we're—thank you," he finally said. Amanda didn't need to know the details. "I appreciate that."

"Of course. We'd be happy to have you anytime; just give me a call."

"Will do. Have a good night."

The door clanged a little too loudly behind him, and he jumped, which made Reid chuckle.

"Your face is all red. What'd she say?"

Oh god, would the ground swallow him up already? "Nothing, just that we could go. She said we make a great team."

Reid pretended to straighten a tie at his throat. "Well, that's because we do. We killed that."

Suddenly, he lifted his hand and gave it a sniff. Then tilted his head and sniffed his shoulder. "Is that… normal?"

Nolan chuckled. "Oh, yes. The smell clings."

Reid glanced over his shoulder, toward the parking lot. "Well, now what?"

"Are you hungry?" Nolan asked, accidentally overlapping his words with Reid's. He chuckled. "Sorry."

Once again, he didn't want the night to end. The sun had only just set; surely he didn't have to say goodbye already?

"I could eat," Reid answered, a smile tugging at his lips. "Have something in mind?"

The words almost got stuck in his throat, but he forced them out. "Room service has quite the selection."

His eyes widened at the same time Reid's did, the implication of his words far too loud to ignore. "No—I just mean, a shower! You could take a shower, for the smell. Oh my god, not that *you* smell, I mean, the cats. Smell. Oh my god." Nolan lowered his head into his hands and sighed.

And suddenly Reid was laughing, and a palm curled over Nolan's shoulder to give him a gentle shake. "I could go for a shower. And some room service. Do you want to call a car, or can I be your taxi for the evening?"

Nolan lifted his head slowly, absolutely certain steam would be curling off the heat from his cheeks. "Do you *want* to be the taxi?"

He nodded, a small grin still playing at his lips. "Yes."

And so it was there, in the gravel parking lot of the pet rescue, that Nolan got to see Reid change again. It was so smooth and fluid, he would've missed it if he'd blinked. But instead, his eyes were wide open. He was awake and alive, and there was a thrill running through him at the idea of flying through the sky again, clutching at the warmth of Reid.

Nolan shook himself back to the moment, back to Reid, still very much human, but with two huge, feathered wings extending from his back.

It had been so dark the last time he'd seen Reid's wings, and now they practically glowed in the light of the setting sun.

Nolan's eyes were surely as big as the moon cresting the trees. "Reid, you're amazing."

The wings were huge, a creamy hue with dark tips,

complimenting the spun gold of Reid's hair like a renaissance painting.

Nolan tried to circle him but Reid shifted away, keeping his hands behind his back as he turned, and Nolan came to a stop at the worried expression on his face. "What is it?" Nolan asked.

Reid's cheeks were flushing, and Nolan decided he liked the look on him, very much so. "Well, there's, like – you know about the feathers, the fur. I have wings, but they come with something else. I didn't show you the first time because it's… well, you're not allowed to laugh."

Nolan couldn't imagine laughing at Reid for anything, but nodded solemnly. "I won't laugh, promise."

Reid huffed, nostrils flaring before he released his hands. At first, Nolan frowned in confusion, because his hands were empty. But then, something caught his eye, twitching behind Reid's back in a familiar kind of manner.

Nolan gasped. "Reid! Is that…"

"Yes, it's a fucking tail!" he blurted, crossing his arms. "Just don't pull it and we won't have any problems."

It was a lion's tail, the flared tip flicking around in that way a cat's did when it was irritated.

Oh dear, was Reid irritated?

Nolan stepped forward, took Reid's hands, and untucked them from his arms. "There's nothing to be embarrassed about. You have wings! I can see them better in this light. You're beautiful."

Reid shuffled his steps, glancing down. "Ah, that's… Thanks. They're just my wings."

He spread them out, the span extending far wider than Nolan had expected, even after having seen them in action.

"Wow," he breathed. "Can I touch them?"

Reid's eyes widened. "Yeah, sure."

As Nolan circled Reid, his tail swished again, and Nolan couldn't help the smile tugging at his lips. The flare of affection in his chest expanded, leaving no room for his own breath.

He reached his hand out and lightly brushed his fingertips over the feathers. "Wow, you're soft," he said. Reid's wings fluttered under his touch and he pulled back. "You're not ticklish, are you?"

Reid's voice was tight when he said, "No, just, uh, startled me, is all." Then he cleared his throat.

Nolan felt honored, suddenly, that Reid was showing him this. Sharing this half-shifted form with him, even though he was clearly hesitant. Well, in Nolan's opinion, he had nothing to be ashamed of, and he kind of wished he could go back in time to whoever had said something to make Reid feel like he had to hide.

Just to talk, of course, as one did.

He paced around and sought Reid's gaze out, finding his brows furrowed in worry over those dark, decadent eyes, and tried to return even a fraction of the moment's significance in just a look.

When that couldn't do it justice, he murmured simply, "Thank you, for this."

And Reid's huge eyes stared up at him, emotion wavering in them, and god, Nolan was so *fucked*.

"You still won't drop me, will you?" Nolan asked, shattering the moment before it swelled into *too big* territory with a clumsy chuckle. He was mostly teasing. Their first night, when Reid had flown him to the top of that building and then back to the hotel, was still vivid as ever in his mind. The way Reid's arms had wrapped around him, enveloped him and kept him safe.

Reid's lips twitched up. "No, I won't drop you."

"Promise?" His stomach flipped.

Reid reached out, grabbed Nolan around the waist, and

pulled him close. He gasped as their bodies formed one line, pressed together from chest to toes. His tail wrapped around their thighs, holding them together.

"Promise," Reid answered, voice soft in the same breath they shared.

Before Nolan could untangle his thoughts to come up with a response, Reid's wings moved, and Nolan grabbed onto him instinctively. His arms slid around Reid's waist, fingers pressing into his back as their feet left the ground.

"Oh god," Nolan said, and slammed his eyes shut. "I forgot how high it was up here," he whispered, words lost to the wind as Reid's wings worked in strong, full beats, propelling them through the sky and over the many tall and small buildings of the city.

It seemed to take longer to get back to the hotel than it had to get to the rescue, and Nolan realized halfway through that Reid was going slowly for him. Instead of diving and plummeting around buildings, he was taking his time, leisurely flapping his wings to get them to their destination instead of racing there in heart-leaping speeds.

His hands tightened around Reid's waist, emotion catching in his throat that he couldn't put a name to.

Nolan wanted to live in this moment forever, wrapped in Reid's arms, feeling safe despite the height they dangled from. He could feel Reid's heart thumping in his chest alongside Nolan's, caught in the intimacy of the moment.

His stomach swooped as the hotel came into view again, and he tried not to mourn the moment before it had even ended.

They landed in front of the hotel again, at the rideshare drop off, and ignored the many curious glances as Nolan finally slid his arms from around Reid's waist. He cleared his throat, and by the time he was brave enough to meet Reid's gaze again, he was human, wings and tail tucked away, standing there with a smile on his lips and his blinding golden halo of hair.

"That wasn't so bad, was it?" Reid asked him.

Nolan shrugged, heart suddenly in his throat. He spoke around it when he said, "The flying thing is growing on me."

"Thought so." Reid held out his hand, as if motioning Nolan forward. "Lead the way."

Nolan did, but not without grabbing Reid's hand first. If he wasn't imagining it—god, he hoped not—Reid's breath caught just a split second before their fingers threaded together.

It was a small gesture, but his heart pounded just the same in his chest. They'd just been close enough to breathe the same breath, and yet a simple touch sent his heart racing.

Thankfully there was no sign of his father or Chance or anyone he knew, for that matter, as they took the elevator to his floor once again.

"Something tells me we've been here before," Reid said as the doors closed on them.

Nolan wheezed out a laugh, meeting Reid's eyes in the reflection of the metal doors. As similar as it had sounded, Nolan's intention had not been to invite Reid to his room to… hook up, or whatever.

The image in his head went like this: separate showers, maybe a borrowed robe or a shirt and pants or something of the like, and then ordering room service, watching something silly on the unnecessarily large television mounted to the wall.

Things had been so tense between them only that very afternoon. The dejection that had unraveled in him when Reid walked away had been more intense than Nolan was prepared for.

Nolan was already smitten with this man. Besotted with his kind eyes and dumb jokes and his transparent love of life.

He was the fucking sunshine, casting rays of light along Nolan's dreary life.

And that was scarier than any height Reid could fly them to.

The doors opened, jolting him from his thoughts, and he tugged Reid from the elevator, hands still clasped.

He only released him to dig his wallet out for the key, and swiped it over the circular lock. The beep echoed in the hallway, and he pushed inside to his room once again.

God, was it really only this morning that he'd left Reid sleeping in his bed?

Unbidden, his attention trailed to the bed in question, long since made up, pillows restacked by the cleaning crew. He hated the pinch of disappointment in his chest at the erasure of Reid, even though the very man was standing just before him.

"So… shower," Nolan said, cheeks flushing as he suddenly floundered. "Do you want to go first?"

The silence was deafening.

"Sure," Reid finally said, voice low and quiet and private, just for the two of them.

Something hot twisted in Nolan's gut, and he swallowed, motioning to the attached room on the right, peeking in to verify that— "Yeah, fresh towels and everything. Uh, there's a robe you can wear, or you can borrow something if you'd like—"

"Nolan," Reid interrupted, and he stopped mid-sentence. "You're freaking out."

"I'm freaking out," he admitted, turning to face Reid. Nolan's head filled with white noise at the sight of Reid's bare chest, the feathers creeping over his shoulders, and god —he swallowed—along his forearms, interspersed with the tattoos.

"Don't freak out," Reid said, stepping closer. He chuckled softly, gaze dipping to Nolan's lips and—

"I didn't invite you here for this," Nolan blurted. Reid's step paused midair, hesitation slowing his movements, and Nolan reached out. "I mean, that wasn't my *intention*. I didn't know, if after everything—"

Reid's expression glowed bright with understanding, and he stepped forward again, pulling Nolan with him into the bathroom. "I know. I know."

And then Reid's lips were on his, and Nolan's breath was weak, and his heart pounded so loudly he was certain it echoed off the enclosed space of the bathroom.

Nolan let the warmth envelop him, let himself relax into Reid. This was happening. Reid tilted his head into the kiss, lifting his hands and cupping Nolan's jaw.

Nolan melted, and then Reid's fingers were making deft work of the patterned button-up. When they parted for a breath, his gaze dipped down to the skin he'd exposed, and Nolan flushed even more, if that was possible.

Then Reid paused suddenly.

"Are these… little cats?" he asked, brushing a thumb over the fabric below a button.

Nolan nodded, discovering it *was* possible for even more heat to fill his cheeks.

"God, you're… fucking wonderful," Reid breathed.

No one had *ever* used that word to describe Nolan before, and it took him a few seconds to process the warmth in his chest.

Maybe once, as a child, had a teacher referred to him that way. The word most certainly had a different effect on him now than it had then.

Nolan knew he wasn't a good person, had never entertained any fantasy notions otherwise. But with Reid's lips shaping those words, he could almost believe it.

Instead of trying to find his own words to respond, he tilted Reid's head up with a gentle touch and kissed him about it. Kissed him with the soft fluttering in his chest as Reid pushed his shirt off his shoulders.

Nolan lifted his hands, letting his fingers trail down the softness of his skin. He broke the kiss with a small smile. "I wanted to tell you, all day, that you looked absolutely devastating. Very smart."

Reid glanced toward the door, the pile of his jacket and the plain tee beneath, then to his matching pants.

"I wanted to impress the rich men thinking of investing in your hotel. Do you think it worked?"

"You certainly impressed me," Nolan admitted.

"Well, that's all that matters, then," Reid said, and while they both knew it was a lie, they didn't mention it, pushing it from their minds in the form of another kiss.

Reid's dashing pants ended up crumpled on the floor alongside Nolan's jeans. His breath was short, heart racing as they bared more and more skin, as they pressed closer and closer and tasted the affection between them, sweet on their lips.

Reid was the one who turned the shower on this time, ducking beneath it and motioning for Nolan to join him, eyes sparkling and dark with desire at the same time.

This was… big. This moment.

Nolan knew this was the point of no return. He was going to fall for this man, this man whose life he was supposed to ruin.

If he stepped into that shower with him, he knew there was no turning back.

Nolan walked into the steam, joining a waiting Reid.

ROOM SERVICE

Nolan joined him under the spray, and suddenly it was like no time had passed at all. Once again, the water slicked their bodies and dripped between them. It was hot on his tongue as it melted into their kiss, as he chased the drops down Nolan's neck, pushing him against the shower wall.

As he slid a thigh between Nolan's legs, felt his hard length against his skin and chased the rush, he realized this was only the beginning. It was only Monday, even though it felt like he'd already lived a whole week in just one day.

He still *had* a whole week with Nolan. Of *this*.

And suddenly he didn't want to wait anymore. He pressed even closer, slotting their cocks together and basking in Nolan's moan.

"You know what I just realized?" Reid whispered.

Nolan's eyes were wide as he shook his head. "What?"

"We have all week together," he announced, dipping his head to take his lips again.

Reid couldn't believe he'd almost allowed himself to miss out on this. Almost let himself walk out of Nolan's life without looking back.

Nolan hummed, the sound tickling Reid's lips. His hips

kicked forward as Reid dropped a hand between them, wrapping around both their cocks and stroking slowly.

He leaned into Nolan even more, holding him against the wall. The water barely reached them in this corner, and chills spread over his skin at the contrast of the chilly air and the mist.

The next thing he knew, *his* back was pressing into the cold tile, sending a shiver up his spine, and Nolan was curling his hands in his hair, tilting his head up, deepening the kiss.

He rolled his hips into Reid's touch, and Reid slowed the pace, squeezing his hand on each upstroke.

"*Reid,*" Nolan panted into the kiss, and god, *that* was hot. Hearing his name on Nolan's breath.

Zings of pleasure danced across his scalp as Nolan tightened his grasp, and Reid's fingers closed around them in turn. Nolan's breath skated across his cheek, and Reid couldn't help himself; he fought the delightful tug in his hair so he could chase another drop of water across his skin, desperately jealous they were closer to him than Reid could be.

He licked and sucked along the line of Nolan's neck, and Nolan tilted his head to the side for more, holding Reid there with a hand in his hair as the other dropped to his hip, holding him in place, pushing him against the wall.

Reid loosened his hold a bit more, just to see what Nolan would do, how desperate he'd get.

He groaned again, the sound deep and needy in a way that made Reid's blood run even hotter.

"Are you intent on torturing me?" he questioned, righting his head and staring into Reid's eyes.

Reid swallowed. "Maybe."

"Like you said, we have all week, yes?" he asked, gaze drifting to Reid's lips, and then lower.

Reid didn't know what to do except nod.

"Good," Nolan simply replied.

His hand joined Reid's between their bodies, framing the hand Reid had wrapped around them, fingers twining around their cocks. He tightened his grip, and Reid gasped at the pressure, hips knocking forward into the touch.

"I've been thinking about you all day. This. Every time I saw you," Nolan confessed.

Knowing that Reid had been on Nolan's mind as much as Nolan had crossed his was... a heady, brilliant thing.

Together they stroked down, fingers sliding over the bumps along Reid's cock, so different from the smooth length of Nolan's. Over the mushroom heads, bunching the foreskin of Reid's, the ridge that was extra sensitive, pulling a moan from his throat that Nolan swallowed.

"It kind of... swells. You know. For..." He cleared his throat. "Breeding purposes."

"What was that?" Nolan asked, leaning forward, eyes wide and blinking water away. "Breeding?"

"I know, like, with us, it defeats the purpose, but it just happens anyway. Just want you..." He sucked in a breath at Nolan's grip. "To be prepared."

Nolan grinned, then ducked in for another kiss and a tug at his lip before sliding his mouth along his jaw, down his neck to suck at his pulse.

"Prepared, huh? As if I don't plan on branding you into my brain. I have to see this," Nolan said, voice low and deep and dragging along his senses in the same drugging way his touch did. "You'll let me see you, right?" Nolan asked, breath hot along his neck like the steam around them.

He dropped his head to Reid's shoulder, releasing the hand in his hair, and Reid's own head knocked into the tile behind him with a thump.

"You'll come for me?" he asked again, and Reid wondered

how the other man ever expected an answer when Reid was barely hanging on as it was. Every touch and breath and even each word seemed curated just to ruin him.

Reid had never wanted to be ruined before, but with Nolan it seemed like it was inevitable, and he welcomed it, especially with Nolan's voice rasping like that, echoing off the tile. Pleasure slid down his spine, heavy and hot and electric.

Like Nolan could sense it, he clasped his hand tighter around them, concentrated his strokes, short and quick and tight around the heads, and Reid arched into him for more. Nolan slid a hand over his hip, pushing him back into the chilled tile with a smack, and Reid shuddered beneath him.

"Stay there," Nolan said.

What the *actual* fuck? Reid wanted to whine, but he choked it back. Who was this? Because it wasn't the endearing, dorky, nervous business guy he'd spent last night with.

This man was whispering little praises between them, *god, you feel so fucking good* and *yes, yes, just like that*, staring between their bodies as he stroked their cocks and made Reid lose his everloving mind. He blew out a hiss that ended on a moan, bouncing around the tiles with their panting breaths.

"Come on, Reid, come for me, let me see you."

"Oh f-fuck," Reid stuttered, pleasure barreling down on him and making his hips kick against the hand Nolan held him still with, abs tensing and releasing as ecstasy swelled beneath his skin and—

"Oh, *look at you*," Nolan murmured, a strike of awe flickering in his voice.

The whimper Reid had been trying to swallow back finally slipped free, sliding into a moan as he came. His eyes fluttered shut as his cock kicked in Nolan's grasp, and then

Nolan's lips were on his, grounding him, holding him here when otherwise he might float right off.

He felt Nolan's breath stutter and his body tense before he groaned into the kiss, spilling over their hands.

Reid's hand dropped, hanging limply by his side, and then in a burst of affection he wrenched the clean hand into Nolan's hair to hold him there, their tongues twining lazily as the last aftershocks faded between them.

They panted as Reid let his head fall back into the tile, squinting against the mist from the shower head as he tried to come up with a word. Any words at all would do.

"What. Was that?"

"Was that okay?" Nolan asked.

Reid *almost* rolled his eyes. "'Was that okay,' he asks, after making me see stars," he drawled instead, staring at Nolan.

Nolan cheeks flushed and *then* he blushes, all virgin-shy after… after *that.*

"I can't believe you," Reid whispered, pushing him under the spray and tasting him again.

After that it was lazy and easy and silly, as they washed each other again and Nolan got acquainted with the feathers on his shoulders and forearms, the soft fur on his thighs and legs.

No one had ever paid such close attention to him before, taken such care with him.

Fuck, it sounded kind of sad when he put it like that. Or maybe it made Nolan all that more special.

He blinked slowly when the water finally shut off, and accepted the towel Nolan handed him.

"Come on, then, I still have to feed you."

Oh yeah. Room service.

As if summoned, his stomach growled and Nolan chuckled, turning to head into the bedroom.

"You're not gonna fall asleep on me this time, are you?" he asked.

Reid flushed, skin still warm from the shower, disguising the color on his cheeks. "No. S'not my fault you were taking forever."

"Mm, you're right. I shouldn't have left you here to fend for yourself."

"Damn right." Reid let himself fall onto the cushy mattress. "In this huge bed? What else was I supposed to do?"

Nolan hummed as he shuffled through the closet.

"So you're one of *those*," Reid mused before letting his head flop back down to the pillows.

"And what is one of *those?*" Nolan asked.

"You unpack and hang everything up instead of living out of your suitcase like a normal person."

"Excuse me?" Nolan's voice rose in pitch in his disbelief. "I'm not a heathen."

Reid snorted again, stretching, until a piece of fabric hit him in the face. He uncovered a grin when he pulled it away, a pair of boxers held between his fingers.

"I'll have you know, I wear a lot of suits, and you can't leave those folded. You'll get creases," he hissed, in a way that Reid thought vampires might hiss towards a crucifix.

"And creases are... bad," he guessed, lips twitching as Nolan stared at Reid like he'd lost his mind.

"Creases are *very* bad. Unprofessional!"

"Did your dad teach you that?" he asked, tugging the borrowed boxers up his legs.

It was silent for a moment, and Reid glanced over at him once he was appropriate. As if they hadn't spent the last thirty minutes being inappropriate as hell.

"Sorry if that's a touchy subject..." he added, sitting on the edge of the bed.

Nolan had his own pair of boxers on and paused with a

shirt in hand, gaze darting to Reid as he was jolted out of his thoughts. "Ah, no, no, nothing like that. I was just thinking about your question. I… don't think he did teach me that," he said, smoothing a hand over the fabric. "I think that's all me," he announced. He held the shirt out to Reid as he continued talking. "Maybe I started it as a way to impress him or something, but I'm afraid it stuck. Pretty sure my therapist would tell me it's a control thing."

"Ouch," Reid winced on his behalf.

"Yeah, I know." Nolan chuckled and donned his own shirt before grabbing his phone and laying back on the bed. "So. Food."

"Right. You still intend to feed me."

"Mhm," he hummed, flicking through his phone. He paused suddenly, lifting his gaze and winking. "Gotta keep up your energy, because *that*," he tilted his head to the bathroom, "was just an appetizer."

Reid's eyes widened. "Jesus christ, Nolan."

Eventually, he ended up with his head on Nolan's shoulder as they browsed the virtual menu for the hotel's room service on Nolan's phone.

It was different, because he wasn't usually a cuddler after sex. Or maybe he *was*, because he'd most certainly never enjoyed it this much.

But the little circles Nolan was tracing into his thigh as they browsed was certainly turning him on to it. Nolan *would* be a cuddler, Reid thought.

And maybe that wasn't so bad.

Once their order was placed, Nolan grabbed the remote and turned the television on.

"This is perilous territory," Nolan warned. "Picking something to watch."

"Did you just use the word 'perilous'?" Reid drawled. "It'll be fine, we can agree on *one* thing to watch."

Except twenty minutes later, they were still scrolling through the third streaming app.

"Oh, I hated this one," Nolan grumbled. "The dog died."

"Well, we don't want anything sad," Reid agreed. There had been enough emotional turmoil for today.

"Maybe an action comedy?" Nolan suggested.

But, "Eh, the CGI in that one is so bad," Reid had to complain.

"It's a comedy, isn't it supposed to be bad?" Nolan questioned.

Reid was already shaking his head, motioning for Reid to continue scrolling. "Not if they're trying to be serious about it."

"The two main actresses in this series hated each other on set," Nolan shared as they flipped through the Drama section.

Reid's mouth dropped open. "No! Really? That kinda ruins it. I thought they were good together."

"Good actresses, not good friends," he murmured.

"Bummer," Reid huffed, and laid his head back down on Nolan's chest.

The strong thump of Nolan's heart was steady beneath his cheek and Reid tried to focus on the scrolling, but Nolan was combing his fingers through Reid's drying hair, and he was pretty sure he didn't care what they watched, as long as Nolan didn't stop.

He imagined it was similar to the way Nolan had pet all the cats at the shelter, and the word that came to mind was *finally*.

There's absolutely no way Reid had been jealous of the felines. Because that was weird, right? Kind of crazy, even.

And yet Reid had spent the better part of his time – when he wasn't washing bowls or getting treats and food – staring at Nolan. At the way he'd given each cat his full attention, letting them get sniffs in and then figuring out where they liked to be scritched, which part of their head or shoulders or neck made their fuzzy little butts lift up to meet him.

So. No. Of course he wasn't jealous of the cats.

But if Reid could purr, he was pretty sure it would be vibrating his throat.

"So. Why cats?" Reid asked suddenly.

Nolan's strokes through his hair faltered, and now Reid wished he'd never opened his big mouth.

"What do you mean?"

"I mean, why volunteer with pets? Why not soup kitchens, or Habitat for Humanity, or—"

"Oh," Nolan said, then hummed. "It's kind of a sad story."

It seemed all of Nolan's stories were kind of sad. Reid's heart squeezed in sympathy.

"I don't mind. I wanna know."

"My dad's not a fuzzy-feeling kind of guy, as I'm sure you know. When I was home one summer, I found a kitten, all muddy and sad looking. I brought him home, but couldn't find Dad, and Mom had already been gone for years at this point. Gosh, I think I was, like… nine? Ten? Something around there."

Reid swallowed. This was not going to be a pretty story.

"I cleaned her up in the kitchen sink, making what I'm sure now was a huge, annoying mess. But I was just happy to take care of the kitten. She was white under all that mud, and had the most pitiful meow." Nolan's throat clicked when he swallowed. "Dad was *not* happy when he came home. Said some bullshit about her being a wild animal, better off on her own, and if she couldn't survive, it was her own fault."

Reid's heart thundered. *This close enough to kicking dogs for you, John?*

"God, Nolan, I'm so sorry."

Beneath him, Nolan attempted a casual shrug. "It's… in the past at this point. George Whittier hates pets. So, it's just my little petty obsession. Taking care of the ones I can, in whatever way I can."

"That's fucked up. I'm sorry he's such an awful person," Reid muttered, voice muffled in Nolan's chest. "I'm glad you volunteer."

"Me too. It's nice. I want a cat of my own, but I travel so much it just seems cruel, to let one get attached to me and then never be around."

"That can be the first thing you do when you tell your dad to shove it," Reid said, with a frustrated edge to his tone. George Whittier was an awful person, and Nolan was better off without him.

"Maybe it will be," Nolan offered, a note of wonder in his tone, and resumed the comforting strokes in Reid's hair.

Reid let loose a low breath. Not a sigh, because that wouldn't be fair to Nolan. If he didn't want his whole life to implode because they'd spent one night together… well, that was more than fair.

And besides, with Nolan's fingers brushing through the strands of his hair, he was content as fu—

A knock on the door made them both freeze, and Reid *just* stopped himself from whining when Nolan slid out from under him to go get the door.

Reid listened to his polite tone and many thank-yous until the door closed.

Nolan cleared his throat as he came in pushing a little cart. "Wanna hear something funny?"

"Hit me," Reid said.

He lifted a small box. "I asked for condoms," Nolan said, lips twitching.

Reid almost bruised a rib laughing so hard.

CLOSET SPACE

The sun woke Nolan up, blinding and bright and warm —no.

That was Reid, asleep next to him in the bed, lips slightly parted with his deep breaths.

Nolan stared for probably longer than polite, watched Reid's face twitch in sleep, counted the even number of breaths.

But the time niggled at the back of his mind. What hour was it? Was he late again?

A stealthy roll and stretch brought his phone to him from the side table, the small unopened box still sitting on the top.

They hadn't done anything that warranted condoms, and if left up to Nolan, they wouldn't be using them anyway, since they didn't have to. But the inside joke had made Reid laugh, so buying them had been worth it.

Instead, they'd finally decided on a movie, eaten, and then fallen asleep before the credits rolled.

But it didn't matter. They still had the whole week.

And yet that didn't feel like long enough, so with time permitting, he rolled back over to stare at his new favorite sight, only to find Reid blinking himself awake, smiling fondly at him.

God, it was rather warm this morning, wasn't it?

"Hello, you," Nolan whispered, afraid raising his voice would shatter the porcelain moment.

"Morning," Reid responded, voice raspy from sleep. His arms slipped from the covers to stretch overhead, biceps straining with the long line of his body in a very cat-like stretch. A muffled groan slipped out of him, and Nolan swallowed tightly.

"Are we late?" Reid asked on an exhale before diving back under the covers.

Nolan tried to focus, but Reid was pulling him into his arms and humming contentedly against his neck. "Not late," he murmured. "You're warm."

Reid shuffled even closer, nudging a knee between his until they were a tangled bundle of limbs under the covers. "You're warmer."

"You're snuggly," Nolan commented, and held tight when Reid tried to pull away. "Just an observation, not a complaint."

"It's not usually my thing," Reid responded, relaxing into their pretzel shape again.

"It's definitely one of mine," Nolan admitted. *With you.*

Reid hummed softly, and Nolan let his eyes drift shut, his head resting atop Reid's as he nudged his nose into Nolan's chest.

"How much time do we have? I'll need to drop by my place and get clothes before the conference."

Nolan hated sacrificing even a moment of time with Reid. "You're welcome to borrow something of mine, if you'd like. Though I don't know if my suits will give you the same... vibe."

"What vibe is that?" he wondered against Nolan's skin.

Nolan winced. "I don't know, effortlessly cool? Charismatic? Colorful? I can keep going—"

"Did you not see the tie you were wearing yesterday? It looked great, like the fuckin' sky or something."

Nolan's cheeks heated, a pleased little notch burrowing into his heart. "Well, that's… it's not like your boots or anything."

"How about I just borrow a shirt? Do you have any more of those cute little printed numbers like you wore last night?" Reid asked, nuzzling a line up Nolan's throat.

Nolan tilted his head back to extend the journey. "Maybe. Maybe not. Depends on whether you keep doing that."

Reid leaned back, brow arched, and Nolan extended his bottom lip in a pout. "No, I don't think I do—" But before he was finished speaking, Reid nuzzled in close, nose trailing up Nolan's pulse. "Actually, seems I might have one after all."

"Thought so." Reid nipped at his skin, slowly but surely working his way down his neck and to the collar of his shirt.

"Don't think we have quite that much time," Nolan managed through the heartbeat in his ears.

"Disappointing," Reid murmured. "I'll have to save it for later."

"Much later," Nolan agreed, already wishing the day's panels were over.

"Or just… later." Reid lifted his head with a decidedly suggestive expression.

"After the convention," Nolan guessed.

"Ehh." Reid scrunched his nose. "Might not be able to wait that long."

He pushed Nolan to his back and followed him, sliding over his hips like he belonged there. "You look really good in your suits, all buttoned-up and professional. You know your numbers. S'kinda hot."

Nolan floundered, staring up at him with his mouth dropping open and closing again when he couldn't find anything to say.

"We can't..." Do whatever they were doing. "*Flirt* during the convention," Nolan breathed, scandalized.

Reid cocked his head to the side, a knowing smile curling his lips. "Sure we could. Why not?"

"Because, all those people—"

"Don't know shit. For all they *do* know," Reid drawled, leaning down until they were chest to chest, his weight comforting and dizzying all at once, "we met at the convention. Who knows. Maybe we even meet today."

"What?" Nolan couldn't think with Reid and his honeyed eyes so close, his lips brushing Nolan's, his words casting some kind of spell on him.

"What if we hadn't met on Sunday? What if all I had to go on was that teal blue tie you wore yesterday?"

"The tie, really? I'm just—"

"That fitted suit, the pants. The way you commanded that whole room of people, with your charts and graphs and numbers."

Nolan wouldn't have given it a second thought, would've thought Reid was just indulging him, if not for the length hardening against his own. "Well, that's just—"

"You're not *just* anything, Nolan," Reid argued, leaning down to nip at his lips.

Humming into the kiss, Nolan chased after Reid when he tried to pull away, already mourning the morning they could've had, if not for the convention looming over their heads.

"And if I wanna have you at the conference, somewhere private, can I?"

Nolan gulped, indecently aroused by the thought, and found himself nodding.

How could he say no to Reid?

"Good," Reid purred, and laid another kiss on his lips, light as a jewel placed upon its cushion.

Nolan groaned and, with a tap of his phone, confirmed what he already knew—they didn't have time.

"Fine," Reid sighed, sounding very put upon in the cutest way. "Pick me out something nice to wear." He flopped onto his side of the bed, clearly unashamed of the tent in his boxers as he covered his eyes with a forearm. "Hurry, before I perish."

"Well, we can't have that, can we?" Nolan mused, and slid from the bed.

There was something thrilling about giving Reid his clothes, watching him pull the chosen shirt over his arms and buttoning it up. The short sleeves framed his biceps more deliciously than they ever would have Nolan's, and the fine, tiny print of—

"Are these bees?" he asked, and the wonder in his voice made Nolan's heart leap with acrobatic agility. Who needed caffeine when he could wake up with Reid?

"Yeah," Nolan said, voice a little tight as he watched Reid fix the collar, mess with the sleeves.

"So fuckin' cute, man." Reid's voice had a distinct quality to it that brought Nolan's eyes back to his, only to find them pointedly fixed on Nolan.

Oh.

"Bees are important to the environment. I bought that shirt specifically because twenty percent of the total went to the conservation of them," Nolan explained.

Reid continued to stare at him. "Do you have a story for every item of clothing you own?" Reid crossed the room and was *right there* and suddenly catching a breath was a bit harder than it had been only seconds ago.

"Well, no, that would be outrageous."

Reid waited a beat.

"Okay, fine, maybe," Nolan admitted.

Reid's lips twitched, and he leaned up to pop a chaste kiss

on Nolan's, who threatened to melt under the casual affection. "Maybe you can tell me one day."

"I'd bore you," Nolan informed him.

"Oh, I highly doubt that," Reid retorted. "If hearing you talk numbers made me want to drop to my knees, imagine what listening to you talk *clothes* would do to me."

Nolan's face was as bright as the pink sunrise, he was sure. "Oh," he choked out, eloquent as ever.

Reid only smirked, pressed another kiss to his lips, and stepped back.

"You still have to put pants on," Reid said, motioning to Nolan's lower half. "Get distracted?"

"Watching you put on my clothes? Most definitely," he answered, voice a little rough.

"Well, you better hurry. First presentation starts in… thirty minutes. See you there?"

Right. They couldn't very well walk over together, could they? What a scandal it would be, to walk arm in arm—even holding hands, in his wildest fantasies—into the convention where Nolan was supposed to convince them to bulldoze Reid's business.

"See you there," Nolan replied.

The room was quiet after Reid left, and Nolan decided promptly that he hated it. He much preferred Reid's humming and puttering around and opening all the drawers and investigating the nooks and crannies to the silence.

By the time he was dressed properly and slinging his bag over his shoulder to head toward the convention, he was already thinking about Reid. Where they'd go to lunch, if he could even be whisked away. What they might do that evening. Would Reid take Nolan to his place? He thought he'd quite like to see the chaos that Reid most likely lived in.

Nolan shook his head as the elevator beeped at him. He was utterly *consumed* with thoughts of Reid.

Nolan didn't know why he was surprised, not when it came to *Reid*.

God, he couldn't wait to see him again.

Nolan had thought Reid was joking when he'd asked about *having him* at the convention, when they'd sorted through Nolan's clothes and found something appropriate for Reid. He grabbed himself a coffee upon entering the convention's hotel lobby, deciding a caffeine boost was necessary after all.

It turns out Reid was most certainly *not* joking.

Not when he raised a hand during the questions portion of Nolan's presentation.

Nolan cleared his throat, hoping his cheeks weren't as red as they suddenly felt. "Yessir, what's your question?"

"Just wondering how this would affect the local economy? Have you considered how your new mega hotel would take out multiple small businesses that serve the community?"

Cheeky little shit.

Nolan loved it.

His father's eyes bored into him, gray and dark like a storm on the horizon, and even though it suddenly felt a lot warmer in the room, he turned his gaze to Reid.

"In fact, I had… not. Would you like to enlighten us?"

Oh, he hadn't expected that, Nolan could tell.

Reid stood and adjusted the shirt around his throat — *my shirt*, Nolan thought with a kick of heat in his gut.

Shit, this was basically foreplay, in front of all these people. His face *burned.*

Reid's voice carried as he talked about servicing the lower- and middle-income members of the community, questioning aloud where those people were supposed to go once another multi-million dollar hotel went up. Because why did it stop there? What was to stop them from building a sixth hotel, a seventh, or even a tenth?

The shirt sleeves tightened around his biceps as he talked with his hands, animating the words with his passion.

The thing was, Nolan was really fucking good at telling people what they wanted to hear. He'd been practicing his whole life. So Nolan could have interrupted, could maybe have corralled the room back into his favor by talking about how the hotel *did* intend to help the community. However, the hotel's policy hardly had the same impact, when it came down to it, so he simply... kept quiet. As Reid's speech extended, and other people started asking questions, it turned into a bit of a town hall, with Reid at the center of it.

The longer it went on, the more beet-red his father's face turned, and suddenly Nolan realized maybe he *did* have a little power in this situation. His father sure wasn't prepared for presentations, probably didn't know half of what Nolan was expected to keep track of. He probably didn't even *remember* the hotel's commitment to the communities they invaded, had hardly been listening when Nolan had sold him the idea based on tax write-offs. He'd agreed only to get Nolan out of his office, more than anything.

So maybe Nolan could help Reid after all.

A few others stood, and Reid was treated to a round of applause from the room. Nolan was fully enamored and a little in love by the time Reid finished speaking.

Nolan was proud of him.

He absolutely sparkled with the victory, and Nolan bowed playfully, conceding to Reid's very sexy competency.

Nolan got it now. After watching Reid talk with such confidence and surety, maybe he did finally understand what Reid meant by finding Nolan hot.

Because Nolan most certainly was a little more than warm under the collar after watching him command the room.

"Well, I think that's all the questions we have time for today. If you'd like to pick my brain, I'll be around," he said, and bid everyone a good day.

The room began dispersing, and Nolan schooled his expression as his father neared, a fake smile stamped on his face, and who else to follow at his heels but Chance?

"What. Was. That?" he asked, spitting the words between clenched teeth in that fake smile.

Not even the low veiled threat in his voice could dull Nolan's mood.

Nolan plastered a smile on his face, meeting his father's furious eyes. "Seems someone opposes the building of a mega hotel atop local businesses. Imagine that."

"You just *let* him talk!" his father argued, stepping closer and framing one shoulder with a hand. He squeezed. Tightly. "He ruined your presentation, and you let him."

"Hardly," Nolan lied, finding it easier than he thought. "What was I supposed to do? Start an argument and look like an asshole? Not a very good look for business, wouldn't you think?" He covered his father's hand with his own, trying to dig a finger or two under his harsh grip. "Take the loss. We'll recoup with the next one."

"Appreciate your dedication," his father bit out. "I'll schmooze, try to soothe some ruffled feathers. You... you just try not to fuck this up."

"I'll do my best," he agreed stiffly. "Do try to be professional, there *are* eyes on us," he reminded him. Specifically, Reid's eyes.

His father dropped his hold instantly, clapping him on the back a little too hard and offering a forced chuckle that made

Nolan grit his teeth. Nolan huffed as the man walked away, Chance hot on his trail.

They were long gone and Nolan had just slid his messenger bag over his shoulder when Reid finally approached.

"Hey there. Sorry about crashing your presentation. I'm Reid," he said, and held out a hand.

A fission of excitement vibrated through him as he shook Reid's hand, playing this little game with him. "Hello. Nolan, but I'm sure you already know that. Impressive interruption, though. You really had them going."

"Dear old Dad didn't seem too bent out of shape about it, though. I'll have to try harder next time." Reid lowered his voice. "He wasn't too mad, was he?"

Nolan cocked his head to the side, shoulder still smarting from the hard squeeze. "He's good at pretending."

Reid looked like he wanted to ask about what exactly that meant, but Nolan changed the subject. "I think I'd like to hear more about your business, if you don't have anywhere to be?"

"I think I'm gonna be wherever you are," Reid said, gaze dipping appreciatively down his body, and Nolan's cheeks flushed. He cast an eye at the room around them, but found no one paying them any mind, to his relief.

"Walk with me," he said, and turned, taking the exit beside the temporary stage. It spit them out in a much less traveled hallway, closed doors lining its length into the multitudes of other conference rooms. They only passed three other people, and Nolan was tracing the names on the doors before he spied the one he was looking for.

With a glance, he made sure the few other people were headed in the opposite direction before he tugged open the door to the small closet, and yanked Reid inside.

"Ah, your office, I take it," Reid teased.

Nolan shut the door with the quietest click before locking it behind them. Convenient.

And crowded, but he'd make it work.

"Thought you might like to… talk business somewhere private," Nolan drawled.

"Is that what they're calling it these days," Reid wondered, and Nolan drew him close before spinning him into the door with a thump to match the banging in his chest.

God, he felt like a fucking teenager. He hadn't felt this way… ever. This lightness in his chest, the soft elation as Reid tilted his head at him, lips quirking.

"Figured any further inquiries would be better handled behind closed doors," he murmured, his attention glossing over the darkening of Reid's chocolate truffle eyes, the bow of his lips, the shape of his jaw beneath the blond stubble.

"Oh, I can think of a few inquiries alri—"

Nolan dropped his mouth to Reid's, savoring the soft scratch of their cheeks together, the brush of their lips, then tongues when it wasn't enough.

Moments later they pulled apart, breaths loud in the small, dark space. "It's rude to interrupt," Reid panted, and Nolan grinned, tilting his head up with a thumb under his chin to get at the pulse pounding beneath the surface.

"Rich, coming from you," Nolan retorted, dragging his lips down Reid's neck to the collar of the borrowed shirt. *My shirt.* "Can't believe you stole my spotlight."

"Are you mad?" Reid asked, and Nolan jerked his head up, eyes intense on Reid's, or what he could see of them, anyway.

"No! Of course not. Never." Nolan slid his hands up Reid's chest, cupping his head and threading his fingers through his hair. "It was actually quite… hot."

Reid snorted. "Hot, huh?"

Nolan leaned in to nip at his neck again, feeling the chills work their way down Reid's spine since they were pressed so close together.

"Definitely. In fact..." Nolan dropped to his knees, thankful the lighting was dim because his cheeks were on *fire*. He'd never done anything like this before, not so close to the public, and most certainly not in a *closet* where they could be discovered at any time. "I think I just have to have you."

"*Oh* fuck," Reid whispered, as Nolan let his hands rest on his thighs.

"Yeah?" Nolan asked. This was his idea, after all. Nolan was just following through.

"*Yes*," he rasped, combing his hands through Nolan's dark hair. "I'll try not to mess you up too much."

Nolan shivered at his words, making him wonder if he wouldn't mind being messed up all that much. He slid his hands up over Reid's thighs, fumbling around with his belt and button and zipper until they were giggling and hushing each other and— fuck, why was it so dark in here?

But then Reid's pants were down around his thighs, and as Nolan's eyes adjusted to the dark, he could *see* Reid.

Glances in the shower, feeling Reid's length against his hand, was one thing. To see him though, especially this close, practically tasting him already, was another.

Reid had been right when he'd said that he was different. At the very least, he was uncut, and Nolan circled him lightly with his fingers, stroking once to reveal the mushroom head, the bump of the ridge beneath. His fingers tightened over all the other little bumps that lined his cock, and *dear god*, Nolan wanted to feel him.

"Be-be careful, when I come, the swelling, it'll—"

"I got it," Nolan interrupted, licking across the tip and tasting Reid on his tongue. He reveled in the choked-off groan, and tilted his eyes up, then spoke with his lips against the head of Reid's cock. "Be quiet, or someone will hear."

"Jesus," Reid hissed, head thunking against the door, and Nolan pinched his inner thigh. "Ow!"

"Do you wanna come in my mouth or not?" Nolan huffed, and Reid's quiet gasp sounded, followed by a low chuckle.

"I love when you're bitchy," he whispered, and Nolan's cheeks flamed anew.

"I do not get *bitchy*—" he attempted to return, but Reid tightened his grip in his hair and his words fell silent.

"Shh. I'm pretty sure there are better things you can do with that mouth."

If Nolan was a stronger man, those words wouldn't have speared him through with heat, wouldn't have made his cock twitch in pants that were slowly tightening.

But he was weak for Reid, so he had the grace not to respond with any of the *bitchy* retorts that went through his mind, and instead laved his tongue across the head for more of Reid's taste.

Reid panted loudly above him, but swallowed any other noises that would give them away as Nolan mouthed at the ridge an inch or so beneath the head.

He tuned into Reid, listening for his breaths and feeling his hands clench in Nolan's hair and the way his hips jerked or his thighs tensed beneath the hand planted there. In the dark, in that closet, feet away from discovery, Nolan started to get an idea of what made Reid's knees weak.

Nolan took the head into his mouth and gently, so fucking gently, teased his tongue around his foreskin.

"Fuck," Reid croaked, fingers twisting into his hair as if he couldn't decide whether to pull Nolan away or yank him closer. "S-sensitive," he breathed.

Taking the hint, Nolan focused his attention elsewhere, sinking deeper as he dragged his fingers down Reid's length until the bump of the ridge beneath the head was resting on his tongue. The weight of him, the taste, the knowledge that

Nolan was the one making Reid feel so good made his own cock throb, blood rushing south until he was lightheaded with it. Or maybe that was just the effect Reid had on him, breathtaking and heart-pounding.

God, he was *already* a mess, and it had nothing to do with the hand in his hair.

A choked sound slipped out of Reid's throat when Nolan sank deeper, lips and tongue sliding along the bumps. He had to wonder what purpose they had other than pleasure. If it was part of the—of the breeding thing.

Reid's fingers tightened against his scalp and Nolan pulled back to angle him out of the way, then dragged his tongue along his length, feeling those bumps press against his tongue, then lower, to suck one of his balls into his mouth. Teasing and experimenting, even though they didn't really have the time for it.

The realization made him wish he'd dragged Reid all the way back to his hotel, conference be damned. So when Reid tugged at his hair, he let Reid drag him back up, and Nolan sucked him between his lips again.

A puff of air exploded from Reid on a gasp, and a little fissure of pride cracked Nolan's chest apart. *He* made Reid feel so good the man could hardly keep quiet, and suddenly Nolan had to make him come. Needed that validation like he needed his next breath. Maybe that wasn't the healthiest line of thinking, but that was the last thing on his mind with the weight of Reid on his tongue.

He slid his lips around Reid, taking more, curling his fingers around what he wasn't brave enough to, and focused on his breathing as he built a rhythm. He curved his tongue around the underside, dragging it against the ridge on every withdrawal and thrust.

"Nolan," Reid pleaded, nothing more than a whisper, and

Nolan glanced up. "Oh god," he breathed, and Nolan *felt* his cock swell against his tongue.

He pulled back until he could suck around the ridge, working his hand over the rest of him with ease, his own spit and Reid's precum slicking his hand and lips and chin and god, it was so messy, and Nolan *loved it.*

Reid's thigh flexed beneath the fingers Nolan dug into his skin, his hands tightened in his hair, and Nolan sucked with vigor, circling his tongue around the sensitive ridge and the head. Reid's muttered litany devolved into barely-there murmurs, and the ones that reached his ears went like *oh god, oh god* and *fuck, Nolan* and *so good, holy shit.*

The praise went straight to his head, straight to his cock, and unbidden, his hips rolled, seeking any kind of pressure and unable to find any good enough.

Like Reid *knew*, he nudged his leg between Nolan's thighs, and his gaze darted up again, finding a filthy smirk on Reid's lips. The toe of his boot nudged at Nolan's ass and when he rolled his hips forward again, he found blissful, decadent friction against the line of Reid's shin.

"God, you're so fucking hard," Reid whispered, eyes sliding shut even as Nolan continued to stare up at him, his hand stroking Reid's cock and his cheeks hollowing as he sucked at the head of him. "Just from my cock in your mouth—fuck."

He swelled once again and Nolan mourned that it was against his hand instead of where he craved to feel him. He nudged his hips into Reid's leg and groaned at the delicious pressure.

"*Fuck,*" Reid hissed through gritted teeth. "I'm—"

Reid pulsed against his tongue as he came, as he swelled and spilled, and Nolan squeezed his hand tightly around him, slowing his strokes. Above him, Reid choked back a moan and cursed, fingers twisting in his hair and holding him still as he slowly worked his hips away from the door, sliding along Nolan's tongue as he swallowed.

"Oh god," he finally said, hands falling away.

Reid pulled him up and Nolan stood on shaky legs and sore knees and gasped into the kiss, sharing the taste across Reid's tongue as they fell against the door. Nolan planted his palms against the surface and leaned his whole weight into Reid's chest.

"I can't believe you just did that," Reid murmured when they parted. "Did you come?"

Nolan had to collect his thoughts first. "And walk around all day like that? No."

Reid's grin was daring and dirty and hot. "D'you wanna?"

Before Nolan could answer, as if there was an answer except *of course, god, please*, Reid spun them around and dropped to his knees, made quick work of his zipper, and—

"Fuck," Nolan gasped out as Reid's fingers wrapped around his cock.

His hips jumped away from the door and Reid pushed him back gently, a hand around his hip as he—

Some odd noise got stuck in Nolan's throat at the first touch of Reid's tongue against him, and he dropped his head to watch as Reid sucked him in.

"Won't take much." He breathed the admission, struck with a sharp heat as Reid's gaze flicked up to his.

And it was that *look*, paired with the sight of his cock sinking between Reid's plush lips, his blond hair tangled in Nolan's fingers, his smarting knees and the taste of Reid on his tongue, that sent him over the edge. In a closet at a convention, hoping no one opened the door.

"Reid," he bit out in a muffled groan, body curling forward as he bowed under the pleasure. "Fuck."

He was left with a warm glow, and Reid shot up from the ground to kiss Nolan again. Between the two of them, their hearts were pounding so loudly he wondered if the entire conference could hear them.

"Told you," Nolan managed to say.

"That was so hot," Reid returned. "God, what am I gonna do with you?"

Nolan sputtered. "Well, hopefully more of that. Later."

Reid grinned, leaning in to nudge at his cheek with his lips before dragging them to his throat. "Definitely more of that."

"Good. I want to take my time with you," Nolan admitted. Reid choked on a breath, but Nolan talked over whatever reply he could've come up with. "Wanna feel you inside me."

"Jesus," Reid hissed, and laid his forehead across Nolan's shoulder. "You realize how stupid this was?"

"Absolutely," Nolan agreed, but he couldn't help it. He wanted every piece of Reid he could get, and maybe it was selfish, but… he was going to let himself have this, cherish it.

"Wanna do it again?"

Reid snorted, pulled back with a wild gaze.

"You're insane," he responded.

Nolan felt a smile curl his lips. "And you like it."

CAUGHT

After they'd tucked themselves away and acted as the other's mirror, trying to lay their hair back down, they slipped out of the closet one at a time, with no one the wiser.

Or so Reid thought.

His phone buzzed as he came to the end of the hallway, and he pulled it out, a message lighting up his screen.

I'm begging you not to fuck this up for me. You'll bring me something, right?

Reid's head snapped up, scanning the long hallway, searching for—John. His grumpy face glared back at him from the opposite end of the hallway, and Reid tried to smooth his hair into order before he gave up. Maybe they could've been a little less obvious about it.

Would it kill you to let me have a little fun? he messaged back, staring across the room as John pulled his phone out to read his response. *I'm doing what you said, spending time with him.*

A little fun? John's message read, before the typing bubble appeared and disappeared and appeared again. *You floated out of that closet on cloud nine. Are you doing research or just getting your dick sucked?*

Reid's heart gave a desperate thump. *Does it matter? this*

was ur fuckin idea! Reid's texts got lazier the more his annoyance festered.

John rolled his eyes at the device and shook his head as he replied. Reid was scowling at his phone when the message arrived. *I guess it doesn't matter what avenue you take, as long as we arrive at the same destination. Just don't let me down, man. I need this job.*

Reid huffed, letting his eyes close for a brief second before he responded. *I know. I'll find something. We have all week.*

That's what he and Nolan kept saying. But they didn't really have all week, did they? They had until Reid found something, reported it to John, and ran a story.

Because surely once the story—Reid *would* find one—was published, and Nolan read it, he'd know it was Reid. He'd know what Reid had done and then that was *it* for them, he knew it. And he hated it. Maybe even hated himself a little for going through with this, but…

With a blink, he was on Nolan's chest again, fingers carding through his hair while his eyes got sticky with sleep, and with another blink he was here. In reality, where he was supposed to betray Nolan.

Maybe they *didn't* have all week. Maybe they didn't have long at all, but Reid would have to collect and save and lock away all the sweet little pieces of Nolan he could savor, and then let him go when he inevitably left.

He walked away from John, thoughts racing and the taste of Nolan still on his tongue.

The rest of the conference that day was boring in comparison. But his little interruption had made the rounds. Familiar faces came up to greet him, to ask him questions, to share in his frustration about the hotel digging up the community's roots. His chest was tight with emotion. The more people he talked to, the heavier he was weighed down.

Not only was he trying to save his own business, he was trying to send a message. A message that all these people, proverbial strangers, stood by: that nothing was worth the community they'd built here, that they'd stick together and weather this one out.

But they didn't know about the pile of unpaid bills on Reid's desk, didn't know how long he'd been sacrificing his own pay so he could keep his employees.

He bit down on the anger of the unfairness. Their support meant something, no matter what form it came in.

So as he spent the day fielding questions and handing out cards and telling people about the restaurant and inviting them to experience it for themselves, he smiled and put on his most welcoming expression. Even to the ones in suits with turned-up noses.

He only looked for Nolan every single fucking chance he got, but the man proved to be elusive up until the very last speaker was finished.

He checked his phone repeatedly, unsure if he should head home, or to his restaurant to check on everyone, or if he should give in and head back to Nolan's hotel, like he really wanted.

Fuck it.

It was a short, hot walk to the hotel down the street, and once the blissful air conditioning welcomed him in, he headed toward the bank of elevators, tapping his foot as he waited.

He chewed at his lips as the elevator took him up to Nolan's floor, and stuck his hands in his pockets so he wouldn't tap them against his thigh or pick at his nails.

By the time he was in front of Nolan's door again, he was a ball of tension and nerves and exhaustion, and maybe he *should* just head home. He didn't think he'd be very good company.

But fuck all if he didn't want to see Nolan. Even if it was just for a moment. To tell him goodnight.

He was lifting his hand to knock before he knew what he was doing, and then there Nolan was, bright and beaming and pulling him through the door without a second thought.

It wasn't until the door shut behind them that Nolan recognized his expression, and paused, a hand still curled around Reid's wrist.

"What is it? What's wrong?"

And Reid kind of hated how Nolan could see right through him, but he kind of liked it too, and he couldn't help but reach for him.

Everything felt too big and overwhelming, and this ease he had with Nolan wasn't helping because it was all so confusing, but—

But.

It was a little easier when he buried his head in Nolan's neck. When he sucked in a breath of the citrus florals of Nolan's scent and Nolan wrapped his arms around him and held him tightly.

He was *so* fucked.

Because he took the first deep breath since their closet affair, and closed his eyes as Nolan's hand threaded into his hair and scratched against his scalp. Like he *knew* what Reid needed and just provided it, no questions asked.

"Want a shower?" Nolan asked.

And it was perfect. The steam relaxed his shoulders, but he had an idea that it was more to do with Nolan's hands on his skin than anything else.

"Want to talk about it?" Nolan asked as they dried off, as he led Reid to the bed and pushed him down on it despite the fact that his hair was still dripping water.

Reid murmured something noncommittal, and Nolan

hummed in response, and then a smile was twitching at his lips.

"Wanna get your wings out? Take your comfy sweats off?" Nolan suggested, and…

Hey. That wasn't a bad idea. And it struck him as a little silly, that Nolan had remembered such a small, inconsequential thing that meant so much to Reid, and suddenly he couldn't breathe.

"Okay," he choked out quietly, and found Nolan beside the bed, out of the way. Reid was prone, head tucked on his forearms, and with a sigh and shuffle, his wings were free and resting along his back.

"There," Nolan said, voice soft and close to his ear as he pressed a kiss to his shoulder. "That's better, hm?"

"Don't go getting a big head about it," Reid grumbled, fighting a shiver at the warm drag of his voice.

"I would never," Nolan drawled, and then puttered around the room until Reid got curious and propped his head up on a hand.

"What are you doing?"

"Looking for—aha! This," he said, and proudly turned, boxers now stretching across his thighs—a shame— and a small bottle held in his hands like a commercial.

"What's that?" he asked, laying his head back down as Nolan rounded the bed until Reid couldn't see him without turning over, and to be honest, he was all melty-warm from the shower and couldn't be bothered to follow him with his gaze anymore.

At least not until the bed dipped, and weight settled across the backs of his thighs.

"You're not allowed to laugh at me," Nolan said, and Reid was taken back to just the night before, when he'd said the same thing about the very tail that now swished around Nolan's thighs.

"I would never," Reid parroted. "What did you do?"

"I had some downtime and couldn't very well find another closet to suck you off in, so I did some research."

"Research?" he questioned, interest piqued, ignoring the flare of heat in his gut.

"Mhm. Can I touch your feathers?"

Reid swallowed. "Sure."

"It was rather annoying to sort through all the care of feathers that *aren't* attached, but eventually I found that hemp oil is good for shining them up," he said casually, calmly, and not like it was the sweetest thing anyone had ever done for Reid in his entire life.

Most birds have a gland that produces oil naturally so they can clean their feathers. Well, Reid's only half-bird, so he didn't get one. Which meant he kept a stock on hand. At home. And maybe it'd been a few months since he'd actually done them up, because, well. He was lazy, he'd admit it. And it didn't interfere with his flying, or the rideshare job he'd taken for some extra money.

Reid's wings fluttered, shivering at the first touch, and he sucked in a breath.

"Alright?" Nolan asked, pausing.

"Yeah, yeah it's fine," Reid said, trying to force more volume into his voice because it threatened to come out as a whisper.

"Are there any places you want me to avoid? Too ticklish or sensitive?"

He shook his head against his forearms, laying his forehead down and breathing through the crater in his chest.

And so began the most delightfully torturous half-hour of his life.

Nolan slicked his hands with the oil, the soft hush of his skin somehow audible over Reid's racing pulse.

It was slow-going at first, and gentle. His touch began so

lightly that Reid hardly would've known he was there, if not for the weight across his thighs. But the more Nolan continued, the more Reid sank into the bed, eyes drifting shut. His chest pushed into the mattress with every breath, and it was comforting to have Nolan's weight pressing back.

The more Reid relaxed, the more confident Nolan became with his hands. His fingers stroked over his feathers, in between them, ruffling and combing until constant chills raced over Reid's skin.

It stretched into a muted kind of pleasure, nothing demanding, just warmth and softness and the sound of their breaths and the hush of skin against feathers.

Reid's worries melted away under the heat of Nolan's fingers.

He was fighting sleep when Nolan adjusted, shifting his weight to one knee and sliding the other between Reid's thighs. Settled across the back of his left thigh, Nolan could reach the tips of his feathers when Reid helped, curling the wing close.

However, he was more concerned with the knee sliding between his legs, a whisper of a touch so light he wondered if Nolan even noticed.

The thought of sleep slowly burned away beneath his steady touch, leading Reid back to this moment as if it had been his destination all along, Nolan guiding him sure and firm.

"Do you wanna talk about it?" Nolan asked, voice gentle as his touch.

"It feels silly now," Reid admitted. "I feel better."

He could sense Nolan's smile before he heard it in his response. "I think you've heard enough of my problems to warrant a little sharing of your own, if that's what you're worried about."

Nolan's warm hand closed around his shoulder and

squeezed once before slipping away to press into the bed. Reid held his breath as Nolan straddled his other thigh, shifting his attention to his right wing, knee brushing his inner thighs.

Great. Now he was horny.

Reid focused on each touch, but remembered Nolan had asked him a question.

"It's not that I don't wanna talk about it," he said, pushing up and glancing over his shoulder. Nolan's hands paused on his feathers, the concentrated furrow to his brow easing. "It's that I want to fuck you more."

Nolan's cheeks flushed red instantly, his gaze darkening. "Oh." He cleared his throat. "Well. That's certainly... Okay. But I won't be able to sleep if you don't let me finish this wing first."

Reid rolled his eyes, an affectionate grin tugging his lips. "Fine, fine. If you must."

Nolan pressed him back down to the bed. "I must, sorry."

If Reid expected him to hurry through the rest of his task, he should've known better. Nolan took just as much time with the remaining feathers as he had with all the others. He worked the oil through the individual feathers, his fingers sure and gentle, his weight a solid presence against Reid.

Warmth slowly gathered in Reid's belly, spreading and burning low with each pass of Nolan's hands, each bit of oil melted into his feathers, massaged into his skin.

"I've been thinking about this all day. About you," Nolan admitted.

An amused hum rumbled from his throat. "Is this a kink? You got a thing for feathers?"

Nolan rolled his eyes, hands firmly pulling at his shoulder to roll him over. "I've got a thing for *you*," he retorted, and Reid noted the blush coloring his cheeks, his own lips curling triumphantly.

Reid was helpless but to kiss him about it. "Do your worst," he murmured against his lips before slotting their mouths together. Nolan melted against him, shucking his boxers before sprawling over his lap, and Reid shuffled back on the bed, making room for him.

Reid reversed their positions, pushing Nolan back into the generous stack of pillows angled against the headboard. Reid fell across his lap, straddling a thigh and groaning at the friction.

Nolan's hands wrapped around his hips and pulled him in against his stomach, cock aching and trapped between their bodies. His mouth latched onto Reid's throat and he tilted his head back, swaying into Nolan like an air current threatened to carry Reid right off.

He found purchase along the top of the headboard, fingers clutching over the wood.

They shifted, and matching groans spilled from their lips as their cocks slid together, slick and hot.

Nolan skated his mouth up Reid's throat, lips catching along the coarse hairs until their mouths collided, breaths harsh and panting across their cheeks.

Nolan's hands slid along his sides, his back, slipping up around his shoulder blades, and hanging onto the sensitive arch of his wings, fingers winding through the feathers. His touch was desperate and demanding, where only moments ago he had been so gentle.

The dichotomy made Reid's head spin.

Reid groaned, his head tipping back and hips grinding against Nolan's stomach, the hard line of his cock.

Nolan hiked his knee up, heel pushing into the bed, slipping along the sheet and jarring against Reid. It forced a moan out of his throat, and he barely choked it back at the last second to muffle the sound.

"That's it," Nolan breathed, reverent and low and just for him. "That feel good?"

Reid nodded, and Nolan's right hand melted down his side and over his left thigh, then yanked his leg up until his knee sank into the pillow by Nolan's hip, dragging him down harder over Nolan's thigh.

"Fuck," Reid whined, head dropping to rest his cheek against Nolan's temple. His tail circled Nolan's wrist, holding him there until his fingers dug into his thigh.

"Don't make me go to the conference with marks," Reid managed to say, as Nolan's lips trailed up and down his throat.

He felt Nolan's lips pull into a filthy grin as they dragged across his skin, over to his shoulder, and he let out a petulant groan. "Right here?"

"Ye—ah!" Reid didn't even finish answering before Nolan struck, lips and teeth sucking and biting at his skin.

The rhythm he'd been grinding fell apart, hips jolting as he stilled, balanced on a thin precipice, frozen with the indecision to grind against Nolan's stomach or lift up into his mouth.

Nolan's other hand still gripped at his wing, and pulled in tandem with the one on his thigh to direct him into a new rhythm.

"Is this how you wanna come?"

Reid couldn't tell up from down, yet Nolan expected him to make a decision like that? As pleasure raced up and down his spine and settled low in his gut and made his cock throb as they slid together in the mess of their own making?

"Uh—" Reid slammed his eyes closed, tried to focus past the *god please more fuck yes right there*.

His cock swelled with the cresting ecstasy, and his hips came to a dead stop, lifting up a bit to get away from the addicting pressure. He knew exactly what he wanted.

"Wanna come inside you," Reid panted, and Nolan hummed and nibbled at his shoulder. "If that's what—"

"Yes, yes, I really fucking want that," Nolan breathed, words skipping across his skin in the wake of chills.

It took everything in Reid to pull back, the air cold as it slipped between their bodies compared to the heat of their skin.

Nolan stretched beneath him, sinking deeper into the pillows as he leaned over to paw at the nightstand. "Look, I'm prepared this time," Nolan teased, the box of condoms they wouldn't be putting to use thumping against the lip of furniture. He reached back in and returned with a small bottle of lube.

"And I'm *very* awake," Reid murmured, sliding down his body. Their fingers collided as he stole the bottle of lube from Nolan and dropped it by his hip, only for it to roll into the dip his knee created in the mattress.

"I sure as hell h-hope so," Nolan retorted, breath catching on the words as Reid lowered between his thighs, making room for himself.

He skated his lips along Nolan's soft thigh, nipping at the sensitive skin and reveling in the shakes and shivers of his reaction. He was so responsive, making little gasps and hums, his thighs tensing under Reid's lips and fingers.

"I think I will actually die, if you don't hurry up," Nolan whined.

Reid hid his grin in the warmth of Nolan's thigh, slid a hand to the back of it, and pushed his leg up and out to make room.

Nolan huffed, and Reid turned that bitchy little sound into a muffled moan by leaning up to take Nolan between his lips.

His hips arched off the bed, and Reid planted a hand over his hip to push him back down.

With deft fingers, he uncapped the small bottle of lube before slicking his fingers and, while Nolan was distracted by the feel of his mouth, slid them between his legs.

He jerked, a full-body jolt that made Reid pull away so he could smile and study Nolan's features, pinched with pleasure as he stroked the pads of his fingers over his hole.

God, he was a marvel. Reid wanted to catalogue every sound, every whimper and moan and grumble of impatient breath.

Nolan's breath exploded when Reid slid into the first knuckle, and he wondered if Nolan's heart was racing like Reid's was. It had to be, right? With each exhale skating past his lips so shakily like that?

Nolan rolled his hips down onto Reid's hand, and he muffled the chuckle against his hip.

"You're good," Nolan said, cheeks and chest pinkening, cock hard and leaking against his stomach. The praise went straight to Reid's head. "Keep going. Faster," he added, with a snarky little tilt of his lips, hand sliding into Reid's hair and tightening deliciously.

"Demanding," Reid retorted, but gave in, eager to feel him, pressing deeper, letting Nolan get used to the welcome intrusion.

When Reid finally pulled back, he added more lube before forging in with two fingers.

"That's—better," Nolan gasped out. Reid's gaze trailed from where he was working him open slowly, up the line of his body, to his flushed cock and pink-splattered chest. His eyes drifted closed, lips parted on his ragged breath.

Reid ground his hips into the bed, searching for any bit of pressure, of friction. He barely found it in the soft cushion of the mattress. To distract himself, he mouthed at Nolan's thighs, pale skin stretching out before him in miles of softness.

Nolan tightened around his fingers, and Reid smirked before chomping down on the inside of his thigh.

"Fuck!" Nolan barked out, thigh twitching beneath his grip.

"You said as long as it wasn't visible, right?"

He laughed out a pleased noise and nodded. "I did say that, didn't I?"

Reid chuckled, sliding the curl of his lips up Nolan's thigh to his hip before nipping the thin skin sharply, just to hear Nolan's breath catch. He pressed deeper, scissoring his fingers, opening him up. Each sound urged him on, each tug of his hair, every time Nolan's body tensed, arching into his touch and his lips. Searching, searching—Nolan jolted, a startled moan spilling from his lips.

There you are.

Reid absorbed all of it, let each passing second sink into his skin and settle, committing it to memory.

Reid was mouthing at the head of his leaking cock, three fingers stretching and twisting and thrusting, when Nolan finally broke.

His hand wrenched Reid's head up, forcing him to meet his wide, wild gaze. "Stop torturing me," he demanded, voice barely a rasp. "You're very fucking good at this. Show me what else you're good at."

Reid's cock twitched at the words, and then he was slipping his fingers free, palming Nolan's hip and shuffling up between his legs.

Nolan reached between them to stroke Reid's cock, and his breath punched out of him at the touch, the skip of pleasure up his spine. "I've been thinking about you inside me since the first night. How you'd feel," he practically purred, voice low and velvety and warm, just like the way he stroked him.

"Me too," Reid admitted, the words forced from his throat

in a desperate admission. The front of his thighs bumped the back of Nolan's.

"Why are we still wondering, then?" Nolan breathed, eyes dark with desire.

"I-I don't, fuck–" Reid didn't know how he was already this wrecked, and he wasn't even inside Nolan yet. An error he planned to rectify.

Reid shifted his tail over, slid it around Nolan's wrist, and held it out of the way under Nolan's heated gaze. Nolan gasped, and Reid waited until he had slicked his length before releasing him.

As if Nolan couldn't wait, he dropped his hand back between them again, and Reid curled his hand around the base of his cock, fingers bumping against Nolan's. Together, they notched him against Nolan's hole, and Reid let out a shaky breath before pressing forward.

Nolan's hand fell away, landing on his hip and squeezing, pulling him in, and in, and in.

Reid planted a hand alongside Nolan's head, gaze tracing his features, watching them crumple. "Oh my god, you feel— you feel—fuck," Nolan panted.

"Yeah?" Reid asked, barely coherent as Nolan dissolved into pleasure beneath him, squeezed around him.

"Move," Nolan begged, and god, with that hitch in his voice, how could Reid resist?

He pulled his hips back, the drag of Nolan around him tight and perfect and—"Fuck," he hissed, as only the head remained.

Reid thrust back in, faster this time, and watched Nolan's head tilt into the pillows, throat working against the moan that spilled out. Nolan's nails bit into his skin, and he hoped Nolan left marks on his hip, wanted to wear the evidence of their night for days to come.

Pleasure rattled up and down his spine, making him grit

his teeth as he fucked in and in, fire raging in his gut as he pulled out and out.

Reid snapped in against him. With his tail, he dragged Nolan's thigh up against his hip, tilted the angle, searching—Nolan tensed around him, stilling momentarily.

"There," Nolan said, the word bursting from him. The hand around Reid's hip tightened, nails digging, hopefully leaving half-moons in his skin. Nolan's head turned, his mouth dragging along Reid's wrist as he panted.

His pulse jumped. Could Nolan feel it against his lips?

Nolan arched into him, meeting him on each thrust, each drag and pull better than the one before.

"I'm not gonna last, fuck—" Nolan groaned. "Touch me."

At first, Reid thought he meant wrapping his hand around him and stroking until he came. Instead, Nolan curled his fingers around his own thigh, taking over the job of Reid's tail, and the implication made his breath explode on a huff.

"Jesus christ, you want—"

"God, yes," Nolan whimpered, and heat speared him, striking in his gut and making his cock swell.

Nolan tensed, mouth dropping open as he felt it for the first time, eyes wide and locking on Reid as if he was lost, as if Reid was the only one who could tether him.

So he did, slipping his tail between their bodies and around his cock.

He was hard and slick and the shush of Reid's fur over him was loud between them, but not as loud as Reid's pounding pulse, their heaving breaths, the slap of their skin as he drove into Nolan.

Reid felt him tightening and squeezing, and watched his expression slip into ecstasy.

It scared him a little, how good this was, how close he felt to Nolan, how much he enjoyed watching him edge closer and closer. Being the one to put that look in his eyes.

"Don't stop," Nolan said, both hands wrapping around his waist and urging him to retain the rhythm. "Wanna feel you."

"Nolan," Reid said, voice breaking on his name.

Reid couldn't be sure what exactly was Nolan's last straw, whether it was the way his voice cracked over the pleasure; or the way his tail twisted on the upstroke; or maybe it was Reid's cock swelling even more, the ridge growing more pronounced, tugging at his entrance on every withdrawal.

Whichever it was that sent him over, Nolan stilled beneath him for a split second, lips parting, before the waves of pleasure took him. He arched beneath Reid, body quivering around him, spilling between them.

Nolan's leg shook, the one curled around his hip, and with a glance Reid confirmed his fingers were digging into the back of his thigh, leaving divots as the ecstasy rocked him.

Reid's hand fisted the sheets beside Nolan's head, hips still grinding as Nolan squeezed around him, his head tilted back and lips parted on a cry.

Reid silenced him, tasting the sound straight from the source, even though it was messy, their mouths bumping over each other before they met again.

When Reid pulled back, Nolan's eyes were cloudy and half-lidded with residual pleasure, hand still holding on, but without the desperate drag of his nails. He stared up at Reid, expression intense and dark.

"God, I can *feel* you," Nolan said, a hint of wonder in his voice. Then his lips twitched. "Feels much bigger than it did in my hand. Keep going."

Reid choked out a half-sob, half-laugh, hips swinging into Nolan again and again, just like he'd told him.

Nolan carded a hand through Reid's hair, bringing him

back down to his lips. Their breath skated across their cheeks, tongues twining, though Reid was finding it hard to focus as he neared the horizon.

It felt kind of like flying, being stuck in the clouds, knowing the other side was just through the fog of condensation, his wings working just like his hips were.

"Come on, come on, come for me," Nolan chanted, voice smooth and silky, unlike the hand in his hair. He wrenched his fingers, strands tangling and sending a shock through Reid's senses, lightning through the sky.

Fuck. In the closet, Reid had been worried about messing Nolan up, but Reid had never felt more of a mess than he did in this moment, the break in the clouds just out of reach.

Nolan lifted his head, nipped at Reid's throat *hard*, and whispered, "Do you know how you look right now?"

Reid had *just* been thinking the same thing about Nolan earlier, and his chest went tight with the idea that Nolan might view him with even an ounce of the same awe Reid felt when he saw him.

"Desperate." Nolan bit at his throat again, tugging his hair to arch his neck back more.

Reid's breath was rough in his throat, his rhythm faltering as pleasure clapped like thunder. A moment of clarity.

"Crazed," followed by a bite.

Leave a mark, please leave a mark.

"Fucking—I'm never gonna get you out of my head. Like this, the way you feel inside me."

Reid whimpered, probably. He couldn't tell, because suddenly he wasn't flying anymore. He was falling. Crashing back through the clouds and fog and just waiting for the ground to come up and meet him.

"Reid," Nolan whispered, and Reid snapped his eyes open —when had they closed?—and met the dark blue of his gaze. "Wanna feel you come, baby, come on."

His voice, quiet and low and gentle, paired with another tug of his fist in Reid's hair, finally sent him over the edge with a shout.

A crash through the clouds. Open air and white light and *ecstasy.* Reid spilled inside Nolan, his cock swelling, and Nolan groaned too. He held Reid poised there, head going limp in his hold, hips rolling forward in no rhythm whatsoever, twitching more than anything, as heat and *almost, almost too much* ravaged him.

"Holy shit," Nolan whispered.

Reid's head was resting on Nolan's shoulder, which began to shake. With laughter, Reid realized, because it made Nolan tense around him, and he grumbled into his skin, damp with sweat.

"Don't laugh," Reid moaned.

"Sorry, sorry," Nolan said, voice still quiet. "That was just… that was…"

"Yeah," Reid answered eloquently. "Yeah." Because saying it twice would surely get across all the thoughts he couldn't voice, right? Reid chuckled, collapsing on top of Nolan, ignoring the mess between them. Another shower would be in order.

"It's not always… like that, is it? Or is it because you're… that's rude, isn't it?" Nolan suddenly cut off, swallowing sharply, cheeks glowing red when Reid lifted his head to look.

"Are you asking me if that was so good because I have a weird dick?"

"Well, I — no, I mean, maybe, but—"

Lifting his head, he stared down at Nolan, searching his gaze, studying the bow of his lips and the sheen of sweat on his forehead.

"No." His voice got stuck in his throat. "It's not always like that."

It was crazy. Falling in love felt kind of like flying, too.

That damning thought was followed shortly by another: *Fuck.*

After his cock deflated—which was a humiliating way to describe it—they showered *again.* The waterfall shower head was certainly worth it.

Reid was comfortable with his head on Nolan's chest, and he sank deeper into the soft mattress and softer man as sleep neared.

"I'm honestly surprised you came back," Nolan said into the darkness. "Yesterday."

Suddenly, he was wide awake. God, was it only yesterday? "What? Why?"

"Well. With the new information brought to light, I would have understood if you hadn't wanted to see me again."

Reid sighed, pressing heavily against Nolan's chest, heart lurching. Guilt festering. "Listen, I mean... maybe that's how I felt at first–" god, that sounded familiar, didn't it? "–but I kept seeing you at the conference and it's… you're not your father. You're not responsible for his actions. You're a separate person."

Nolan was quiet for so long, Reid wondered if he'd heard him at all. "Wow," he finally said, voice quiet, filled with awe. "No one's ever said that to me before."

Reid hummed. "It's true. You're only responsible for *you.*"

"I'm glad you asked that question today, during my presentation. I'm glad it went the way it did."

Reid remembered watching Nolan's father palm his

shoulder, the barely-there wince marring Nolan's features. "Even if it pissed off your dad?"

Nolan let loose a heavy breath. "Especially because of that. Sometimes I feel like I could burst with the unfairness of it all. I wish..."

Glancing up at him, Reid noted the furrow in his brow, the pinch of his lips. He patted Nolan's chest. "What do you wish?"

"I wish this whole thing would fall apart. I don't want to *do* this anymore. I wish there was a way to ruin it," he admitted softly.

Reid's heart thumped.

Maybe this was it. Maybe Reid should say something. Right now.

Just admit the whole thing. Tell him about his friend John, the article.

Nolan would help, he just knew it.

Reid didn't even necessarily have to mention his own involvement in it.

But that felt... wrong. It *was* wrong, to lie to someone as wonderful as Nolan.

And maybe he *should* have taken that moment to confess, but he was frozen with the fear of Nolan's rejection, especially after their night together. He didn't want to hurt Nolan. And he also didn't want to *be* hurt. And even though it was all his own doing, it would hurt if Nolan turned him away.

When it came down to it, he was a coward who kept his mouth shut.

"You never know," he said instead, voice rough with forced lightness. "Maybe something will."

"The night is still young?" Nolan asked with a chuckle.

"Something like that."

GLOW

Wednesday.

Midweek.

He spent most of the day unfortunately glued to his father's side. A business lunch, meetings, schmoozing. All under the watchful eye of his father, and Chance, his assistant. It was clear they'd rather him not be there *almost* as much as Nolan would rather escape.

Each moment was spent wishing it was already over, that the clock would strike five-fifteen, the moment of the last presentation.

Because he had a date.

With Reid, at his restaurant.

He had barely paid attention all day, instead reliving every moment of last night, every touch and the damning words Nolan had breathed to life, his guilty admission whispered in the safety of Reid's presence.

As his father droned on about the hotel to a group of suits, his mind drifted. He wondered if this was what he really wanted. Did he *truly* expect to do this for the rest of his life?

It suddenly seemed an awfully long time to remain miserable.

"Don't forget about the brunch mixer this Friday," Chase reminded him. "Noon, in the Gold room."

"Yes, I know," he responded, as if it wasn't on the itinerary of the convention's app.

Before he could stray too far, the day was over, and he rushed back to his hotel to change, as he had promised to meet Reid at his restaurant.

It was nearing six p.m. by the time his rideshare dropped him off. He went through the large wooden doors and located Reid next to the host stand.

The restaurant was *alive.*

That's the only way he could describe it. The warm tones were welcoming, waiters and hosts were scurrying around, and the low hum of the patrons added a buzz to the room that made chills race up his arms.

"This is lovely," Nolan said softly, leaning into Reid as he rounded the podium.

Reid's grin was priceless, and his employee was looking at him as if he'd never seen him before. "C'mon, we've got a table in the back."

He wasn't kidding. They wound their way through tables and chairs and booths until the loud hum of the crowd was more like a murmur, and they were tucked away in another room that was empty, spare a few large booths for groups.

"All for us?" Nolan asked, a little shocked.

"Yeah. We don't book this back room often anyway, so it's no big deal," Reid assured him.

"You sure?" Nolan asked, sinking into a booth.

Reid cleared his throat, following Nolan in and sliding close until their thighs touched. "Positive. Hi."

"Hi," Nolan breathed, then Reid was leaning in and Nolan couldn't help but meet him halfway.

The kiss was chaste and sweet and far too short, Reid's beard brushing Nolan's cheeks with that delightful tickle again. He followed him for a second and third kiss, cupping his cheek until Reid chuckled.

It was bright and everything he needed.

"How was the conference today?" Reid asked.

Nolan wrinkled his nose. "Awful. I'm much happier right here."

Reid stared back at him for a long moment after that, before clearing his throat and motioning to the menu before them.

"Alright, then, Business Man, do your worst."

"Me?" Nolan asked, arching a brow. "What's this got to do with me?"

"Well, you've been to quite a few fancy places, I imagine. I wanna know if I can keep up."

Nolan let his gaze wander around the room, taking in the decor and greenery and warm lighting and exposed brick. "You've already got them all beat with the atmosphere."

"Oh yeah?" Reid asked, voice low and gaze focused on his menu. But Nolan could see the rising color in his face.

"Absolutely. There's none of that… fake, *we're better than you* air here. It's refreshing," Nolan admitted with a soft smile. "Now, what's *your* favorite thing on this menu?"

"That's cheating," Reid said, scandalized. "I'm not telling you. You're on your own," he declared, leaning back in his seat and crossing his arms.

A waiter appeared, collected their drink orders, and promised to return shortly. When he left, a comfortable silence settled over the table.

"Did you have a hand in creating all these dishes?" Nolan skimmed the menu, noting the array of different foods. There was surely something on there for everyone, from vegetarian options to vegan to steak and potatoes.

"I did, actually. I cooked for us a lot, growing up. It was my… thing, I guess. When I opened this place, I experimented a bit. The menu looks totally different now than it first did."

Nolan liked the image he built in his mind of Reid cooking and playing and having fun in the kitchen. It fit.

"You'll have to give me some pointers. I'm afraid the microwave is the most used appliance in my place," Nolan confessed, realizing only after the words had left his lips how they sounded. As if this intense affair between them didn't have an expiration date. As if the end of the week wasn't looming closer by the hour.

"That's unacceptable," Reid retorted, shaking his head. "You don't have a cook or something?"

"Why would I have a cook?" Nolan asked with a thrum of amusement.

He shrugged. "Dunno. Don't rich people have those?"

Nolan's lips twitched.

"I think we had one growing up, but I don't have one now."

"Well, you must not be *that* rich," Reid said with a put-upon sigh. He shuffled in his seat before making to stand. "What am I even doing here, then—"

"Oh, shut up," Nolan grumbled, and pulled him back into his seat, tugging him close in the booth. "If it's money you want, you should've gone for the Senior Whittier," he retorted.

Reid shuddered dramatically at the suggestion, and then watched Nolan peruse the food options, gaze heavy but quiet.

When the waiter returned, he had barely made a decision. Reid's eyes crinkled with his amusement as Nolan pointed to an item on the laminated card stock and handed back the menu.

Reid's pick was fast; he didn't even have to glance down at the menu.

"I'll get your order in, boss—I mean, sir," the waiter said, a lopsided grin on his face at the blunder.

Reid rolled his eyes playfully. "Thanks, Evan."

Nolan watched the exchange with a slowly growing smile, and when the kid was gone, Reid huffed. "Bunch of old ladies back there, probably gossiping."

"About us?" Nolan guessed.

After sipping his cocktail, Reid nodded. "Yep. Usually don't bring dates here."

Nolan's cheeks flushed at the simple admission that this was a *date*. Oh, he had it bad.

"And why is that?" He played with the silly umbrella in his drink, a piña colada. Three cherries. Another drink Reid had affectionately pestered him into selecting. Apparently, they were one of the special cocktails from the bar. It was a lovely relief against the sweltering heat outside, even as the sun began setting.

As his question sank in, Reid looked embarrassed, if Nolan could believe it. "Don't know, actually. Just never considered it."

"And why me, then?" A little fishing never hurt anyone, did it?

Reid's cheeks flushed even *more*, a delightful glow on his face as he pointedly avoided eye contact, staring down at the rim of his glass with sudden interest. His lips moved in a mumble of something too low to catch, and Nolan grinned, leaning forward.

"What was that?"

Reid's eyes flashed to his, and Nolan forgot how to breathe.

"I want you to like it," he said, just loud enough for Nolan to hear. "M'proud of it."

Oh, Nolan could kiss him.

So he did, taking advantage of the empty room, leaning

into his space with a hand on his knee. The warmth of Reid's lips was hot in comparison to his own, chilled from the frozen drink.

"You should be proud of it," Nolan told him, pulling back to meet his gaze before settling properly in his seat. "This is wonderful, Reid." His hand lingered on his knee.

"You haven't even tried the food yet," he argued, lips curling into a smile.

"You make people feel good, Reid. That's what's wonderful."

"It's just food," he said with a shrug, pulling away.

Oh, uncomfortable with praise and seeking it all the same? Interesting.

Nolan nudged his shoulder. "It's an experience. A memory. And you know it."

"Yeah," Reid agreed wistfully, tilting his glass back and forth. "I guess this place is pretty special," he finally admitted, eyes lifting up to trace the walls of the room.

Nolan drew a pattern into his knee and hummed his agreement.

"The trick is to do simple meals, let them shine on their own. They might post a picture on Instagram, sure, and presentation is important, but the taste is what they'll remember the most."

In Nolan's eyes, Reid glowed even brighter, enough to rival the sunset, as he explained his favorite dishes, brave enough to talk about them now that he wasn't swaying Nolan's decision on his entree. He spoke about their creation, the final decisions, and how proud he was for balancing the costs with the list price on the menu.

This place meant so much to Reid. It was his life, his passion.

The more Reid gushed and shared his love for this place,

the brighter he shined, casting light on all the guilt hidden in the planes of Nolan's chest.

How was Nolan supposed to take that all away from him?

He'd never hated his father, and himself, more than he did in that moment.

The mains arrived, and Nolan's mouth watered at the smell of his risotto and scallops as it was set before him.

It really did look like some of the better dishes at his father's favorite expensive places.

Seated on a creamy bed of risotto were five steaming, perfectly seared scallops, and the grilled vegetables lined up around it were vibrant.

"Reid, this is beautiful," he hissed as the waiter turned away.

"You sound surprised," Reid mused. "Why do you sound surprised?" He arched a brow in suspicion, and Nolan rolled his eyes.

"I knew you were impressive, but even this is beyond my expectations. It's lovely."

Those red cheeks reappeared again, and Nolan made it his mission to make this man blush as many times as he could. After all, it only took a compliment.

"It's not like I cooked it, man, come on—"

"You created it and made the recipe, didn't you? Taught the cooks the presentation?" Nolan already knew the answer, because the man had explained as such only moments ago.

He shrugged and finally nodded.

Nolan squeezed his knee again. "Accept the compliment, Reid."

"If you're just trying to get in my pants, it's totally working," he murmured, and Nolan laughed.

"You mean I was supposed to be trying?"

"Oh, shut up." Reid said it softly, fondly, and Nolan finally removed his hand so they could get to eating.

Because after dinner, came—

"What about dessert?" Reid asked once they were finished, reaching over the flower in the tiny vase and grabbing the drinks and dessert menu.

"Besides you?"

Nolan was just as shocked as Reid was at the blatant line, and heat rushed to his face as the moment stretched on. Reid's eyes were dark as Nolan cleared his throat. "Even I've heard about the crème brûlée," Nolan informed him. "Especially after yesterday, when you were the talk of the entire convention."

His brows furrowed, lips pursing in doubt. "Oh, come on, now, that's an exaggeration."

"It's really not," Nolan pressed, turning in the booth to face him. "Honestly, I passed several groups yesterday raving about your food."

In the moment, just the sound of Reid's name had made Nolan's chest tight with affection, and it bloomed into pride the second he'd realized what the groups were discussing.

"Really?" Reid asked, disbelief in his voice.

"Really. Honest truth," Nolan swore. "It's part of why I was so excited you invited me here."

Like they were in orbit, Reid leaned into him, too. "What's the other part, then?"

"I'd think it's obvious by now," Nolan began, "but I quite like you, Reid. I want to learn everything I can about you."

If Nolan was a decent person, he would've left well enough alone days ago. Why be cruel and drag this out when they both knew it only ended one way? He was a greedy, terrible person, already threatening Reid's business, his life. And apparently that wasn't even enough; no, Nolan wanted every piece of Reid the man was willing to divulge. He'd take every crumb he was offered and stow it away for safekeeping. Because if each crumb *was* as delectable as the crème brûlée—and it had proven to be thus far—he wanted to savor them for as long as possible.

And if a tiny, quiet part of him wondered if there was another solution, he ignored it completely. Didn't even give thought to… quitting. Leaving it all behind. His lonely apartment and his sculless job, his terrible father.

Maybe if he was brave, he could mold any kind of future he wanted from this moment. But Nolan was no fucking sculptor.

After the dessert was cleared, the restaurant did too, and Reid left him briefly to lock up after the night shift. He returned with two glasses of ice water and presented them with a flourish.

"Don't tell night shift."

"I'll take this secret to my grave," he vowed, and accepted the crisp, clear glass.

They talked for what felt like forever, and yet it passed in the blink of an eye. They were facing each other, legs pulled up in the curved booth to better see one another. Reid still glowed long after his rival, the sun, had set, leaving him the brightest thing around.

When a lull in the conversation finally provided an opportunity, Nolan tilted his head and bravely asked Reid the question he'd been pondering all day.

"Would you want to be my date to this… schmoozing party? It's a brunch on Friday, after the conference concludes. I do have to give a little speech, but my father is mostly having me attend so he can have photo evidence framing him as the perfect dad. After that, I'm usually left to stand in the corner and hate my life for a few hours. Want to make it a little more bearable for me?"

It was selfish to ask Reid to suffer alongside him for a few hours, but, well, maybe it wouldn't be suffering at all, if Reid was there.

"After that enthusiastic invite, how can I decline?"

Nolan smiled, sipping his drink. "Good. I look forward to it."

"Won't your father have something to say about you bringing… me?"

"Oh, I'm positive," Nolan nodded. "But he won't do it where there's an audience, so I don't care."

"You really mean that?"

Reid stared at him for a moment, and Nolan tried to imagine the direction of his thoughts. Lights flashed through the window, briefly illuminating his features.

"Of course I do," Nolan said softly, leaning against the table, reaching out to rest his hand on Reid's forearm. "Listen, Reid, I've been thinking—"

A loud crash interrupted, and Nolan and Reid shared a wide-eyed glance. Glass shattered, echoing around the empty restaurant like a threat, followed by the thunk of something heavy.

"Stay here," Reid said, and before Nolan could argue, he was gone.

For once, Nolan didn't listen, and followed right after him.

SHARDS

"Reid!" Nolan hissed behind him. "You can't just – oh, no."

His voice broke off as Reid came to a stop in the main dining area.

A window had been shattered, and the culprit lay on the ground in front of a booth. A brick.

Glass littered the booth and its table, as well as the floor.

"Shit," Reid breathed, covering his face with his hands. "Are you okay?" he asked, turning toward Nolan.

He was a little pale, yet flushed at the same time, eyes wide. "Y-yes. I'm fine. I can't believe this," he said, moving a little closer.

Reid pulled him back by the shoulder. "Stay here," he told him.

Nolan nodded, and once Reid was certain he would stay put, he disappeared to the back to get a broom. He returned, the remnants of the window framing the perfect view of the sidewalk and street outside.

"Fuckin' kids," Reid muttered, bending down to sweep the shards of glass into the dustpan. It was probably just kids. Like usual.

Warm air spilled in through the broken window, the streetlamp glaringly bright with no glass to soften it.

"Here," Nolan murmured, and sat a trash can down beside him with a thump. "I'm so sorry this happened," he said.

"S'not your fault," Reid said, dejected. Where was he going to get the money to replace an entire fucking window panel? Again? "That's what I get for wanting natural light." He tried to lighten the mood. "Besides, it was bound to happen sooner or later."

"What do you mean?" Nolan asked. He leaned over to pick up the brick, and Reid glared to make sure he didn't cut himself on a stray piece of glass, but didn't stop him, and swept more glass into a small pile.

"This isn't the first time it's happened, and it won't be the last. That's the second time this year. Which... Just frustrating that it's happened at all, y'know."

"What? Why haven't the police done anything?" Nolan asked.

Reid glanced up at him. "The police don't give a shit about some vandal. It's just fuckin' kids, anyway."

"Oh," Nolan said, hands twisting in that anxious way they sometimes did.

"Yeah, like I said, shit happens. Someone graffitied the front windows last time. Bunch of dicks all over the wall. I would've laughed if it hadn't been such a bitch to clean off." Eventually, he'd learned to just use a razor to scrape it away instead of smudging it around with soap and water. The paneling, though? It had taken him days.

"How often does this happen?"

Reid shrugged, another dustpan's worth of glass tinkling as he dumped it into the trash. "Truthfully? It's a new thing. I don't know what's gotten into the kids these days, but some-times... sometimes it's enough to make me wanna close up shop, y'know? If even the community doesn't respect and love this place… what's the point?"

Nolan remained quiet, and suddenly Reid was angry. Pissed, actually. Why was the community so against them? Why was everything so *difficult*?

"It's not just me, either," he admitted bitterly. "Chippy's? Their freezers went down last month, so they had to throw out all of their stock. All of it. The owner sold his truck just so they could keep the place open." He huffed, chest tight and warm with frustration. "That's why I can't stand people like your dad. They're sharks. They sense the blood and swarm, throwing offers at us we almost can't afford to turn down."

"God… that's awful. I never realized…"

Nolan sounded so dejected, and Reid exhaled slowly, shaking his head. "No, no. I know. I'm sorry, I didn't mean anything by it. It's just hard, sometimes."

Nolan's fancy shoes entered his line of sight, but before he could tilt his head up, Nolan was kneeling down, motioning for the broom and dustpan.

"Go have a drink, I'll finish this up."

"But—"

"No arguing. I've got it. I won't tell night shift you dirtied another glass after they did the dishes, either."

His hand covered Reid's on the handle, warm and sure and just the anchor he needed in that moment, amongst the swirling depths of outrage and doubt and confusion.

"Okay," he finally agreed, standing with a crack of his knee or hip or some other ancient part of his body, and made his way to the bar.

He watched as Nolan swept the glass together, then bent to retrieve it with the dustpan before starting with another area.

Reid went for the bourbon, the burn in his throat similar to that of the anger within him, but instead of fanning the flames higher, it seemed to douse them. He slumped against the bartop.

Eventually, Nolan joined him at the bar, and laid a comforting palm on his shoulder. "Do you have some trash bags we can tape across the window?"

It jolted Reid out of his reverie, and he nodded. "Yeah, good idea."

He gave Reid the unofficial tour of the back rooms, his office. Flipped over an envelope with red letters stamped across its front. Ignored the sympathy coming off Nolan in waves, and led him back out into the main area, tape and bags and some scissors in hand.

It went much faster with two people, whereas the last time Reid had done this, he'd had only himself to count on.

The warm air was once again shut out, this time by an attractive display of black plastic across the front of his restaurant.

"I'm really sorry," Nolan said again.

Reid grabbed the dustpan and broom, the extra bags, and the tape, and returned them to their locations, ending in his office.

When he turned after placing the tape on the desk, he stopped to find Nolan filling his doorway.

"Are you okay?"

It was like Nolan could see right through him, and the care in his voice, the worry, made him crack.

He shook his head slowly, eyes slamming shut against the heat of tears behind his lids, and the next thing he knew Nolan was wrapped around him. A hand on the back of his neck pushed his head down into Nolan's shoulder.

Reid sucked in huge, gasping breaths, filled with the citrus scent of Nolan. Bright and jarring and addicting and perfect.

Slowly he lifted his hands, slid them around Nolan's waist, and held on tightly.

"It'll be okay," Nolan promised. But he didn't know that. He didn't know about the stack of unpaid bills and the notices in red letters. He didn't know that Reid lived above the restaurant because he'd had to sell his place to cover some of the expenses. He didn't *know* how hard it was.

Reid focused on his breathing, and swallowed his tears and his worries.

"I started this restaurant because of my mom," Reid admitted, the words soft and sorrowful in Nolan's neck.

Nolan stroked a hand up his back, warm and comforting. "Yeah?"

He nodded and sniffled. "Yeah. We were poor. Couldn't afford a whole lot. And I spent my whole childhood wishing for *more*, never able to see that she did all she could. I'd wished we had a place like this to come to. To feel fancy, even if it was for one night."

"Oh, Reid," Nolan whispered. "You were just a kid."

"I know. And kids aren't supposed to feel the financial strain of their parents. And Mom was so good at taking care of us, we never knew. But I think I did, deep down. I mean, she worked two jobs and was never home, and my older brother got a job as soon as he could find someone to hire him, to pay him a little under the table. And meanwhile, I... I just wished for more, without appreciating what I had."

"That's part of being a kid. That's every kid's experience."

But Reid hated it. He felt so guilty it kept him awake most nights. "I think I made her feel like she wasn't enough. And I *hate* that," he said, voice breaking. "Fuck."

He pulled away, pressed the heels of his palms into his eyes, and leaned against the desk.

"I never got to tell her I was sorry. That I appreciated

everything she did for us," he muttered, crossing his arms and staring down at the floor

"But you made this for her," Nolan said gently, motioning to the building around them. "A place for families to come together, to feel special together, like you said."

But not for long. Not if your father has any say in it.

Reid was afraid of failing. Again. Failing this restaurant like he'd failed his mom, and then he really would be left with nothing.

Nolan didn't understand that Reid was one, just *one* costly accident away from losing it all.

This deal couldn't go through. It *couldn't*. He had to find something on Nolan's dad, anything. But he hated betraying Nolan, too. Hated lying to him, hated the idea that he might find out, hated that he might find himself lacking because of Reid's actions.

Reid couldn't stand the thought of making another person feel like they weren't enough.

Especially Nolan.

Reid swallowed sharply and tugged Nolan closer, turning him toward the desk and wrapping his arms around him.

Nolan huffed at the sharp squeeze, but his arms curled around Reid and held on tightly.

Reid was aware of the press of their bodies, the hands branding into his shoulder and spine, the thump of a heart against his own.

"Sorry if that was scary," Reid said softly.

Nolan shrugged. "It's alright. No one was hurt."

Just the thought, the idea of Nolan being hurt, made his chest ache.

"D'you wanna curl up in bed? This will all be here tomorrow."

Reid shook his head in the crook of Nolan's neck. "Not yet."

He tightened his arms around the man, drew in a breath filled with his scent, and pressed a kiss to his throat. Then his clean-shaven jaw. His cheek. Finally, his lips.

Reid knew what this was: a distraction. He knew Nolan knew it, too, and yet the man played along. Met him halfway, their lips and tongues and shared breaths like little anchors to hold Reid *here.*

But he wanted more, and he pressed for it, dragging a hand between their bodies.

Like Nolan had said, their problems would still be problems tomorrow.

So, why not? Worry tomorrow. Fuck his throat tonight.

"I know what you're doing," Nolan breathed out.

"And? Any objections?" he asked, pausing with his hand halfway down Nolan's pants.

"Are you sure?"

"Yes. The last thing I wanna think about is…" He pulled out his hand and waved it toward the front of the restaurant. "All that. What I want to think about…" He sank to his knees, watched Nolan's eyes darken. "Is your cock in my mouth."

One of Nolan's hands lifted, threaded through Reid's hair, and held him still. It struck a spark of heat in him, and he waited patiently. Whatever Nolan was looking for in Reid's eyes, he either did or didn't find it, but he nodded regardless.

The hand in his hair gentled, and Reid practically ripped the zipper open, revealing the slowly-growing bulge beneath his boxers.

"A stronger man would say something about how you're deflecting with sex," Nolan warned.

Reid hummed and pressed a kiss to the patch of skin he bared when he tugged the boxers out of the way. "Good thing I'm into weaker men," he drawled with a chuckle.

"This doesn't seem fair."

Pushing to his feet, Reid brushed a tender kiss across his

lips. "This isn't about thinking, remember? Just... be with me?" *Since we don't have that long anyway.*

"Reid..." Nolan whispered, the sound a little hurt. Maybe he'd finally realized it, too– that no matter what they said, the week was slipping between their fingers faster than they could hold onto it. They needed every moment they could get. "Okay," he finally said.

Reid dropped to his knees again, ignoring the ache in favor of the taste of Nolan across his tongue.

Every sound that came out of Nolan was *hot*, and loud, and he realized maybe it was a good thing Nolan had come so fast in the closet. His lips parted and sounds poured out as Reid worked his tongue over his cock, lapped at the head like those fucking ice cream cones they'd gotten the first night, dipped his tongue in the slit to chase more of his salty flavor.

"So you do always make so much noise," Reid said after a few moments, mouthing against his length.

Nolan snapped his mouth closed, and Reid pulled off completely. "Don't *stop*. You sound so hot."

With a huff, Nolan said, "Well, now I'm embarrassed, so..."

Reid quirked a grin up at him. "Is that a challenge?"

"What? No—*oh*," Nolan moaned as Reid took him in deep without hesitation. Nolan was just so responsive, and Reid *wanted* to make him feel good, wanted to hear more of those noises fall from his lips.

The hand in Reid's hair tightened, his hips rolling forward of their own accord. If he hadn't been preparing to take Nolan in further at that same second, it might have taken him by surprise. But they were in sync, like always.

He wondered if Nolan knew as well as Reid did that it wasn't always like this, so effortlessly easy and fun. Part of him wanted to ask, but another part of him *knew* already that Nolan felt the same way. It was in the cast of his eyes when

Reid glanced up and found molten heat and something sweet there, too.

The realization made him redouble his efforts, dropping a hand to Nolan's balls as he followed his lips along the hard length with the other.

Nolan must not have been embarrassed anymore, because the sounds that slipped from his lips were downright pornographic and only encouraged Reid, desire sliding right down his spine in a jolt of need.

Focusing on his breath, Reid slid his mouth lower, took more of him in, and eventually let his hand press flat to Nolan's abdomen, giving himself more room.

As Nolan registered what the press of his touch meant, his own hand slipped against the desk, sending a stack of envelopes tumbling to the floor.

"Fuck, sorry," Nolan breathed, a chuckle rumbling out of his chest. "God, you're good at that."

Reid pulled back, lips curling into a smile that he dragged the head of Nolan's cock against.

"Christ—"

"No god here," Reid said, lifting his gaze. "Just me."

Nolan's hand wrenched in his hair, dragging a groan from Reid's mouth this time, as he parted his lips and let Nolan guide him.

"Touch yourself," Nolan said, his voice as heavy as the weight on Reid's tongue. "Can you come with my cock in your mouth?"

Reid moaned an affirmation, hands fumbling at his button and zipper, desperate to get his fingers around—

"Good. Don't," Nolan said, directing him back with the hold in his hair. Only the head of him remained between Reid's lips. "Don't come until I do."

Fuuuck.

Reid melted at the words, and he let Nolan drag him deeper on his cock, swallowing around him.

He worked his own length slowly, collecting the precum pooling at the head to ease the glide. It felt so fucking *good* to sink into his knees and ignore the bite of pain in favor of the way Nolan filled his mouth. The weight of him, the scent, the taste and the feel and the way he sounded, miles above Reid as everything fell away but *Nolan.*

His whispered, desperate praises kept Reid tethered to the earth, if only so he could hear the next words that tumbled off his lips.

"—look so fucking good on your knees for me."

Reid had to pull his hand away from his cock, pleasure pulsing through him.

God, where did Nolan get off saying things like that? It made Reid want to stay here forever.

"—just look at you, *fuck,*" Nolan said, reverence in his voice. Reid glanced up past the watering in his eyes and felt Nolan pulse against his tongue.

Reid wrapped his fingers back around himself, stroking slowly, trying to keep pace with Nolan.

Nolan's other hand lifted away from the desk, threading in his blond hair alongside the first, and Reid's eyes drifted shut again as Nolan held him still, dragging his cock over Reid's tongue.

He pressed back in with a slow, careful thrust of his hips, and Reid reached up, grabbed a hold of one thigh, and pulled him closer, faster, more, everything.

"Reid," Nolan whined, sounding close to ruin, and Reid only hoped Nolan would join him soon because he was well past it.

The next press of his hips was more calculated, slightly quicker, and Reid breathed when he could, focused and sank into the moment like warm molasses.

Nolan grew braver, encouraged by the tug and pull of Reid's hand on his hip, and finally, *finally* was sliding down Reid's throat like he wanted. It was messy, spit and precum spilling down his chin, and he loved that it was Nolan making a mess of him.

He stroked his cock in time with Nolan's thrusts, feeling the rhythm devolve as his moans and litany of words got all jumbled up.

"—don't come yet, fuck, you feel—wait for me, be good and wait for me," Nolan chanted.

Reid's blood rushed in his ears. He curled his tongue so Nolan would glide over it with every thrust, and earned a resounding curse.

"So fucking perfect, god, Reid—" His rhythm skipped, and Reid's cock throbbed and he squeezed around the base to halt his race toward the edge, but then—

Nolan's hands tightened in his hair, and he moaned, hips stuttering. "Your mouth—I'm gonna come, Reid, come with me, please—"

He'd hardly circled his fingers back around his own swelling cock before he was coming, spilling over the tight squeeze of his hand to follow Nolan over the edge.

Reid gripped his thigh tighter, swallowed around him, and Nolan's cock pulsed across his tongue as he came down his throat.

With a groan, Reid thumped his head against Nolan's thigh, riding the waves.

Nolan pet his hair and Reid breathed and the pleasure eventually faded into a muted hum, a memory just out of the corner of his eye.

"Reid?" Nolan murmured.

When Reid pulled back to lift his head up, Nolan sank down to pull him to his feet. They collapsed in the desk chair, which squeaked alarmingly under their combined weight.

"I can hardly remember my own name," Nolan said softly, offering him a tissue from the box on Reid's desk.

Reid felt a little silly, gathered in his arms like this, but he laid his head on Nolan's shoulder and breathed him in and forgot to care as he wiped his hand clean.

"It's Nolan," Reid offered helpfully, and then they were both chuckling.

Reid couldn't help but kiss him, taste him, feel him. He felt lighter than he had all day, like he'd simply float off if Nolan didn't keep hold of him. It was a pressure in his chest that he welcomed, but one that almost spilled up his throat and off his tongue in an admission far too early to breathe life into.

So he let Nolan taste it on his tongue, hopefully, and maybe without words he'd know just what Reid meant. And Reid thought maybe he did, because he cupped his cheek and stroked a thumb over his facial hair and he imagined it said the same things Reid was too scared to say to Nolan.

Ruin, indeed.

DISCOVERY

The last thing Nolan wanted to do was move, but he didn't want to risk the chair any longer.

"Show me your place. Come on," Nolan said, urging Reid to sit up. "It's time for bed."

"But—"

"This will all still be here tomorrow. Lead the way, please."

Maybe it was the polite *please* that made Reid give in, or maybe it was the idea of Nolan going with him. Either way, they made themselves decent again and after cleaning up the mess, Reid led Nolan out of the office and to the stairs at the end of the hall. With the keys he unlocked the door and motioned for Nolan to go ahead, then locked up behind them.

It was only a single flight of stairs, but Reid looked exhausted by the time he got to the top and shifted past Nolan to let them in.

Reid's place was… open, like it had been one giant room and remodeled to fit a person.

The vibes matched his restaurant, though, all dark, warm colors and low lighting, the walls covered haphazardly in posters and art and photos to make it feel cozy.

As soon as the door was shut, Nolan pulled him into a hug.

"I'll stay until you fall asleep, yeah?" Nolan asked softly.

Reid nodded and sighed heavily into his shoulder, and just for a moment, they simply existed. But despite how desperate they might be for time to stop, it continued on, and so Nolan pulled away, tugging on Reid's hand.

He led him to the bed, and waited for Reid to strip down to his boxers while Nolan stepped out of his shoes. Reid burrowed under the covers, then held up one end of the sheets, and Nolan shuffled in next to him.

It was comfortable and smelled like Reid, all earthy, green spice, and Nolan pulled him in closer, his back to Nolan's front. Reid's throat clicked as he swallowed.

Quiet.

All he could hear was Reid's breath, in and out, slow and even.

Tomorrow was Thursday. Today, technically, since it was so late.

His chest squeezed tightly. The week was coming to an end, whether they were ready or not. Nolan wished he could stay right here, wrapped around Reid.

When had it changed from *we have all week* to this pit in his stomach?

It took him a second to catch on to it, but Reid was still in his arms. Like, really still.

"Breathe, Reid," Nolan said softly, the breath of his words shifting Reid's hair.

Reid sucked in a breath, and Nolan pressed a kiss to the back of his head. "Stop thinking. Sleep."

Nolan stroked his hair and whispered sweet things to him, promising they'd figure it out one way or another, that the problem would still be there after Reid slept on it.

And none of it was a lie. He'd figure out some way to stop

this, some way to keep Reid from losing his restaurant, his *home.*

Reid's breaths eventually became less timed, less forced, as Nolan talked and ran his fingers through his hair. They turned heavy and deep, and he went limp in a way that could only mean sleep.

Nolan knew he should slip away and make his way back to the hotel so he didn't end up late for the next morning's presentation.

But he didn't want to leave Reid.

Five more minutes.

The elevator was slow and boring as it chimed through floor after floor. Nolan swore Reid's warmth still lingered, even so long after leaving his bed and locking up behind himself like Reid had shown him.

He could still taste Reid on his lips, and he wondered if he'd ever be able to step foot in another elevator and *not* think of the man.

Not think of the way Reid's hands felt against his skin, his breath in his ear, his... tears on his shoulder and his heart-breaking little gasps as he cried.

Maybe the elevator had nothing to do with it, and Reid was just branded into his mind and on his body.

As the floors ticked by, Nolan's mind turned over and over. The broken window. The conference. The stupid speech Nolan was supposed to give on Friday at the brunch mixer.

His heart sank.

Nolan couldn't give that speech. Nolan *refused* to be part

of this. He couldn't assist in taking the restaurant away from Reid. Not when it was all he had. Nolan thought about the red letters stamped across those envelopes, spread out across the floor after he'd slipped against the desk, staring back at him.

He'd been so close to blurting it out, confessing to Reid everything he was feeling. It was too big for words, and yet he was ready to try making them fit anyway.

A fluttering began in his chest. He didn't *have* to give the speech. He could make Chance do it. And Chance sucked at speeches. Or maybe there was something he could say, some way he could ask his father for help. Hell, maybe they could find another location, another—anything.

Deep down he knew his father wouldn't ever help, would scoff at the idea and tell Nolan what an idiot he was to throw away all their work for a guy.

But it was *Reid.*

And fuck. Nolan dragged a hand down his face. Fuck it all if Reid hadn't somehow become more important than all of it. He didn't care how crazy it sounded.

Nolan didn't know if it would work, if his father would hear him out or turn him away, but all he knew was that he had to try.

The doors parted, opening to his floor, and he stepped out, not bothering to hide the silly, dopey grin on his face as the night replayed in his head, as hope twined through his ribs, as he began making hasty plans.

"—*that* business!"

Nolan slowed as he exited the elevator, and his gaze cut to the ice and vending machine room, where he'd heard the familiar voice of his father's assistant.

What was Chance doing up so late?

Trailing closer to the door, he listened carefully to the

short, snappish words. Chance sounded *very* upset, and there were few things—besides Nolan—that upset the man.

"—by Nolan's fucking boyfriend! Do you realize how you've possibly just complicated this for us?"

Nolan's heart pounded at the sound of his name. *Boyfriend.* Chance had to be speaking about Reid – there was no other option. How did he know?

Even as he hovered outside the door, Chance lowered his voice, and Nolan could only hear mumbles. Then a huff. "Fine!" More muffled words, but Nolan picked up the most damning ones.

Money. Account. Tomorrow.

Then the door was opening, and Nolan froze like a deer in headlights. At the last second, he reached his hand out as if he'd been moving to open the door.

"Oh! Hello, Chance. You can't sleep either?"

He sneered. "What are you doing here, Nolan?"

"I came for some ice chips," he lied. "Helps me focus on rehearsing for presentations. How's your night?"

"It's… normal. And you?" he asked in a tone that suggested he did not care how Nolan's night was.

"It's been rather eye-opening," he admitted, heart racing almost as quickly as his mind.

Chance's eyes narrowed.

"And a little scary," he continued, dedicating himself to the bit. "You know, I was having drinks at a bar earlier this evening, and someone threw a brick through the window! Can you believe that?"

Chance tried very hard to not stiffen. He did not succeed. "Sounds tragic."

Nolan sighed. "Oh, no one was hurt; thank you for your concern. But, goodness, can you believe the time and repairs that go into something like that? Almost enough to want to shut the doors and never open them again."

Chance's eye twitched.

"Then again, I suppose that would be a relief for the Whittiers, wouldn't it? One more business ready to sell. Makes it easy to just… swoop in and take it."

"Yes, that would be convenient, wouldn't it?" Chance said, eyes dark and harsh and scarier than Nolan had ever seen them.

Bingo.

Despite the victory, Nolan's stomach twisted.

"Well, have a good night, Chance. See you in the morning," he said, and stepped past him to go into the ice room.

"Nolan," Chance called, and he turned, trying not to let his worry show on his face. "Where's your ice bucket?"

Nolan glanced down as if surprised not to find the item of reference in his hand.

Playing dumb, he frowned. "I assumed they would be in the ice room. Are they not?"

Chance rolled his eyes. "They're in your room. You're supposed to bring it with you."

"Oh. That's kind of silly, isn't it? Why wouldn't the ice buckets be in the ice room?" he rambled, changing direction and following Chance past the elevators as if to retrieve it.

But that was as far as they went together, because Chance had booked their rooms at opposite ends of the floor. Nolan originally thought it was so they'd have to see as little of each other as possible, but now he wondered if it was to keep Nolan from overhearing something he wasn't supposed to.

As soon as Chance was out of sight, Nolan raced to his room, key already in hand as he swiped it against the round lock, waiting for the beep. He closed the door quietly behind him and sat at the small desk, cracking open his laptop.

His mind raced, possibilities of the worst kind revealing themselves, the pieces slowly coming together as dread filled him.

It's just kids.

Nolan had a very damning notion that it wasn't just kids at all, and it steadied his resolve.

He *would* help Reid. Any way he could, even if it meant digging up his own father's buried secrets.

He pulled up tab after tab, creating a log of businesses the company had bought only to bulldoze over, making room for each hotel.

Small businesses. Family-owned. Making just enough profit to keep the business afloat, at least until unexpected expenses started piling up. Broken windows. Graffiti. Power outages. Poor food safety ratings, claims of bugs even amongst the thoroughly spotless kitchens.

His father was very creative, it turned out.

Nolan had never been privy to the brokering side. The deals, the contracts. He was only good for making slideshows and talking to people and looking like a happy father-son duo for the papers. Giving the company a good name.

"Oh, god," he breathed, and sat his head in his hands. As he dug deeper, it was like the unearthed dirt piled up on his chest. He tried to breathe past it, but he felt like he was suffocating in articles and information and the realization that he, Nolan, had *helped* his father cheat all these people. Like Reid.

He had to tell Reid.

Packing away his laptop in his bag, he grabbed his phone and stuck a Do Not Disturb sign on the door. He texted Chance and his father, some lie about a stomach bug, and left the hotel at the impossible hour of four a.m., under the cover of the silent city.

He would not be attending the conference that day.

And Reid was keeping his damned restaurant. Nolan would make sure of it.

BREAKING NEWS

Despite Nolan's best attempt, Reid had awoken when he'd left. The kiss goodbye had been far too brief, but Reid let Nolan slip away into the night without him.

And unfortunately, Reid's mind wouldn't let him have peace.

So that's where he was at the god-awful hour of not-quite four a.m. In his office, poring over recent earnings and trying to figure out where he could pull money from to cover the window repair.

The night was passing him by, but he hadn't been able to convince himself to rest. Maybe it was a kind of torture, forcing himself to clean up the desk and sit in the chair and see visions of him and Nolan in this very office until his eyes crossed.

So yes, he was desperately awake when his phone buzzed on the desk.

John. At this hour? He answered the call with a frown.

"Is everything alright?" he greeted.

"Reid! Are you awake? You won't believe what I found."

"No, I'm still asleep," he drawled. "What is it?"

"Smartass." He heard the grin in John's voice, and his

stomach dropped. "I found it. I found the dirt. The whole business – Reid, it's collusion. Whittier has been hiring people to sabotage the businesses."

Reid frowned. "What do you mean?"

"I spent all day reaching out to some of the businesses that were bought out by Whittier. In the months before they sold, business became increasingly hard for them. I'm talking... power outages resulting in inventory going bad, broken windows, robberies. They all have the same kind of story. Like you."

His stomach dropped. Did Nolan know about all this? No. He couldn't. There was no way Nolan would accept something like that.

"What good does that do?"

"It makes it hard for them to say no to him. If they have no other options but to sell or go under. They choose Whittier every. Fucking. Time."

Leaning back in his chair, Reid rubbed at his tired eyes, heart suddenly racing in his chest.

"A brick was thrown through the restaurant window earlier tonight," he admitted. "And to be honest, fixing it is not in the realm of things I was prepared for."

"And they *know* that. That's the game they're playing, setting you up for failure so that when they give you another lowball offer, you'll have no choice but to take it."

There was a knock at the front door. Usually Reid would just ignore it, since it was so late, but something made him stand and exit the office. It was like he was being pulled to the door.

"Someone's here," he said absently into the phone.

"What? Who? It's past four fucking a.m.," John grumbled. "Wait, don't answer it. What if the Whittiers sent him?"

Through the frosted glass of the door, he could make out

a build he'd know anywhere by this point, and the same fuschia shade of Nolan's shirt.

"Something tells me he came of his own accord," Reid muttered. "I'll call you later, John."

"Wait, Reid—"

Reid ended the call and opened the door, his stomach fizzing in a nauseating mix of excitement and dread.

"Nolan," he breathed.

"Reid, something is very wrong," Nolan began.

Reid stepped back, stomach dropping at the frantic edge to his words.

"What is it?" he asked, though he had a feeling he knew.

"My father..." Nolan locked the door behind them, collapsing against it and slamming his eyes closed. The bag around his shoulder was heavy, banging softly against the door. "He's been—I've..."

"Do you want a drink?" Reid offered, already heading toward the bar.

"Okay," he agreed, deflated.

So this was it.

Reid had to resist the urge to wrap his arms around Nolan and squeeze. Instead, he... well, his hand hovered over the basic bottle of bourbon, but at the last second swerved and grabbed the whisky. Then he turned and carefully grabbed two lowball glasses from the shelf.

Nolan watched him silently as he placed his bag on the chair, leaning against the bar, brow furrowed as his thoughts raced.

"I'm not sure this is really a cocktail occasion," he murmured, lips quirking up sadly.

"It is if we want it to be," Reid answered simply, ignoring the thump in his chest. He added a twist of an orange peel and three cherries before sliding Nolan's cocktail across the bar.

Nolan took a hesitant drink and hummed in appreciation before his lips turned back down.

"I know about your dad," Reid said softly.

"What?" Nolan asked, gaze snapping to his. "How? When?"

"Just a few minutes ago, actually." Reid sipped his drink and set the glass down with a soft clink. It was almost funny, the celebratory cherries with nothing to celebrate, and he wanted to laugh, but the sound got stuck in his throat.

"This is... god, this is *terrible*, Reid," Nolan breathed, and then he was walking away from the bar. At first, Reid thought he was heading toward the door, ready to leave, to... to what? But he turned at the last second, retracing his steps in an anxious pace.

"What are we going to do?" he asked, a shrill note to his voice that made Reid wince. Nolan dragged his palms down his face, pausing to cover his mouth as he returned on his route. His words were muffled when he spoke next. "We — we have to tell someone, right? Oh my *god*." Nolan's expression crumpled, eyes slamming shut. "Collusion? All these years. All the different cities."

Reid stepped around the bar, hands lifting to frame his shoulders, but he stopped at the last second, hovering inches from his shirt. His lips parted, but nothing came out.

Nolan knew what to say, though; in fact, he couldn't *stop* saying anything at all, unaware of Reid's hesitant frame in front of him as he rambled. "All the businesses he bought were manipulated in the same way. That's not... that's not right. We have to tell someone. But who do we tell? What do we say?"

"Nolan, I have to tell you something." Reid tried to catch Nolan's gaze with his own, but he was still out of reach even though he was inches away.

"The police? What would they do? Should I get a lawyer

first? Oh, god, that's hundreds of people that he – that I—"
He choked suddenly, eyes watering.

"Nolan, hey. Hey, I—"

"You know I had nothing to do with this, right?" he asked,
eyes landing on Reid's. It almost startled him, Nolan's intensity, and Reid pulled his hands back.

"I know someone we can tell," he said, words practically
rushed into one. He sucked in a deep breath as Nolan's eyes
widened.

"You do? Who?"

"A reporter. We can have him print it, run it as a story."

Nolan nodded, searching his face. "Okay, that's great!
That's – we can gather evidence and he can run it. So why
do you look like you're about to tell me something not
great?"

Reid didn't know where to start. *I like you a fucking lot?
Sorry, I started hanging out with you to get dirt on your dad?*

"When I met you that first night, I had no idea who you
were," he began because the start was a good place, yeah?

He swallowed, stomach swirling with nerves. He felt like
he'd done something wrong, because he *had*.

"I know," Nolan said sincerely.

"And after I saw you at the conference, I really thought it
was best if we just – cut ties and ran, y'know?"

Hurt flashed through Nolan's eyes, and he let his attention fall to the bar. "Yeah, I remember. But then you came to
my room—"

"Before that," Reid interrupted, "I had lunch with John,
my friend, the reporter. He said he was gonna lose his job
unless he found a really good story to write, to impress his
boss with."

"Oh," Nolan said, taking a step back.

Reid's chest tightened, his breath short, like Nolan was
stepping away with all the oxygen in the room.

"And we knew there had to be... something. Something I could find about your dad."

"*Oh*," Nolan said again, and sat down on the bar stool with an oomph.

Reid panicked, feeling like he was losing Nolan even as he sat not a foot away from him, and babbled on. "And that's maybe how I justified it, getting involved with you, because I felt so stupid, I mean—you're *here* to take this away from me," he said, waving his hand around at the bar. "But I couldn't – it didn't feel possible that that was all we were. I couldn't *stand* the idea that we ended there. I *wanted* to get breakfast with you that first morning. I wanted to walk you to your stupid conference and wish you luck, but when I woke up, you were gone and I was late. All fucking morning, all I could think about was your number burning a hole through my phone, asking you to dinner and planning what I wanted to show you next."

Nolan swallowed audibly, his sky-blue eyes darkening like a storm, lifting to Reid's. "Me too. I couldn't focus for anything," he said sadly.

"But then I figured out who you were, and I just – I felt like I was throwing this all away for a guy. So, yes. I agreed to John's stupid plan, and I went out with you, lying to myself, telling myself that I could do this without... And then you took me to the stupid rescue and god, Nolan..." Reid ran a hand through his hair, feeling crazed. "There's no one else *like* you, and—"

"Without what?" Nolan interjected.

Lost, Reid stared at him. "What?"

"You said you were telling yourself that you could do this – pretend to like me, pretend to be interested in me with ulterior motives – without...?"

Each word was a dagger to the chest, and Reid's throat

felt tight as the words scraped past his lips. "Without falling for you."

"And did you succeed?" Nolan asked, his tone short.

Reid shook his head. "No." His voice was small, about as small as he felt. "No, I didn't."

"Oh," Nolan said, again, and Reid wished he could come up with some other syllables.

And then he did. "So, even though you might have initially hung out with me for the article…"

"I hung out with you because I wanted to. The article was an excuse. Just a big, stupid excuse to see you again. I'm sorry."

It didn't matter that Reid hadn't wanted this in the beginning. That he'd used the article as an excuse to spend time with Nolan. That his own guilt was the reason he couldn't let himself have something nice for once. Someone nice. Because in the end, Nolan had become the collateral of his indecision.

"Okay," Nolan breathed, pain still scattered across his expression.

The only thing that mattered was how the chips fell. But instead of chips, they were splinters, and Reid's hands were all bloody from trying to catch them before they hit the ground.

Nolan hated his father, hated being used to further his image and make the business look good, hated being a pawn.

And that's exactly what Reid had done: used him.

Reid was no better than Nolan's father, in the end.

He could apologize a thousand times and it still wouldn't change that fact.

"Okay," Nolan repeated, and he nodded, determined.

"Now what?" Reid couldn't help but ask. He'd do anything.

"Well, now we just need proof."

Reid swallowed, gaze falling to the brick still sitting at the end of the bar. "And how do we get that?"

"Oh, I have proof."

Reid paused, slowly turning to stare at Nolan. "You do?"

"I mean, I can get proof. Easy."

Easy, huh? Something told Reid it would be anything but.

PAWN

"How?"

"This might surprise you, but I actually did a bit of research before running over here in a panic," Nolan admitted, and tugged his laptop out of the messenger bag, ignoring Reid's gaze.

The whole ordeal actually smarted quite a bit. In a way that made his chest tight and his stomach churn. His heart kind of hurt too, but he didn't think it was appropriate to have a heart attack at the moment, so he chalked it up to heartbreak.

Which was.

Fine.

Everything was *fine*.

His father's entire business was built on a plot of lies and manipulation, and the man he was maybe possibly almost certainly in love with was using him to uncover it all.

He couldn't *breathe*.

But he spoke anyway.

"I heard my father's assistant, Chance, on the phone," he choked out. "Once I returned to the hotel. Something about not hitting *your* business because it's a conflict of interest now. Chance was acting more weird than usual, so that's what made me suspicious."

"But speculation isn't enough," Reid countered.

"I said I did my research, didn't I?" he asked, powering up his laptop. His tabs slowly loaded in, revealing spreadsheets and deals and agreements and all the fine print that went with it.

"This is a list of the businesses he's bought out since the beginning. A simple search turned up some small articles from local papers, as well as complaints about increased vandalism in the area."

"Your dad?"

"I think it's safe to say so," he admitted. "There's not a trail of crime that leads to all of them, but I bet with a few phone calls, we could verify the timelines from the owners. That's why I need you," Nolan said, pulling up the list of numbers he'd compiled.

"Me? What for?"

Nolan leveled him with a stare. "Do you think they'd rather commiserate with another victim of my father's scheme, or the son of the man that stole their businesses from them?"

Reid winced. "Okay, yeah, I see your point." He glanced over Nolan's head to the clock behind the bar.

"What about the conference today?"

"They'll have to find some way to survive without me. Something tells me they won't have that much trouble." Absently, he wondered if his father would even check in on him. Probably not.

"And so we're… today?"

"Yes. We need to find all our evidence before they realize we know," Nolan said, scrolling through the phone numbers.

The sun was rising, cresting over the city and casting

Reid's restaurant in a soft morning glow. They had the entire day to find what they needed.

It took him a moment to recognize the silence in the room. Unlike before, when he and Reid were alone together, this silence was heavy, pressing. It wasn't comfortable and easy.

"It's still early. We can't call these people at six a.m. They'll get pissed before they even figure out why we're calling," Reid said softly.

Nolan had already realized this. But to do nothing would drive him mad, so he aimlessly flipped through all his documents, poring over the fine print and hoping to find something more concrete than a list of complaints.

While damning as a whole, it was conjecture, and his father likely knew this. Probably had a plan in place to refute it. Probably had enough money to make it go away.

They needed something *solid.*

Money. Account. Tomorrow.

There had to be a paper trail. Somewhere.

"Do you want breakfast? I can whip something up real quick," Reid offered.

Nolan's chest squeezed tightly all over again at the hesitant tone in Reid's voice. If cooking is what Reid needed to feel better in this moment, he wasn't going to deny him.

"Yeah, that would be nice," he said, fingers pausing on the mouse pad of his laptop. "Thanks."

But then he was alone as Reid disappeared to the back, alone with his thoughts, and at the moment they weren't very good company.

His hands fell into his lap, shoulders slumping as he stared at the screen, unseeing.

Nolan had thought himself lucky. Lucky that someone like Reid was giving him the time of day, even after the disaster that many of their… dates had been.

Because that's what they were doing all along, weren't they? Dating.

Maybe without so many words, but what else did you call it?

It suddenly made much more sense why Reid kept showing up at his door night after night.

A flash, a memory of warm hands and soft touches and softer kisses. Reid arching beneath him.

Had that all been a lie, too?

Almost as soon as the notion had crossed his mind, he dismissed it.

The man had said it himself. Reid had fallen for Nolan.

But Nolan didn't know if that was better or worse.

His screen went dark from inactivity, pulling him from his thoughts, reminding him of his purpose.

Right. There was no time to dwell on it, at least not now. So he swallowed back the tightness in his throat and continued searching through local news reports for more ties to his father's shady dealings.

The scent of whatever Reid was concocting in the kitchen drifted out, a tease, and despite the way Nolan's stomach still swirled, it grumbled as well.

Reid returned a handful of moments later with avocado toast and eggs and bacon filling two plates.

"Wow," Nolan breathed. It was hard to believe this was the first time Reid had cooked for him. Because it felt natural to accept the plate from him, as if they'd done this a thousand times before in a thousand other lives.

Now his throat hurt again.

It was pretty, a work of art in the form of a simple breakfast, and he remembered Reid talking about fancy meals without fancy pricing. Because everyone deserves to feel special every now and then. "You're truly impressive."

Reid's cheeks darkened as he ducked his head, as if swerving to avoid the compliment. Or Nolan's gaze.

"Thanks, man."

They ate, more of that uncomfortable silence making his skin itch. He tried not to think of the obvious. Like: what did this mean for them?

It wasn't until this moment that Nolan realized, while he'd considered that the week would come to an end, he'd never been able to envision *leaving*. Even though he'd have to leave Reid, eventually. But it just didn't *fit* in the image he'd slowly been creating as the days went by too quickly.

And if, in the meantime, he'd actually been considering… *not* leaving? Staying, saying goodbye to his father and his job and the company and his lonely apartment for good? Well, that was just crazy, wasn't it? Uprooting his whole life for a man he'd known less than a week?

Reid must have been having the same thoughts. If he'd fallen for Nolan, like he claimed.

"What are you thinking about so loudly?" Reid asked, voice soft and yet sounding like a gunshot in the silence.

"I don't think you want to know," Nolan admitted.

"I do, or I wouldn't have asked," he retorted. "Are you… mad?"

Nolan swallowed, the bite of perfectly fluffy egg going down like chalk.

"Reid. You lied to me. Or at least omitted the truth, which is…" He trailed off. This wasn't Reid's fault. "How I feel about the matter doesn't change that what my father is doing is *real*. And putting an end to it takes precedence. So I think – I think we should focus on that."

"Yes. Of course," Reid said. Nolan didn't miss the way his fingers tightened around the fork in his hand. "What do you need me to do?"

"Call your friend to meet us, so he can start writing his story."

"Okay. But finish eating first."

Nolan did, because wasting a single bite of this delicious meal that Reid had prepared for him was unacceptable.

Nolan was trying very hard not to think of Reid's role in all of this. If it wasn't for his father, would Reid have come back at all?

He would laugh if his chest didn't feel cracked open.

Nolan Whittier, just a pawn in other people's games.

Well, it was about damn time he played his own.

Starting with his father.

REHEARSAL

Meeting Reid's friend did not go well.

"I don't like you," John said the *moment* Reid left them alone to go collect coffees.

Nolan frowned, glancing up from his laptop in the secluded corner of Reid's restaurant. They were stowed away in the large back room again, the silence of the closed restaurant loud in its presence. Between the three of them, the entire table was covered with spreadsheets and phone numbers and checklists and articles. The chaos of their mission was spread out amongst them, and for the moment, the only witness to John's harsh tone.

"Excuse me?" Nolan said, brow furrowing.

"I'm glad you're helping Reid," John responded. "But that doesn't mean I like you."

Nolan tried not to show how bothered he was by the other man's words. He probably wasn't doing a very good job of it as he stared down at a bank statement.

"Well, sorry to hear that." He intended distant politeness, but even Nolan heard the bitchy note to his own tone.

John practically growled, and Nolan lifted his eyes to the other man once again. "I may not like you, but Reid does."

Nolan sucked in a sharp breath.

"And god knows why, but he does. He's different around you." John's lip twisted into a snarl. "He's like, glowing, or some shit."

Was it warm in here? Nolan's cheeks were hot.

"I know you're under the impression that he hung out with you to get dirt on your dad... God, I can't believe I'm about to say this," John moaned, rolling his eyes. "But that was my idea. I had to beg him to do it, with a healthy little guilt trip."

Nolan narrowed his eyes, his displeasure obvious, and John nodded, dropping his eyes to the paper he was trying to smooth a wrinkle out of. "Yes, I know, not my best moment, but I'm desperate, man. Look, all I'm trying to say is, don't... hold a grudge. He was just trying to help me out. And trust me when I say whatever is going on between you two is as real to him as it is to you. I've never seen him like this."

"Like what?" Nolan asked. Because he wanted to hear it, wanted to hear how Reid was maybe just as lost as Nolan was.

"All... smiley and happy and shit. It's gross." John wrinkled his nose, turning his gaze back to the laptop.

Maybe Nolan was a gullible, hopeless idiot, but the admission filled him with a little hope. A match strike against his ribs.

Nolan had said just the other night that he wanted to ruin everything for his father, and, well, Reid had technically just gotten a head start, right?

Nolan was still going back and forth with himself in the back of his mind while he scrolled through statement after statement, searching for the final nail in the coffin of his father's business.

He and John exchanged nothing of substance while their fingers tapped away at their keyboards. That was how Reid found them, hunched over and focused, as he balanced a cardboard tray of coffees.

Glancing up, Nolan caught the small smile on Reid's lips as his cup met the table.

"And a caramel macchiato with three extra pumps of caramel for you," he said with a smile that, even to Nolan, appeared soft and affectionate. When Nolan shifted his gaze away from sunshine personified, John was glaring at him.

He's different around you.

"The extra caramel makes a difference," he said, just to have something to say. Had what he uttered even made sense?

It must have, or if it hadn't, Reid chose not to dwell on it as he sat between them and got started on his list of phone calls.

Their knees brushed, and Nolan couldn't find it in himself to pull away.

John's words repeated in his mind as they continued compiling evidence. Reid's chipper, polite tone was a welcome soundtrack, filling the quiet as he interviewed the people Nolan's father had fucked over.

A headache pinched his temples as Nolan searched for the last piece that would solidify everything they suspected.

The day faded in the form of empty coffee cups and dishes from the kitchen. Nolan didn't think he'd ever been this well-fed as the sun tracked across the sky, time slipping away with it.

All week. We've got all week.

How many times had they repeated that phrase? Let the words offer comfort amongst the passing minutes?

As the clock ticked on, Reid and Nolan didn't have a single moment alone together. It gave Nolan time to think – to obsess over every exchanged laugh and analyze every shared touch, chaste or not. A background track running on repeat in his head as the numbers blurred together.

Despite it all, Nolan found what he was looking for. John almost cried as he sent the story to his boss.

They celebrated with fruity drinks as the sun melted behind the skyline, casting the space in a tangerine glow.

His father never checked on him, never texted. It was for the best, because what would Nolan say, anyway? By tomorrow, it wouldn't matter.

John left after the first drink, and Nolan helped Reid clear their borrowed table. Then Nolan was out of excuses to stay.

"Thank you for your help today," he said, standing and stalling in limbo in front of the table.

Reid huffed a laugh. "I should be the one thanking you," he retorted. "Are you going back to the hotel?"

That would be the obvious next move, probably. "Yeah."

"Right. Of course." Neither of them moved. "So, noon tomorrow, huh?"

Noon. The brunch mixer where Nolan would expose his father as a colluding, evil little man.

"Yeah. It feels… easier than I'd thought it would, in a way." Nolan cleared his throat.

They seemed to be tiptoeing around something. Reid probably knew what it was. Nolan certainly knew what it was. But he wasn't brave enough to ask.

Thankfully, Reid was. "So you're just going to hide in your hotel room for the next…" He glanced at the clock on the far wall. "Eighteen hours?" Reid's gaze was startling as it tracked back to Nolan.

"Guess so," he said weakly.

"Alone."

Nolan swallowed. "Sounds right."

We have all week.

Well, all week had passed and here they were, with the

last bit of it stretching out before them, close enough not only to touch, but to grab and hold onto.

Was Nolan ridiculous to deny himself that? It *felt* ridiculous, suddenly, when faced with walking away, to deny himself the presence of the one person he wanted to be with most. To deny himself someone that made him happy.

But Reid had lied, had hidden his real motive, and that meant… something, right?

Was it worth enough to warrant missing out on this time with Reid? Time that they had considered precious, had been desperate to grasp onto the entire week. And now he was just going to… give it up?

"I'll see you tomorrow," he heard himself say, a poor substitution.

Reid stared at him, those honey butter milk chocolate—Nolan finally remembered the truffle—eyes flicking over his face rapidly.

"Stay," Reid said.

That match struck against his ribs again, but this time, the spark took.

"Okay," Nolan agreed.

Reid's apartment was just as silent as the restaurant had been, almost eerie without the buzz of patrons below.

The bed was soft beneath them, more comfortable than any five-star hotel's, or maybe Nolan was biased, because his head was currently on Reid's chest. He didn't plan on moving anytime soon.

What was the point in even being upset about any of it? When Reid's heart thumped steadily beneath his ear, when his hand dragged fingertips across the back of Nolan's bare shoulder, skin cooling despite the warmth they shared?

And yet.

"What would have happened? I mean, if... if I hadn't found out about my father when you did?"

Reid was quiet, and Nolan couldn't help but slip his eyes open, trying to read the emotions on his face.

"Well... I guess you would've gone to your conference this morning. I would have met up with John. Had him write the story."

"Would you have ever spoken to me again?" Nolan asked, even though it hurt his throat to voice the words. *Once you got what you wanted.*

Surprise stilled Reid's hand. "What? Of course I would have." Nolan felt him move, yet still startled when his hand touched his cheek, directing his gaze up.

"I would've called or texted or found you, told you everything that was happening. Nolan, this might surprise you, but I do actually listen when you talk." Reid stared down at him, adam's apple bobbing as he swallowed. "Even if we weren't so... entangled," he settled on before continuing, "at the very least, I know you had nothing to do with your dad's decisions – his collusion – and there's no reason I wouldn't have given you a heads-up." His brows furrowed, a spark of indignance glowing in his gaze. "In fact, he's dragged the business that's supposed to be yours one day through the mud. This is just as much your fight as it is mine."

Relief filled Nolan. The question had been burning in Nolan's mind for hours, and with just a few words, Reid had tamed the flames.

"I have a question of my own," Reid admitted.

"What is it?"

"What happens after?" Reid asked, his expression nervous, reminiscent of their first night.

"After... tomorrow?" Nolan clarified, though he knew, even before Reid nodded.

After Nolan exposed his father and his assistant. *After* Nolan protected Reid's business, and in the process, damned his own.

In front of his father.

To his *face*.

"I can't think about that right now," Nolan said, shaking his head. "I can barely think past tomorrow, getting up in front of all those people and—oh, god," he said, sitting up and swallowing sharply. "I'm gonna be sick."

"No, you're not," Reid said, palming his shoulders and holding him still. "Just breathe. I know how big this is."

Nolan shook his head. Reid didn't understand, *couldn't*. "No, you don't. You really don't."

Because in Reid's eyes, Nolan was doing the right thing, the only option. But Nolan saw the other facets. He was losing his father at the end of all this. Despite how decidedly... terrible George Whittier was, at least he was there. Hell, he was the *only* one there. He'd been all Nolan had for what felt like forever.

After all this, Nolan was going to be alone.

If he succeeded. If his father didn't somehow weasel his way out of it.

Drawing in a deep breath, Nolan counted to five and reached up, taking Reid's hands from his shoulders and holding them in his own, turning slightly on the bed to face him. Two of his fingers rested over Reid's wrist, and—call it selfish, if he must call it anything at all—Reid's pulse was racing almost as fast as Nolan's was, and he found relief in that.

"You're afraid of him, aren't you?" Reid asked. "There's no way he could even lay a finger on you, not with me there."

His words were spoken carefully, softly, as if afraid to spook a particularly wild cat.

Nolan blinked. "He doesn't hit me," he said, slowly.

"He doesn't have to hit you to scare you," Reid retorted, expression wide-eyed and sympathetic.

And, well, that was somehow *not* what Nolan needed to hear in that moment, and yet the *exact* thing he needed to hear.

"Fine. He scares me," he whispered. "What if he tries to drag me down with him, turn it around somehow? Would someone even believe I'm that much of an idiot, that this was happening around me and I remained oblivious?"

Reid hummed. "Give 'em a few minutes, they'll figure it out."

Despite the situation, Nolan laughed. "That wasn't nice," he muttered petulantly as Reid dragged him back down to the sheets. Nolan went willingly.

"So, we don't talk about tomorrow," Reid decided aloud. "Only now."

Nolan sank into Reid's shape, his warmth. Stared down at him and melted under the heat of his affection.

"Think you're up to the task of distraction?" Nolan asked softly.

Reid grinned, and kissed him.

BIG DAY

As soon as the sun was awake, so was Nolan.

It would've been nice to spend the morning in bed, maybe watch a movie, distract himself as the hours ticked by with laughter and teasing and lots of kisses.

Instead, Nolan slid from the bed and crept to his laptop, cracking it open and sitting on the small couch, dragging a knitted blanket into his lap.

If he was going to take his father down, he needed to make a spectacle of it. The facts could do most of the talking, but Nolan wanted... he wanted his father to know it was *him*.

From a business standpoint, he could justify it, sure. It was smart to align himself against his father, make it *very* well known just how much he disapproved of his father's actions.

From a petty standpoint, maybe for once he just wanted to see that look on his father's face, the realization that it was Nolan who'd beaten him at his own game.

Eventually, Nolan's fingertaps woke Reid, whose smile slowly grew as Nolan told him the new plan over coffee. Reid made a few phone calls on his behalf, and once it was *time*, he felt less frantic and only slightly panicked.

Nolan helped Reid pick an outfit as they stood in front of

the rack of chaotically-organized clothes. Lots of graphic print tees, jeans, and a million different colored button-ups.

It was domestic, Nolan thought as he shuffled through the clothes, Reid's gaze a spotlight on his shoulders.

They didn't talk about it.

Reid went with Nolan back to the hotel, eyes peeled for his father. They made it safely. Nolan got dressed.

"Which tie do you think says *fuck you* the most?" Nolan asked with false bravado.

"The fuchsia one, obviously," Reid answered, closer than Nolan had expected.

His hands slid around Nolan's waist, holding him still, and pulled the bright tie from his hand.

"Doesn't seem like… too much, does it?" Nolan asked.

"Seems like a party tie."

He doubted his father would see this afternoon as a celebration.

"C'mere," Reid said, and pulled him face to face. He looped the tie around his neck and began tying it for him, fingers moving slowly but deftly. He squinted at Nolan's collarbone, hands hesitating before unlooping and relooping the shiny fabric.

"Fuck," he muttered. "This always looks so romantic in movies."

"Do you know what you're doing?" Nolan asked, lips twitching and heart swelling with such warm fondness he couldn't breathe.

"In theory," he answered, distracted. Reid tilted his head, tongue sticking out from the corner of his lips in concentration.

God, he was cute.

It hit him again with a kick to the solar plexus, how tragic it was that their time together was dwindling to nothing.

They didn't talk about it.

Not as Nolan surged forward to kiss the concentrated line of his lips, not when he re-tied the tie with Reid's head resting on his shoulder so he could watch. Not when they made their way out of the room, together this time, toward putting this whole thing behind them.

As the hotel came into view after the short walk, Nolan was sweating from more than the heat. Reid held his hand anyway.

"You sure you wanna do this?" Reid asked softly.

If he said no, Nolan knew there'd be no judgment from Reid. In fact, they'd probably just turn around and spend the afternoon at Reid's place, watching his phone flood with notifications as the business imploded.

"No, I—I want him to know it was me."

His final *fuck you* to his father. Was it dramatic? Yes.

Was it terrifying, to be led through the lobby, clutching Reid's hand and his lanyard, knowing in just moments it would all be over? Abso-fucking-lutely.

Was it all a little easier with Reid by his side? Nolan squeezed his hand. Yeah, it was.

Reid released his hand as they drew closer to the party, the hum of cheerful murmurs spilling into the carpeted hall-way. Nolan put the lanyard over his neck and sucked in a deep breath.

"You've got this. And if not, I'm right here," Reid promised, low in his ear.

His father's eyes latched onto him as soon as Nolan entered the room. George Whittier's gaze was intense and angry, despite the smile he put on for the person in front of him.

Nolan steeled himself as he approached, stuffing his fear down deep, pulling on his frustration and fury like a set of armor.

"Nolan, glad to see you're feeling better," his father said

after breaking away from his discussion. He lifted his hand to grip Nolan's arm, but Nolan shifted away first, feeling Reid at his back in silent support.

"Have you heard the news?" his father asked. "It's everywhere, it's—"

Nolan smiled. "It's fine. Don't worry, I'm gonna take care of everything," he said. "That's what this brunch is for, right?" he asked his father, whose brows were bunched in confusion. "To celebrate the business? Let's fucking celebrate."

He patted his father on the shoulder, a shitty, patronizing touch, and it felt good to be on the opposite end of it for once. "Is Chance here?" he asked. "Wouldn't want him to miss the big speech."

"He's over there." His father motioned to the side, where Chance was hissing into a cell phone. Nolan pitied whoever was on the other line. "Trying to salvage this shit show."

"Leave it to me," Nolan said, and ignored Reid's chuckle, terribly disguised as a cough.

Reid took the flash drive and motioned to the projector, while he headed over to the table stacked with tech stuff. Nolan took to the stage without a glass to toast with and picked up the microphone, which screeched at his touch, bringing the room's attention to him.

"Good afternoon," he greeted, voice light and friendly, casual. "I'm Nolan Whittier, and if you didn't just sneak in for the free drinks and food, you'll probably recognize me from some of the presentations this week."

The crowd chuckled appropriately, and Nolan smiled, stomach swirling. "It's good to see you all here, and I want to thank you for giving us your time and attention this week. This project is quite a big undertaking, but rest assured, we've done this before. Hundreds of times, in fact. And it's all thanks to my father, George Whittier."

The crowd cheered, though he recognized the unsure glances a few of them shared. Good.

"I hope you'll forgive me for giving one last presentation, but this one might even be the most important of the week." He had the room's full attention now, and sucked in a breath to steady himself before speaking. "George Whittier, of Whittier Hotels," he began. The projector clicked, and the first slide appeared on the screen behind him. He moved out of the way, standing stage right.

"Born in 1955. Father to one – you'll never guess who." The crowd chuckled at the photo that appeared with the next slide, controlled by Reid. He caught Reid's gaze, strong and wide and proud from behind the computer at the tech table.

Nolan steeled himself, wondering if everyone could hear the deafening thump of his heart.

The photo was old, one of the many fake, staged photos of Nolan, his father's arm around his shoulder as they grinned at something off-camera.

"George raised me to believe in integrity," he continued, voice tight, heart racing. "Hard work and perseverance. You know, all that good stuff. Never giving up, working toward a goal with single-minded focus.

"The first branch we ever opened—" He paused as the slideshow transitioned, a clipart skyscraper rising up from the screen to rip the photo of him and his father apart. It was stupid and dramatic and silly and perfect, and confused murmurs rose throughout the crowd.

"—was a huge success," he carried on over them, speaking louder. The slideshow transitioned again, coins falling from the top of the screen to pile over the bottom, filling the pixels with gold. Then a photo of the first hotel. "Some might call him ruthless, doing anything he could to get to the top. No matter who –" His gaze flicked to Reid, softening at the fierce pride glowing from his eyes. "– or what stands in his way."

Again, the photo changed, this time to the happiest photos he could find of the first businesses they'd ever bought out. A little girl on the shoulders of the owner, with his giant grin at the line hovering outside the door of his candy shop. "This is the first business my father ever purchased, bulldozed over –" At this point, a clipart bull-dozer rolled onto the screen, pushing aside the photo of the happy father-daughter duo. "–to make room for…" Again, the photo of the utilitarian hotel, all steel and glass and heartlessness. "This," he said, clear disdain in his voice.

Disappointed gasps sounded throughout the room, and his father stiffened where he stood. If hadn't caught on thus far, he was about to.

"This is another business that stood in the way of my father's hotel," Nolan announced, and Reid flashed another family-friendly photo. Then another, like polaroids landing in a pile. One after another. "These are *all* businesses that had to be bought and torn down, their roots pulled up and tossed out in order to make room for hotel after hotel.

"That's sad enough as it is," Nolan said, filling with disbe-lief that he'd been so blind for so long. It spilled out in exas-peration. "But the worst part is… he didn't even do it *legally!*"

The crowd gasped as a whole, and *oh*, this was so climac-tic, and his father was vibrating in place, rage pouring off of him in waves. He nudged Chance, who picked his mouth up off the floor and stomped over to Reid.

Nolan spoke faster. "Oh, yes, yes, the owners signed on the dotted line, accepted the plainly awful, unfair terms. They really had no choice. You see, leading up to each deal were months and months of bad luck. Broken windows." On the screen, multiple photos flashed of the businesses his father had hired someone to damage, their windows shattered. "Vandalism, break-ins, robberies, ruined produce, power outages. Even doctored health inspections." As he spoke, Reid progressed through the slideshow, even as Chance tried to fight him for the controls.

His mic went dead with a click, the cord hanging from Chance's fist, and Nolan spoke louder, practically shouting to be heard in the back as voices rose around them. Then John was there, holding Chance back and helping Reid, who bounded to the stage.

Nolan frowned, setting the mic down.

At the back, police officers paused at the entrance, taking stock of the goings-on, then hurried to the struggling duo by the controls. The crowd parted like the sea for them, living for the drama.

Reid stepped up onto the stage with Nolan, and handed him a… megaphone.

Reid winked. "Mine's bigger."

God, Nolan loved this man.

He flicked the megaphone on and held it to his mouth to be heard, then paused and waited for Reid to arrive back at the controls, giving the officers and a pissed-off Chance a wide berth.

When the slideshow moved to the next slide, photos of Reid's broken window splashed across the wall. "And don't think it ends there." His voice echoed around the room, over the chaos.

Nolan let his gaze fall to his father as he spoke and watched the realization strike across his features, inspiring anger in its wake. "Your city hasn't been spared his collusion. That pizza you're all enjoying? From Crustworthy's, a business standing in my father's way. The ice cream at the back? Chippy's, who last month lost *all* of their stock in a freak power outage, setting them back *months* in costs.

Those were no accidents, I assure you, and I have the proof."

He wasn't going to post the details of the bank statements on the screen, but the damage had been done anyway. He'd save them for the lawyers.

The gasps around the room were the perfect backdrop to the extra officers arriving, parting the crowd again as they headed for their colleagues and Chance.

"I do offer my apologies for the dramatics and for wasting your time this week. It seems your city is better off without Whittier Hotels, after all."

Nolan turned off the megaphone and set it on the side of the stage before exiting. Where was Reid—

His father's curse of outrage was lost amongst the discord, but Nolan knew the sound of anger in that voice, had heard it all his life. And yet, he'd never heard it quite *this* angry. He turned his head toward the crowd as his foot met the last stair, his father barreling for him, a snarl on his face.

George Whittier fisted the lapels of Nolan's suit, shaking him roughly. "Do you have any idea what you've done?" he shrieked, spittle flying.

His face was dark red with fury, a vein in his forehead standing out in stark relief.

Nolan lifted his hands palm out and tried to remain calm, his father's rage palpable. "Isn't Chance embarrassing himself enough?" Nolan asked. "Surely you're not going to make a scene as well?"

"I spent my whole life—" he began with a growl, but Nolan interrupted him.

"Yes, I know! And I'm glad I don't have to waste mine, too!"

His father's eyes widened, and Reid saw the notion cross his face, knew what was going to happen before he released Nolan's collar to crank his arm back, fist tearing toward—

Nolan blinked at the fist stopped inches from his face, the tail wrapped around his father's wrist, and an infuriated Reid standing next to them.

"I don't think that's wise," Reid said sharply.

He'd brought the officers with him, and they stepped up, speaking softly to George.

"You sure you wanna do that, pal? You might want to take a breather."

His father's fist loosened from Nolan's lapel, and he shook Reid's tail off. Reid winced, flicking his tail away as it curled behind his back in that irritated manner.

"Alright, alright," come on, one of the officers said, placing a hand on George's shoulder.

George huffed, and spun on the officer, smacking his arm away. "Get your hands off me!" he shouted. He slowly advanced on the officer, lifted finger pointed in his face. "Do you have any idea what he's just done? I have every right to be—what are you—ow!"

The other office grabbed George's wrist, and yanked it behind his back, before grabbing the other one. The metal clink of the handcuffs locking seemed deafening.

"What are you doing? Stop this right now! Do you know who I am?"

The officers ignored his sputtering, and the room's scandalized murmurs grew in volume as he was led away.

Nolan tried to calm his nerves, turned his back on the curious throng of people. Reid clasped his shaking hand gently between his own for support. Before Reid could even get a word cut, Nolan surged forward, pressing their lips together.

Reid was shocked into stillness for a split second before he wrapped his arms around Nolan, and Nolan's stomach swooped, similar to the moment when he first took flight with Reid.

When they parted for breath, Reid's voice was filled with disbelief. "I can't believe you just did *that.* That was fucking awesome."

"Me! You stopped—with your tail! And the cops. I—I don't even know what to say," Nolan stumbled over his words. "Holy shit." He pressed a hand to his chest, heart still thumping. "Oh, god."

"Hey, hey, just breathe. It's over. You did it."

It's over.

Just like this week. Just like his father's business.

But it was just the beginning of a legal battle, and he knew his father would come well-armed.

Reid had the proof, and it didn't lie. But Nolan had a sinking feeling he wouldn't be able to come out of all this unscathed.

His fear didn't excuse him from taking ownership of the part he'd played in ruining those people's lives, the ones whose businesses and livelihoods were plastered across the screen.

The best week of his life might be over, but he could guarantee the worst months of his life were about to follow.

"It's just beginning, Reid," Nolan responded.

GOODBYE

Nolan's hotel room was cold, the air cranked up to relieve them from the heat of the walk back.

Despite the chill, Reid tracked a bead of sweat trailing down his spine as he sat on the bed, staring across the room at the man who occupied it.

Nolan was packing, pulling each shirt from the closet and meticulously folding them before placing them in his suitcase. One by one. Even his boxers were manipulated into a tiny square before they went in their spot.

Reid curved his fingers over the edge of the bed, willing Nolan to look at him, to calm his hectic thoughts by saying… anything.

Anything was better than the oppressive silence that lingered.

Nolan was readying for his flight back across the country to his home. To a legal battle that would go on for who knew how long.

And then…?

Reid didn't know whether to give into the rising panic in his chest, brought on by the idea of never seeing Nolan again. He was too scared to ask, unsure if he even had a right to.

What would he do if Nolan's answer wasn't what he wanted to hear? Beg him to come back?

The man had just seen his father arrested, effectively killing the family business. The last thing he needed to worry about was some guy in a city hundreds of miles away.

But Nolan had to be thinking the same thing, right? This whole week couldn't have been for nothing.

But Reid also couldn't let himself forget his role in all of this. Betraying Nolan, even if it had all worked out in the end.

He got to keep his restaurant.

Reid let his gaze land a little heavier on Nolan's frame as he paced from the closet to his suitcase on the dresser and back again, a different item of clothing in his hands each time. He was methodical in his movements, precise and coordinated.

Oh. Reid recognized this, suddenly.

Nolan was freaking out, just like Reid was. Just like that first night, when he'd been freaking out about Reid staying the night. Now he was fretting about leaving.

Or maybe it's the fact that, oh, I don't know, his dad just got arrested?

"Are you okay?" Reid finally asked.

Because this wasn't about him, wasn't about how he wanted to keep Nolan, too. This was about Nolan and how his entire life was about to change. Reid wanted to be there for him however he could, even if it looked differently than how he desired.

Nolan paused, one hand in his bag, facing the closet, shoulders tense.

Reid's throat hurt, and he hoped his eyes weren't as shiny as they felt when Nolan slowly turned around.

"I think I'm still processing. It hasn't really hit me yet,

even though I have a meeting with my lawyer as soon as I get home."

"You did the right thing," Reid said, because it felt right, even though he may not have been an unbiased voice.

"Oh, I know." Nolan nodded sharply, gaze trained down at the floor as he chewed his lip. "I don't doubt that. He deserves whatever he has coming. It's just... I never thought I'd be here. Staring down a future without him. Even though we don't have the best relationship, he's always been there, even if it was just as a voice in the back of my head. I don't hear it anymore, and it's a little scarier than I'd thought it would be."

Reid's chest ached at the hurt in Nolan's words, the fear in the admission.

"He's still your dad. I get it."

"But he's still a terrible person," Nolan added. "And I mean, now that he's not here anymore, I can do what *I* want to do, instead of what's expected of me. I mean, he's not here to yell at me about it!" Nolan inhaled, a high-pitched little gasp, and he lifted his head to Reid. "I'm... I'm going to adopt a pet. A cat!" he exclaimed. "Now that I won't be traveling all over the country at his whim, I can finally have a cat," he rambled. "And my father would've hated it, which is honestly even more of a reason to finally get one. It'll most certainly make my apartment feel less lonely."

Right. Nolan's home, across the entire country.

But what about us? He wanted to ask, but choked the words down a throat tight with emotion.

"What will you name him? Or her?" he asked instead.

"Oh, I don't know," Nolan shrugged. "It'll depend on their personality. And most cats from shelters have names already. I wouldn't want to change it if they're elderly. Too confusing for them. It'll be so nice to have a *cat* around, though, Reid! My apartment is so quiet, too quiet. I hate it there. It's nice, but the cat will make it feel so much better. I have a view, too, and the birds!" he rambled. "The cat will love seeing the birds in the window." Nolan collapsed on the bed beside Reid. "Oh, I can't wait to show you, I mean, pictures don't do it justice, but I do have a really lovely view of the sunrise—"

Reid couldn't help it – his breath caught, the sound almost a squeak as he tried to silence it.

Nolan turned his head at the noise, caught sight of Reid's expression, and pushed himself up. "What is it?"

If Reid said anything he was probably going to cry, so he shook his head and swallowed.

Nolan's frown deepened. "Wait, we're not – did you think we were breaking up?"

From Nolan's tone, the correct answer would be no.

"Are we?" Reid whispered anyway.

Nolan shook his head, so vehemently Reid wondered if his brain rattled. "What? No! No, of course not."

Relief filled him so immensely he couldn't breathe. "Oh," he managed.

"Reid, we just saved your restaurant!" Nolan cupped his cheek and pulled them face to face. "Why would I ever want to break up?"

"I don't know," Reid admitted. "Because of what I did?"

Nolan's fingers tightened around his jaw and gave him a little shake. "Don't worry about that. Are you in love with me, like you said?"

Reid nodded, eyes burning with the threat of tears.

It was hard to resist them, especially when Nolan beamed at his admission. "I love you, too."

And it was just... that easy.

For Nolan to trust him, to trust that Reid loved him and wouldn't hurt him.

Reid cleared his throat. "Right. Of course, breaking up

would require us to have been dating first," Reid drawled, probably ruined by his welling eyes.

Nolan sputtered. "Were we not? But we – oh, I see. You're teasing me."

"Glad you caught that," Reid sputtered out on a watery laugh.

"I'm going to long-distance date the hell out of you," Nolan promised.

His hand slid to the back of Reid's neck, and pulled him close. Their lips brushed once before returning for more, ignoring the smear of salt tinging the kiss.

"And then," Nolan said, trailing his lips to his ear. "Then, when I come back, I'll be the best boyfriend you've ever heard of."

Reid's stomach flipped. "You'll come back?"

"Of course," Nolan said, nodding, mouth slipping over Reid's cheek. "Of course I'll come back to you. And my cat, too."

Reid's chest tightened with overwhelming affection, and he breathed his first easy breath in what felt like hours.

"I've heard long distance is difficult," Reid murmured a moment later.

Nolan pulled away to meet his eyes. "Please. We were *made* for difficult. I mean, if you can help me take down my family's business, figuring out FaceTime will be nothing."

"You don't even know how to use FaceTime, grandpa?"

Nolan paused. "I admit nothing. But I wouldn't turn down a tutorial, no."

Reid snorted, kissing him again because he could. "Couple other things I could show you, too."

When Nolan smirked, Reid felt it against his lips. "I like the sound of that. Care for one last use of that waterfall shower head?" Nolan pushed to his feet and held out a hand to Reid.

And even though Nolan would leave tomorrow, and his chest hurt at just the thought, Reid would see him again, even if it was through a few hundred pixels on a screen.

So for now, he would just have to commit every inch of Nolan to memory.

Reid laid his hand in Nolan's, and let himself be pulled from the bed.

"I thought you'd never ask."

BANANA SHARK PT II

6 *months later*
Reid was sweeping the front step of Essie's Place, freezing in the chilly winter air, yet still wincing under the sun's bright light.

Excited voices neared, and he stepped out of the way to make room on the sidewalk for a gaggle of teens to pass.

"He's been there for *hours*, I'm telling you. I've never seen anyone play so long. It's just Frogger."

Reid's heart thumped, and he cleared his throat. "What's going on?"

One of the kids turned to him, calling out as he walked backwards. "Some weirdo is hogging the Frogger game at the arcade. It's been *hours*."

"What for?" Reid asked.

They shrugged. "Dunno, but he has, like, thousands of tickets already." The kid rolled his eyes and turned back around. "We'll come back another day."

Reid watched them walk off, unable to slow the galloping pace of his heart. *It's just Frogger.* It could be anyone. It didn't *mean* anything—

Reid dropped the broom and startled as it clacked against

the concrete like a gunshot, but didn't bother picking it up before he took off. His boots pounded against the sidewalk as he darted through the crowds of bored teenagers and winter shoppers.

"Sorry, excuse me," he called out as he cut through a larger group. The arcade came into sight, the bright blue letters of the sign like a beacon. He almost broke out into a run.

There was no proof it was Nolan. But who else would hog the only game in the arcade that Nolan was good at? It couldn't just be a coincidence.

He entered the building, and had to come to a stop to let his eyes adjust to the darkened interior. It was empty. Which was normal, he supposed, for the midday hour. The tacky carpet blurred as he stepped inside, rounding the corner to—

Nolan's familiar head of dark hair was bent over the game machine, single-minded focus and intensity in the line of his shoulders.

Reid froze, unable to take another step, unable to believe that Nolan was *here*. After all this fucking time.

He still looked good as ever, even bundled up in what looked like a patterned collared shirt and a coordinating sweater. God, what a dork.

Reid fucking loved him; his chest was about to burst with it.

My dork, he thought, shaking himself and finally gathering the courage to approach him over the frog jumping noise.

"D'you think you should let someone else have a turn?" he asked softly.

Nolan stiffened, head jerking over his shoulder so fast Reid feared he'd put a crick in his neck.

"Reid!" he said, voice cracking in his mix of disbelief and excitement.

The frog on the screen got run over by a car, and the ending music blared from the ancient box. The highest score rankings came up, and every single line was filled with NOL.

"You can't be here! I don't have enough tickets yet," Nolan practically whined, finally turning around to face him.

Reid's lips twitched, despite the desperation he felt to toss Nolan against the side of the game and kiss him. Suddenly, he was in range, too; he hadn't even realized his feet were carrying him toward Nolan. "Oh. Well, okay then," he said, turning on his heel and pretending to leave.

Nolan's hand gripped his bicep and spun him back around. "Don't leave!"

"Okay," Reid agreed again. Before he could convince his brain to get with the program, a bored man about their age in a polo bearing the arcade's logo came up, one arm tucked behind his back.

"Listen, man. That's the third group of kids you've scared off today, and look, just—" He pulled the banana shark out from behind his back and shoved it at Nolan. "Take the damn stuffie and leave. I'm keeping your tickets and we'll call it even."

Nolan gaped. "But I'm only seven hundred away—"

"I *know*. That's why I'm cutting our losses. You've spent more than enough on Frogger to make up for the cost of the fucking shark. Leave."

Before Nolan could refute again because of his pride, Reid reached out and swiped the banana shark from the man. "Thank you. We'll be happy to get out of your hair."

"But Reid—" Nolan began. Reid interrupted by grabbing his hand, threading their fingers together and pulling him away, toward the back exit he knew each of these buildings had, but didn't use.

It was like no time had passed at all as they squeezed their hands together, like Nolan had never left and like Reid hadn't been waiting for this day for months.

The sunshine was bright as fuck, and Reid stumbled to a stop just as they breached the doors. Nolan crowded into his back and took advantage of the movement, burying his head in the back of Reid's neck, wrapping an arm around his waist.

It made Reid's breath stutter, his heart slamming against the cage of his ribs.

"Hi," Nolan whispered softly, and Reid melted.

"Hi," he said. "Fancy meeting you here." Reid laid his hands on Nolan's arms.

"I was going to surprise you."

Spinning in Nolan's arms, Reid held up the banana shark between them. "Nolan, you're *here*. I'd say that's a pretty fucking awesome surprise."

"But I didn't get the – the shark!"

"Uh, love, I'm holding it in my hand."

Nolan's cheeks went red at the name. "I didn't win it, though."

"You did! You played Frogger all day, from what I hear." Reid couldn't stop smiling.

"You heard?" Nolan questioned, head tilting to the side.

The courtyard was rundown, grown-over, and private. Reid had been meaning to repurpose it, turn his half into outdoor seating. But that required renovations, like tearing out his exposed brick wall, and summer had come and gone, and now that Nolan was here, Reid was thankful for his procrastination.

Reid pushed him against the wall, squishing the stuffie between them.

"I thought you were at home today." In fact, Nolan had sent him a picture just that morning of the senior cat he'd adopted lounging in the sunlight against the window. "You sent me a photo of your damned cat!"

Nolan grinned deviously. "I know."

"You're *here*!"

"I know," he laughed, and god, Reid had heard that laugh through the phone for months, letting it keep him awake far into the night as they talked and talked to try and make up for the miles between them, but it was so much better in person.

"God, I missed you," Reid said, practically whimpering as he crushed his mouth to Nolan's again.

"I missed you, too," Nolan breathed in between kisses.

He rocked his hips away from the wall, grinding his hard length into Reid and making his breath catch.

"In front of Banana Shark?" Reid whispered, scandalized. "Here?"

"Unless you don't want to—"

"Now, hey, I didn't say that," Reid interrupted, slipping his hands down to circle his hips and pull him forward.

"You gonna make us walk home with come in our pants?" Nolan asked.

"Babe." Reid pulled back, brow arched. "I can fly, remember?"

"Then what are you waiting for?"

Reid groaned, letting Nolan taste it straight from his lips as Reid thrust against him.

"God, I can't believe you're here," Reid groaned. Pleasure raced up and down his spine, arching anew each time he ground forward, the friction and pressure of Nolan's weight and the hard line of his cock beginning the circuit all over again.

"This is so much better in person," Nolan whined, head tipping back against the wall.

Dropping his head, Reid licked a stripe up his neck, ending in a nip over his pulse, feeling it race against his tongue.

The past six months had been a wonder, teaching Nolan all about the notion of sexting. Turns out, he'd been a natural.

"Six months, Nolan," Reid breathed against his throat. Nolan's hands traced up his back, threading through his hair despite the ponytail, and tugging deliciously.

A moan slipped out, just at the gentle pull, and Reid let Nolan guide his head back. "I know. But it's done. Everything's over, finally," Nolan promised. "Except us. And we've got time to make up for."

"Starting now?" Reid asked, with a punctual grind against Nolan.

"Starting—fuck, now," he agreed. "You're so hot. I missed you so much."

Their rhythm grew desperate, barely in sync, but each grind was better than the last, sending them both closer as they panted into each others' mouths.

"Clearly," Reid teased, grinding harder, faster. "It's like the closet all over again. Anyone could find us out here."

"Shut up," Nolan said, no heat except *need* in the words. Reid felt a shiver dance up Nolan's spine, since they were thigh to thigh, hips to hips, poor Banana Shark crushed between their chests.

"Nah, you like it. Like the idea of being discovered, anyone finding us like this—"

Just as Reid was about to tip over the edge, head falling back with pleasure, words spilling out faster than he could track them, the knob on the door beside them began to turn.

"No—" Nolan gasped.

"Fuck off," Reid shouted, slamming his palm into the door, holding it closed before it could even begin to open.

There was a long silence from the other side, followed by a groan. "C'mon, guys! I just want a cigarette. You're… you're both banned after this!"

"Look what you did!" Nolan hissed, thunking his head back into the wall, frozen.

Reid grinned, stamped it into the skin at Nolan's neck, and resisted the urge to rut against him. "We have Banana Shark already, so it's fine."

"Well, I mean, if you're interested in making up for lost time… I have an apartment."

Reid paused, eyes narrowing in suspicion. "You already have an apartment?"

Nolan froze suddenly. "Maybe. Unless I shouldn't?"

"Why didn't you say anything?" Reid asked, looping his arms around Nolan's neck and pressing their bodies together.

"It seemed awfully presumptuous for me to show up again after six months and not have a place to stay."

"You could've—" Reid tried to imagine the both of them fitting inside his tiny storage room turned studio apartment. "Okay, I get it. Is it nice?"

"Well, I could just show you," Nolan offered, dragging a hand down Reid's arm. "I could use a lift."

"Lucky for you, I happen to know a guy."

Nolan arched a brow, lips twitching. "Oh, that's so kind of you. I don't know how I'll ever repay you for—"

"Oh, shut up," Reid said, affection filling his chest and spilling into his voice as he rolled his eyes. "Let me take you home."

When they parted, Banana Shark almost slipped, and Reid dropped his hand to catch the plush.

"Oh, no," Nolan gasped.

Reid couldn't help the laugh that burst out of his chest at the flat stuffie, one eye on each side of the bend.

"Poor shark, he didn't last a day," Nolan cried.

"No, no, he's fine!" Reid insisted, and placed a hand on either edge of him, pushing his palms together to re-fluff him. When that didn't work, Reid tried placing a hand at each end of him and smushing him together.

"Oh, god, he had to witness *that*, and now you're manhandling him?"

"Look, he's perfect," Reid announced, offering Nolan the once-again plush figure with one hand beneath it and one hand behind, like it was an accessory he was advertising. "I give you: Banana Shark."

"Are you going to take care of him, or should I worry for his well being?" Nolan drawled.

"Please, of course he's in capable hands," Reid retorted. "Speaking of, where's your cat? Not back in…"

"And leave her there? Of course not. She's at my new apartment." He arched a brow. "Do you think you two can get along?" Nolan teased.

"I'll manage just fine," Reid declared, and let his wings out.

"Oh, I missed these," Nolan sighed, reaching over his shoulder to brush at one of the feathers within reach. Then he gazed out at the area behind Reid, eyes widening. "Oh, is this the little courtyard you've been talking about? It certainly has potential."

The whole time he talked, his fingers stroked over one of Reid's feathers.

It sent chills over him. "Where's your place?"

Nolan called out the address, and Reid tried to picture it in his mind. He knew the area and could probably get them there.

"We're gonna flatten Banana Shark again," Reid warned, and placed the plush between their bodies before pulling Nolan in against him.

Nolan sighed and curled his arms around Reid, then buried his face in Reid's neck. As his warm breath tickled his skin, Reid chased off a shiver.

"Alright," he said weakly. "Hold on tight."

His wings pumped, disturbing some of the leaves and debris still littering the courtyard, his stomach swooping as their feet left the ground. It never went away for Reid, the excitement of flying, but usually it was nothing more than a little flip of the stomach right in the beginning. He hardly noticed it anymore.

Funny that he was noticing it now, with Nolan.

The flight was quick and easy, and landed them smack in the middle of the city.

Nolan pointed the building out to him, and Reid carefully lowered them to the ground. There was no doorman to greet them, so once Nolan caught his bearings with a "wow, forgot how high up you usually go" and a nervous laugh, he led them both through the lobby and into the elevators, Banana Shark still clutched in his hand.

I love him.

Reid followed Nolan in and slammed his palm against the shiny wall on the opposite side of Nolan's head. His eyes went wide, and an honest-to-god whimper fell off his lips.

Reid grinned, joy fizzing inside him like a shaken soda. "I love the sounds you make," he said, voice little more than a rumble.

Nolan melted against him, hands gripping hard at his hips, pulling him in, grinding together.

"Your hair's longer," Nolan groaned, sliding a hand up his chest and around the back of his neck to undo the ponytail, the twist falling to the elevator floor as it jerked into motion. "Oh, god, this isn't fair. Look at you."

Reid lifted his gaze from the thumping pulse in Nolan's

neck to his blown, blue eyes, half his vision obscured by the blond tendrils hanging down past his chin.

Nolan's lips parted and he gathered the hair back, fingers tangling in a messy, tight hold.

"I can't wait to hold all this back from your face when I fuck your throat later."

Reid groaned, need barreling over him no gentler than that damn pixelated car over the frog. Nolan tugged him closer, pressing his head into the dip of his shoulder to muffle Reid's stuttered groan.

"Fuck," he groaned as Nolan continued to rut against him.

Reid closed his teeth around Nolan's shoulder and bit down, grinning as he felt Nolan shudder against him.

That's what you get, he thought smugly.

Reid dropped a hand from the wall to tip Nolan's face up, then brushed their lips together, feather-soft, before Nolan opened beneath him. Reid licked into his mouth, their tongues twining as the elevator came to a stop.

They parted for a breath, and then stepped away when the doors separated. With pride, Reid watched Nolan's fingertips dig into the plushie.

"Floor seventeen," he breathed, holding out a hand for Nolan to continue past him. "You do that on purpose?"

"Just a happy coincidence," Nolan said, digging his keys from his pocket and leading the way. They walked all the way to the end of the hall before he finally unlocked the very last apartment.

Nice.

One less wall of neighbors for them to possibly disturb.

His eyes widened as he stepped into the space, taking it in. Nolan was watching him with an eager expression.

Beyond the love of his life waited his rather empty—for now—apartment.

"Holy shit," he breathed. "I know you said your shares of the stock sold well, but…"

"Is it too much?"

It was certainly nicer than Reid had expected. The front door opened to the large living area, currently filled with boxes; a randomly placed couch; and a cat tower, sans cat.

To the left awaited the kitchen behind the bisecting breakfast bar, with three panels of windows casting afternoon light across the empty floor. Past the collection of Nolan's belongings was a nook cornered by windows, and a hallway leading to what he supposed were the bedrooms.

"Wow, so you *just* got here?"

His voice echoed around the empty space.

"Yeah." Nolan motioned to the pile. "I had most of it shipped ahead of time, but I'm still waiting on a few pieces to arrive."

"This is *really* nice, Nolan," Reid breathed, moving to the kitchen first to appreciate the new shiny, silver appliances.

Oh, he could see himself making breakfast here *many* mornings in a row.

Not that this was his *place.*

A first bedroom was located past the kitchen, windows along its right-hand wall. It was nice, but empty.

A spare, then?

His attention flicked to Nolan, who'd come to lean against the entryway to watch Reid's reaction.

Their gazes danced like that for a while, unable to believe the other was real. Lips curling in a smile, Reid was unable to contain his endless bubbly and fizzy excitement. Nolan was *here.*

Part of him was afraid to let Nolan out of his sight, as if he might disappear again if Reid turned his back.

The other part of him just *wanted.*

"So," he began, trailing a finger over the pristine counters. "D'you have a bed yet?"

"Oh, I thought you'd never ask," Nolan practically purred, and wasn't that supposed to be Reid's thing?

Nolan grabbed his hand, touch electric, and dragged him through the empty apartment, past the nook—

"Can't believe there's an actual little reading nook in those windows, man—"

"You can appreciate it later," Nolan growled.

"You could fuck me in it," Reid retorted, and Nolan came to a stop right in the middle of the short hallway.

Reid could practically hear him weighing the connotations of that, but then he moved forward, fingers tightening in Reid's. "Next time."

"Presumptuous of you," Reid muttered, failing to hide the smile in his voice.

The bedroom door was ajar, and Nolan pressed his hand to it, opening it before pausing once more. "Right," he said softly, disconnecting their hands to pat Reid on the chest. "Reid, this is Sunny."

Sunny, the yellow-orange tabby, ancient and bedraggled and all the cuter for it, winked at him from the middle of the bed, one eye missing.

Reid stilled, waiting for Sunny's hackles to raise, but she only stared at him, bored and sleepy.

"She's so much cuter in person," Reid whispered.

"Isn't she just the sweetest? Look at her permanent scraggle. So edgy."

Sunny's long hair refused to lay flat. It stuck up in every direction, keeping her adorably disheveled. "Can't believe you just said 'edgy'."

"That's what you're surprised about?" Nolan chuckled as he crossed to the bed to greet the cat.

"Right, okay, old girl, goodbye, we'll spare you the trauma," he cooed, patting Sunny gently on the head before ushering her off the bed with easy nudges.

She chirped, which really came out as a raspy exhale, and eyed Reid with one big, suspicious yellow eye before scuttling past, tail twitching playfully. Her footsteps echoed on the wooden floor, followed by the jingle of the cat tower as she claimed the other room.

Reid shut the door behind the cat and finally looked over the bedroom. Just as bare as the others, all white paint and simple hardwood floors, a few boxes stacked against the walls and on top of the dresser. The windows were truly the best part, the city stretching out before them, cold winter light shining through.

"It's beautiful, honestly. Can't wait to see how you decorate it." He'd seen glimpses of Nolan's old place through their video calls, but this was a fresh slate. Something that was all Nolan's.

"I'll start with this, of course," Nolan retorted, and sat Banana Shark on the dresser. The plush immediately tilted to the side, wonky from being squished.

Nolan left it there with a fond sigh, and turned to Reid, sidling up to him, palms coming to rest on his chest. "And I figured… *you* could help me with the rest."

Reid grinned. "Well, of course. I'll help you unpack, and we'll have you settled in no time!" Then they could christen each piece of new furniture—

"Reid, stay with me," Nolan said, sliding his touch to his shoulders and giving him a gentle shake. "I'm saying, you could help me with decorating…"

Reid stared at him, brain stuttering. "Yeah, no problem, I got—"

Nolan shook his head. "Because it'll be half yours! I'm asking you to move in with me! Fuck," Nolan huffed, rolling his eyes affectionately before those big blues came to rest on

Reid again.

Reid had gone motionless.

"You want me to move in?" he asked, and Nolan nodded.

"Yes! You silly, adorable man—"

Without giving him time to finish his rant, Reid pressed forward and kissed him,then kept directing him until Nolan spilled down onto the mattress, and Reid into his lap.

"I can't believe you got this place," Reid said, breaking the kiss but pressing his lips into Nolan's cheek, on the tip of his nose, over his forehead. "And you want me here, too? That's —" He couldn't even think of the fucking word for it. He pulled back, thoughts racing. "Are you sure? Don't you want some time to settle in and—"

"I wanna settle in with *you*. Leaving was awful, but spending all these months away from you has been worse. I missed you so much. And maybe it's crazy, but now that you're *here*, I don't want you to leave. So… stay?"

This could totally blow up in their faces. He should say no, play it safe. But another part of him wanted all of Nolan that he'd offer.

Hell, the guy had already changed his entire life. Put his dad in jail after suing the shit out of him. Moved to a new city. What was moving in *together?*

He chuckled, the giddiness bursting out of him in a laugh. "Yeah, yeah. Yes. I'll stay."

Nolan grinned, blue eyes sparkling as he framed Reid's face with his hands and pulled him in for another kiss.

"Thank god. The commute isn't even that bad for work, right? Just whip out your wings and—"

Reid shuffled his hips over Nolan's lap. "The only thing you should be whipping out is your—"

Nolan covered his lips with his own, muffling their laughter, but Reid heard the clink of his belt buckle anyway. Their tongues twined and his heart raced. He felt airborne as

Nolan's fingers warmed against the skin of his stomach, working his button open.

"You're right, we've got to christen the bed of *our* new apartment, after all," Nolan teased, pulling away for a breath.

Reid's hips rolled into Nolan's, brushing their quickly-hardening cocks together. "Say it again," Reid demanded, wrapping a hand around both of them.

Nolan licked his palm and nudged Reid's hand out of the way, leaning in close to nip at Reid's lips. "Which part? *Our* apartment?"

Reid nodded, groaning as Nolan's fist tightened around them in short strokes, low burning embers sparking anew in his gut with each touch.

Nolan chuckled and Reid felt it in his bones, threaded his fingers through Nolan's dark hair and held on. "So easy," he murmured darkly, in that voice he'd been practicing over the phone for the past six months. To hear it whispered so close to his skin was undoing Reid.

"Is it that I bought it for us, taking care of you like I love to?" Nolan asked, nipping at his throat and swiping a thumb over the heads, collecting the precum to make the glide even smoother.

From silly, useless but lovely flowers sent every week to delivered food or a new shirt he just had to see Reid in, Nolan had been spoiling him, and he didn't care to say so.

Reid latched onto Nolan's words, and shook his head once he'd arranged them into sense. "No, it's not that," he panted. Though the idea that Nolan thought of him, included him in his future without a single doubt, made his breath run short.

Nolan hummed thoughtfully, lips buzzing against his pulse, strokes slowing and curling all the way to the base before drawing back up in a mind-numbing rhythm.

"Is it… that we'll be here together, to begin the next chapter of our lives in this apartment?"

Reid's steady grind into Nolan's palm stuttered, his gaze lifting. "As romantic as that sounds, that's not it, either," Reid breathed, rolling his hips, trying to chase Nolan's maddening touch.

After months filled with "good morning" texts and video calls and read receipts, he'd be able to wake up next to Nolan, the love of his fucking life, and whisper the words into his skin instead.

His hips jerked. Maybe there *was* something to it after all.

Nolan was quiet in response, his hand trailing from Reid's hip, up his side and over his chest, and around the back of his head where he combed his fingers through Reid's long hair. "I know what it is. This apartment is ours, just like you're *mine*, hmm?"

The words shot through him like a bolt of lightning, and he stiffened against Nolan. He would've nodded, but the tight hold in his hair restricted his movement, and he melted into Nolan's touch.

"Yeah, that's it," Nolan crooned, hand resuming the steady strokes. "The possessiveness. Should've known."

Reid moaned, hips canting into Nolan's every touch, cock swelling as the eye of the storm neared, his pulse like thunder in his ears.

"This place is *ours*, and you're *mine*, and I'm never leaving you again," Nolan promised, hand tightening and holding him in place, gaze intense and watchful as his hand squeezed and twisted on the up stroke, fingers grazing the ridge of the head.

Reid stiffened, a flash of light striking him as pleasure rolled through him, the landfall he'd been anticipating since he'd suspected Nolan had really come back to him. He spilled over Nolan's hand, the glide turning slick and wet for a few strokes until Reid could open his eyes against the gales of pleasure.

"Should've waited for me," Nolan tutted darkly.

"Can't wait to do this with you every fucking day," Reid whispered, grip harsh on his shoulders. Nolan's hand fell from his hair, shivers dancing over his scalp and down his spine, and Reid used his new freedom to lean forward, cursing the button-up and sweater combo because he wanted *skin*. He found it at Nolan's pulse, just beneath his ear, and hummed into the sensitive skin.

Nolan still stroked them despite Reid's softening state, refusing to release him even as Reid's hips twitched with the urge to tear himself away.

"You're mine, too," Reid choked out, and closed his teeth around the sensitive skin of Nolan's neck.

At the words, the bite, Nolan stiffened beneath Reid, cock pulsing until his hand finally fell away from the flood of their joint release.

Reid slumped against Nolan, sucking in his scent, knees aching and thighs shaking from the oversensitivity. With a groan, he uncurled himself from around Nolan and collapsed beside him on the bed.

Nolan joined him in a tangle of limbs, their pulses slowing and breaths evening, his head resting on Reid's shoulder.

"Well," Nolan said a long moment later. "I certainly look forward to more of that."

"I fucking love you," Reid blurted.

Nolan's smile was dazed and its light was like a beacon, leading him home. His North goddamned Star.

"I fucking love you too."

Reid's head snapped back with the force of his laugh, and his gaze caught on the spread of windows. "Hey, look outside, it's snowing."

The oppressive heat was gone, and winter was officially beginning.

As their sweat-slicked skin cooled, Reid finally got Nolan out of his many layers, and sighed contentedly as their skin met.

Eventually, he'd open the door so Sunny could possibly join them, if she was brave enough.

But for now, he counted Nolan's heartbeats and watched the snow fall from *their* bed.

AFTERWORD

Meowdy!!
Nolan got Sunny (missing one eye) because she reminded
him of the cat at the shelter from chapter eight, Secret Date.
In my head, Reid and Sunny dance around each other for a
week or so, but one day Reid wakes up from a nap with her
on his chest. They're both purring. Sunny likes the
vibrations, and Nolan gets a video of them at some point.
I hope you enjoyed their story.
Please tell other readers if you loved it in a review!
This will not be the last of the Cautionary Tails series. Stay
tuned.
Much love,
Lana

ACKNOWLEDGMENTS

Super thanks to Mems, my sensitivity reader, for keeping the children in mind. (He knows what I mean)

Thank you Meg for cheer reading and always being excited about my characters.

Hugs to Sonny for bringing the covers to life, as well as providing me with cat pics, which are detrimental to the creative process.

And thank you to all my Patrons for your support!

ALSO BY

Visit my website to learn more about my books and how to get your paws on signed paperbacks.

www.lanakoleauthor.com

Cautionary Tails Series

How Not to Date a Demon

How Not to Date a Dragon

How Not to Date a Griffin

How Not to Date an Angel

Short & Sweets

Seasonal Spice & Everything Nice 1

Seasonal Spice & Everything Nice 2

Seasonal Spice & Everything Nice 3

Monster Vacation Series

The Abdominal Snowman

Tentacle Difficulties

In the Sweetverse w/ Kathryn Moon

Baby + the Late Night Howlers

Lola & the Millionaires Part One

Lola & the Millionaires Part Two

Lyric & the Heartbeats

Fighting Instincts

Bad Alpha

All Packed Up

Faith + the Dead End Devils

Knot That Serious

Ashley & the A-Listers

Crystal Clear Series

Illusion of Escape

Illusion of Death

Illusion of Darkness

The Unlocked Series

Chaos Unlocked

Betrayal Exposed

Misery Undone

Truth Revealed

Hope Lost

Death Defied

Standalones

Feline Good

LANA KOLE WRITING AS LOGAN GREY

Heartbelt Records Series

The Deeper You Go

The Longer You'll Stay

Love in Progress

ABOUT the AUTHOR

With a southern twang that's all charm, Lana Kole hails from Tennessee with their four feline roommates. Lana's most likely busy writing stories, but not without a cat purring in their lap. Their work brings life to characters who don't fit the mold, romance as sweet as it is sexy, and worlds better than this one.
Author of paranormal, sweet omegaverse, monster romance, and queer love stories with a happily ever after.